Edmund Fowle

A New Easy Latin Primer

Edmund Fowle

A New Easy Latin Primer

ISBN/EAN: 9783337387884

Printed in Europe, USA, Canada, Australia, Japan

Cover: Foto ©Andreas Hilbeck / pixelio.de

More available books at **www.hansebooks.com**

A NEW EASY LATIN PRIMER.

BY

REV. EDMUND FOWLE,

AMESBURY HOUSE SCHOOL, BICKLEY, KENT,

AUTHOR OF

"Short and Easy Latin Book," "Short and Easy Greek Book,"
"Gods and Heroes," "Schoolboy's First Book of Easy Poetry,"
etc., etc., etc.

LONDON:

SWAN SONNENSCHEIN, Le BAS & LOWREY,
PATERNOSTER SQUARE.
1886.

PREFACE.

—◆—

THIS little Book is an attempt to supply a want that is still universally felt—a Latin Primer sufficiently full and yet sufficiently easy for our Preparatory and for the Lower Forms of our Public Schools.

It has been thought well to follow in many particulars the lines of the P. S. L. P.

AMESBURY HOUSE, BICKLEY, KENT.
January 13*th*, 1886.

** Certain matter will be found repeated in these pages, but this has been found necessary, so that each of the four parts, when published separately, may be complete in itself.

PART I. ACCIDENCE.

PART I. ACCIDENCE.

CONTENTS.

·

A

NEW EASY LATIN PRIMER.

PART I. ACCIDENCE.

LATIN ALPHABET, etc.

The Latin Alphabet is the same as the English without *w*.

The letters have also two forms like the English: (*a*) the Capital or Ancient; (*b*) the Small or Modern.

The Alphabet also, as in English, is divided into: (*a*) Vowels, (*b*) Consonants.

a. Vowels sound by themselves, and are: a, e, i, o, u, y.

b. The *Consonants* must be joined with Vowels to have any sound; as, b (be), c (ce), f (ef).

The *Consonants* again are subdivided into

1. Mutes.   b, c, d, g, k, p, q, t.
2. Nasals.   m, n.
3. Liquids.   l, r.
4. Spirants.   f, h, j, s, v.
5. Double.   x, z, made up of cs, ds.

There are *six Diphthongs* (two vowels with a combined sound): *æ, œ, au*, in common use; *ei, eu, ui*, seldom used.

Latin is spelt by syllables, the quantity of which is long ‾, short ‿, or doubtful ⊻.

The stops in Latin are the same as those used in English.

PARTS OF SPEECH.

The Parts of Speech are eight.

1. Substantive	⎫	declined.	5. Adverb	⎫	undeclined.
2. Adjective	⎪		6. Preposition	⎪	
3. Pronoun	⎬		7. Conjunction	⎬	
4. Verb	⎭		8. Interjection	⎭	

The Substantive, Adjective, Pronoun, Verb change their meaning by their endings. These changes are called *Flexions*, and in making these changes Nouns are said to be *declined*, Verbs *conjugated*. The other parts of speech, sometimes called Particles, have no flexions.

GENDER, NUMBER, CASE.

1. The Noun consists of *Substantive, Adjective,* and *Pronoun.* These have for the most part Gender, Number, and Case. There are

Three Genders:
(*a*) Masculine, (*b*) Feminine, (*c*) Neuter.

Two Numbers :
(*a*) Singular, a *table;* (*b*) Plural, *tables.*

Six Cases, known in English by their *signs,* in Latin by their endings or flexions.

Nom.	Answers	Who or what ?
Voc.	Used in speaking to persons.	
Acc.	Answers	Whom or what ?
Gen.	,,	Of whom, of what, whose ?
Dat.	,,	To or for whom or what ?
Abl.	,,	By, with, or from whom, or what ?

PARTS OF SPEECH EXPLAINED.

1. *The Noun Substantive* is the name of anything; as, a *pen, Cæsar, Corinth.* Names of persons and places are Proper Nouns—all others are Common Nouns.

2. *The Noun Adjective* is joined with a Substantive, to show the quality of the Substantive. Hence it is said to *qualify* a Substantive.—A *good king;* a *bad pen.*

3. *The Pronoun* is sometimes used instead of (pro) a noun. Hence its name. Sometimes it qualifies a Noun— *This* boy is the son of *that* good gentleman, and *he* is a good boy *himself.*

4. *The Verb* tells us
(*a*) What a thing or person *is.*—The boy *is* good.
(*b*) What a thing or person *does.*—The boy *loves.*
(*c*) What a thing or person *suffers,* i.e. what is being done to one.—The boy *is loved.*

5. *The Adverb* is added to a Verb or Adjective, or another Adverb, to qualify its meaning; as, The boy runs *quickly.*

6. *The Preposition*—from præ and pono, *to place before,* is placed before a Noun, to mark its relation to another word; as, The boy was hurt *by* the dog. The boy is *without* knowledge.

7. *The Conjunction* (from cum, *together,* and jungo, *to join*) joins together words and clauses; as, The boys *and* girls. Winter *or* summer. The dog bit the cat *and* ran away.

8. *The Interjection* (a word as it were thrown in among other words, from inter, *among,* and jacio, *to throw*) is an exclamation—*Lo!* it thunders!

STEM AND ROOT.

STEM.

The Stem of a word has been defined as "that part on which the changes of flexion are based," *i.e.*, it is that part of the word which remains after the variable endings have been taken away.

In Nouns the Stem is found by throwing away *rum* from the Genitive Plural of Declensions I., II., V., and *um* from the Genitive Plural of Declensions III., IV. Thus

The Stem of *Mensa* is *MensA*.
  ,,   ,,   *Dominus* is *DominO*.
  ,,   ,,   *Lapis* is *LapiD*.

The Stem of *Nubes* is *NubI*.
  ,,   ,,   *Gradus* is *GradU*.
  ,,   ,,   *Dies* is *DiE*.

But before a Noun can be declined, when the last letter of the Stem is a vowel, as in mens*a*, domin*o*, nub*i*, grad*u*, di*e*, this vowel must be cast off, and the case-endings can then be added to what remains, which is called the Clipt Stem.

For all practical purposes the part of the Stem needful for declining a Substantive can be found by throwing away the Genitive Singular termination of the five declensions.

ROOT.

The Root of a word must not be confounded with its Stem. It is really that part which kindred words (words of one family) have in common. Thus in the words *acies, acus, acuo,* the common root is *ac*, sharp, but their Stems would be respectively *acie, acu, acu.*

SUBSTANTIVES.

A Noun Substantive is the name of anything ; as, a *pen*, *Cæsar*, *Corinth*.

There are five Declensions of Substantives, known by the ending of the Genitive case.

1. æ (diphthong), Mensa, mens*æ*.   3. is,   Nubes, nub*is*.
2. i,   Dominus, domin*i*.   4. ūs, Gradus, grad*ūs*.
5. ei, Res, r*ei*.

NOTES ON THE SUBSTANTIVES.

Peculiarities of the Substantives are given at length (pp. 168–183). We need only give here two or three simple notes.

1. Nom. and Voc. cases are alike in both numbers, excepting some of those of the Second Declension ; as, dominus, Voc., domin*e* ; filius, Voc., fil*i*.

2. In Neuter Nouns the Nom., Voc., and Acc. are alike in both numbers, and in the plural they end in *a*.

3. Some words of the Second Declension in *er* keep the *e* throughout; as, *puer, pueri :* some drop it; as, *magister, magistri*.

4. In the Third Declension note should be taken of *nubes, nubis*, which does *not* increase in the Genitive case, and *lapis, lapidis*, which does. Those which increase in the Genitive Singular have their Genitive Plural in *um* instead of *ium*, with exceptions.

5. Words of the Third Declension have in the nominative various terminations (or endings), as *nubes, lapis, opus, mare*. All other cases depend on the Genitive singular.

The following Substantives are declined (see over) :

Mensa, mensæ (f.), *a table.*   Lapis, lapidis (m.), *a stone.*
Dominus, domini, (m.), *a lord.*   Opus, operis (n.), *a work.*
Magister, magistri, (m.), *a master.*   Mare, maris (n.), *the sea.*
Regnum, regni (n.), *a kingdom.*   Gradus, gradūs (m.), *a step.*
Nubes, nubis (f.), *a cloud.*   Genu, genus (n.), *a knee.*
Res, rei (f.), *a thing.*

DECLENSION OF SUBSTANTIVES.

FIRST DECLENSION.

S. N.	Mensă (f)	a table		P. N.	Mensæ (f.)	tables
V.	Mensă	O table		V.	Mensæ	O tables
A.	Mensam	table		A.	Mensas	tables
G.	Mensæ	of a table		G.	Mensārum	of tables
D.	Mensæ	to or for a table		D.	Mensis	to or for tables
A.	Mensā	by, with or from, a table		A.	Mensis	by, with or from, tables

SECOND DECLENSION.

S. N.	Dominus (m.)	a lord		P. N.	Domini (m.)	lords
V.	Domine	O Lord		V.	Domini	O lords
A.	Dominum	lord		A.	Dominos	lords
G.	Domini	of a lord		G.	Dominōrum	of lords
D.	Domino	to or for a lord		D.	Dominis	to or for lords
A.	Domino	by, with or from, a lord		A.	Dominis	by, with or from, lords

S. N.	Magister(m.)	a master		P. N.	Magistri (m.)	masters
V.	Magister	O master		V.	Magistri	O masters
A.	Magistrum	master		A.	Magistros	masters
G.	Magistri	of a master		G.	Magistrōrum	of masters
D.	Magistro	to or for a master		D.	Magistris	to or for masters
A.	Magistro	by, with or from, a master		A.	Magistris	by, with or from, masters

S. N.	Regnum (n.)	a kingdom		P. N.	Regna (n.)	kingdoms
V.	Regnum	O kingdom		V.	Regna	O kingdoms
A.	Regnum	kingdom		A.	Regna	kingdoms
G.	Regni	of a kingdom		G.	Regnōrum	of kingdoms
D.	Regno	to or for a kingd:		D.	Regnis	to or for kingdoms
A.	Regno	by, with or from, a kingdom		A.	Regnis	by, with or from, kingdoms

THIRD DECLENSION.

S. N.	Nubes (f.)	a cloud		P. N.	Nubes (f.)	clouds
V.	Nubes	O cloud		V.	Nubes	O clouds
A.	Nubem	cloud		A.	Nubes	clouds
G.	Nubis	of a cloud		G.	Nubium	of clouds
D.	Nubi	to or for a cloud		D.	Nubibus	to or for clouds
A.	Nube	by, with or from, a cloud		D.	Nubibus	by, with or from, clouds

THIRD DECLENSION.

S. N.	Lapis (m.)	a stone	P. N.	Lapides (m.)	stones
V.	Lapis	O stone	V.	Lapides	O stones
A.	Lapidem	stone	A.	Lapides	stones
G.	Lapidis	of a stone	G.	Lapidum	of stones
D.	Lapidi	to or for a stone	D.	Lapidibus	to or for stones
A.	Lapide	by, with or from, a stone	A.	Lapidibus	by, with or from, stones

S. N.	Opus (n.)	a work	P. N.	Opera (n.)	works
V.	Opus	O work	V.	Opera	O works
A.	Opus	work	A.	Opera	works
G.	Operis	of a work	G.	Operum	of works
D.	Operi	to or for a work	D.	Operibus	to or for works
A.	Opere	by, with or from, a work	A.	Operibus	by, with or from, works

S. N.	Marĕ (n.)	the sea	P. N.	Maria (n.)	the sea
V.	Mare	O sea	V.	Maria	O seas
A.	Mare	the sea	A.	Maria	the seas
G.	Maris	of the sea	G.	Marium	of the seas
D.	Marī	to or for ⌊the sea	D.	Marĭbus	to or for ⌊the seas
A.	Mari	by, with or from,	A.	Maribus	by, with or from,

FOURTH DECLENSION.

S. N.	Gradus (m.)	a step	P. N.	Gradūs (m.)	steps
V.	Gradus	O step	V.	Gradūs	O steps
A.	Gradum	a step	A.	Gradūs	steps
G.	Gradūs	of a step	G.	Graduum	of steps
D.	Gradui	to or for ⌊a step	D.	Gradibus	to or for ⌊steps
A.	Gradu	by, with or from	A.	Gradibus	by, with or from,

S. N.	Genu (n.)	a knee	P. N.	Genua (n.)	knees
V.	Genu	O knee	V.	Genua	O knees
A.	Genu	a knee	A.	Genua	knees
G.	Genūs	of a knee	G.	Genuum	of knees
D.	Genu	to or for ⌊a knee	D.	Genibus	to or for ⌊knees
A.	Genu	by, with or from,	A.	Genibus	by, with or from,

FIFTH DECLENSION.

S. N.	Res (f.)	a thing	P. N.	Res	things
V.	Res	a thing	V.	Res	O things
A.	Rem	a thing	A.	Res	things
G.	Rëi	of a thing	G.	Rērum	of things
D.	Rëi	to, or for ⌊a thing	D.	Rēbus	to or for ⌊things
A.	Re	by, with or from,	A.	Rēbus	by, with or from

B

GENDER OF THE SUBSTANTIVE.

There are three Genders; a Substantive must be either (*a*) Masculine, (*b*) Feminine, (*c*) Neuter. Some also are Common, *i.e.* Masculine or Feminine.

We give two common General Rules:

I. Certain classes of things are of certain Genders.

Masculine.	Males.	People.	Mountains (*most*).
	Months.	Winds.	Rivers (*most*).
Feminine.	Females.	Countries (*most*).	
	Islands.	Cities and Trees (*most*).	
Neuter.	Indeclinable Nouns; as, fas, nefas, nihil.		
Common.	Words applicable to either sex; as,		
	Conjux, *husband* or *wife*.		
	Hostis, *an enemy.*		

II. Genders of Substantives are in a general way also known by the terminations in each Declension.

First.   Feminine, in *a* and *e;* Masculine in *as* and *es*.

Second. Masculine, in *us* and *er;* Neuter in *um*.

Third.   (*a*) *Masculine* terminations: *o, or, os, er, es,* increasing in gen., *ex* (not *x*).

        (*b*) *Feminine* terminations: *is, as, aus, x* (not *ex*) *s* preceded by a consonant, *es* not increasing in genitive.

        (*c*) *Neuter* terminations: *ar, ur, us, c, a, t, l, e, n.*

Fourth. Masculine in *us;* Neuter in *u*.

Fifth.   Feminine.

But to these rules there are many exceptions (see pp. 158–167.)

GENDER OF THE SUBSTANTIVE.

EXCEPTIONS.

DECLENSION I.

Nouns in *a* denoting Males, are Masculine ; as, poeta, *a poet.*

So also are

Hadria, *Adriatic Sea.*　　　　　　Scurra, a *buffoon.*

DECLENSION II.

A few in *us* are Feminine :

Alvus, *the belly.*	Humus, *the ground.*
Arctus, *the Bear* (constellation).	Pampinus, *vine-leaf.*
Carbasus, *fine flax.*	Pirus, *a pear-tree.* (*a*)
Colus, *a distaff.*	Sapphirus, *a sapphire.* (*b*)

Vannus, a *winnowing fan.*

A few in *us* are Neuter :

Pelagus, *the sea.*	Vulgus, *the common people*
Virus, *poison.*	(*generally*).

DECLENSION III.

Exceptions are numerous (see pp. 158–167).

DECLENSION IV.

A few in *us* are Feminine :

Acus, *a needle.*	Manus, *the hand.*
Anus, *an old woman.*	Nurus, *a daughter-in-law.*
Domus, *a house.*	Porticus, *a portico.*
Idūs (pl.), *the Ides.*	Socrus, *a mother-in-law.*

Tribus, *a tribe.*

DECLENSION V.

All are Feminine except *dies*, which is common in the Singular, but Masculine in the Plural, and *meridies*, *midday*, which is Masculine.

(*a*) And names of plants.
(*b*) And names of jewels.

ADJECTIVES.

A Noun Adjective qualifies a Substantive, as—

A *good* boy.	A *tall* tree.	A *happy* child.
A *bright* day.	*Cold* weather.	A *sad* state.

Adjectives are divided into *three* Classes; those which have in the Nominative .

1. Three terminations.   2. Two terminations.   3. One termination.

1. Adjectives of three terminations end in

us, a, um, as bon*us,* bona, bon*um, good.*
er, a, um, as ten*er,* tenera, tener*um, tender.*
er, is, e, as ac*er,* acr*is,* acr*e, sharp.*

2. Adjectives of two terminations end in

is, e, as trist*is,* triste, *sad.*
or, us, as melior, meli*us, better.*

3. Adjectives of one termination have various endings; as,

Felix, *happy.*
Ingens, *immense.*
Præstans, *excellent.*

The following sample Adjectives are declined;—

Bonus	bona	bonum	*good.*
Tener	tenera	tenerum	*tender.*
Acer	acris	acre	*sharp.*
Tristis	triste	*sad.*	
Melior	melius	*better.*	
Felix	*happy.*		

ADJECTIVES OF THREE TERMINATIONS.

	Masc.	Fem.	Neut.		Masc.	Fem.	Neut.
S. N.	Bonus	bonă	bonum	P. N.	Boni	bonæ	bona
V.	Bone	bona	bonum	V.	Boni	bonæ	bona
A.	Bonum	bonam	bonum	A.	Bonos	bonas	bona
G.	Boni	bonæ	boni	G.	Bonōrum	-ārum	-ōrum
D.	Bono	bonæ	bono	D.	Bonis		
A.	Bono	bonă	bono	A.	Bonis	all genders.	

S. N.	Tener	tenĕra	-ĕrum	P. N.	Teneri	teneræ	tenera
V.	Tener	tenera	-erum	V.	Teneri	teneræ	tenera
A.	Tenerum	teneram	-erum	A.	Teneros	teneras	tenera
G.	Teneri	teneræ	teneri	G.	Tenerōrum	-rārum	-rōrum
D.	Tenero	teneræ	tenero	D.	Teneris		
A.	Tenero	tenera	tenero	A.	Teneris	all genders.	

S. N.	Acer	acris	acre	P. N.	Acres	acres	acria
V.	Acer	acris	acre	V.	Acres	acres	acria
A.	Acrem	acrem	acre	A.	Acres	acres	acria
G.	Acris			G.	Acrium		
D.	Acri	all genders		D.	Acrĭbus	all genders	
A.	Acri			A.	Acribus		

ADJECTIVES OF TWO TERMINATIONS.

	M. F.	N.		M. F.	N.
S. N.	Tristis	triste	P. N.	Tristes	tristĭa
V.	Tristis	triste	V.	Tristes	tristĭa
A.	Tristem	triste	A.	Tristes	tristĭa
G.	Tristis		G.	Tristĭum	
D.	Tristi	all genders	D.	Tristĭbus	all genders
A.	Tristi		A.	Tristĭbus	

S. N.	Melĭor	melius	P. N.	Meliōres	meliōra
V.	Melior	melius	V.	Meliores	meliora
A.	Meliōrem	melius	A.	Meliores	meliora
G.	Meliōris		G.	Meliorum	
D.	Meliori	all genders	D.	Meliorĭbus	all genders
A.	Meliore (i)		A.	Melioribus	

ADJECTIVES OF ONE TERMINATION.

S. N.	Felix (m. f. n.)	P. N.	Felĭces (m. f.)	felicĭa (n.)
V.	Felix	V.	Felices	felicia
A.	Felĭcem (m. f.) felix (n.)	A.	Felices	felicia
G.	Felĭcis	G.	Felicium	
D.	Felĭci	D.	Felicĭbus	all genders
A.	Felĭci (rarely Felīce)	A.	Felicibus	

NOTES ON THE ADJECTIVE.

There are some Adjectives declined like *tener, tenera, tenerum,* which however drop the *e,* as—

Niger, nigra, nigrum, *black.*

There are eleven other Adjectives declined like *acer. Celer* keeps *e* before *r.* It has also *ium* in the Gen. Plural; *um* only when used of the ancient body-guard at Rome— Celeres, Celerum.

1. Alacer, *lively.*	5. Paluster, *marshy.*	8. Saluber, *healthful.*
2. Campester, *level.*	6. Pedester, *pedestrian.*	9. Silvester, *woody.*
3. Celeber, *crowded.*	7. Puter, *rotten.*	10. Terrester, *earthly.*
4. Equester, *equestrian.*		11. Volucer, *winged.*

Adjectives of one termination have various endings—

rapax, *rapacious.*   præstans, *excellent.*   ingens, *immense.*

NUMERAL OR PRONOMINAL ADJECTIVES.

There are some Adjectives which are however declined like *bonus* or *tener* or *niger,* excepting that they have no Voc. and make the Gen. Sing. to end in *ius* and the Dative in *i. Alius* also makes ali*ud* instead of ali*um* in the Neut. Sing.

Unus, *one.*   Uter, *which (of two).*
Solus, *alone.*   Neuter, *neither (of two).*
Totus, *whole.*   Alter *one (of two).*
Ullus, *any.*   Nullus, *none.*
Alius, *one (of any number).*

The numeral Adjectives, duo, *two;* tres, *three,* are thus declined:

N. Duo	duæ	duo	N. Tres	tria
A. Duos (o)	duas	duo	A. Tres	tria
G. Duorum	-arum	-orum	G. Trium	
D. Duobus	-abus	-obus	D. Tribus	
A. Duobus	-abus	-obus	A. Tribus	

NUMERALS.

Numerals are divided into—

1. Cardinal numbers—those on which the other numbers hinge (cardo, *a hinge*) ; as, unus, *one;* duo, *two.*

2. Ordinal numerals—denoting numerical rank (*ordo*) : primus, *first;* secundus, *second.*

3. Distributive numerals—giving or *distributing* so many apiece or at each time. *Pueri scripserunt binas epistolas :* The boys wrote two letters apiece.

4. Numeral Adverbs—denoting the number of times anything happens or is done. *Puer bis locutus est :* The boy spoke *twice.*

The general rule for writing compound numbers is—

1. In numbers less than twenty.

   (*a*) Small number first, without *et. Tres decem* (13) (written as one word, *tredecim*).
   (*b*) Larger number first, *with et. Decem et tres* (13).
   (*c*) *Duo de viginti* (18).   *Unde viginti* (19).

2. In numbers over twenty.

   (*a*) Just the reverse—small number with *et.*
   Romulus reigned thirty-seven years : *Romulus regnavit septem et triginta annos.*
   (*b*) Larger numbers without *et.*
   To men are assigned *thirty-two teeth :* Dentes *triceni bini* viris attribuuntur.

3. In numbers above one hundred the larger comes first, with or without *et. Centum (et) septem* (107).

4. The *thousands* are expressed by prefixing the numeral adverbs to *mille,* as, *bis mille, ter mille* (chiefly in poetry) ; or by prefixing the cardinals to *milia,* as, *duo milia, tria milia.*

N.B.—Mille, a *thousand,* is an indeclinable adjective. Milia, *thousands,* is a neuter plural substantive, and is declined like *maria;* so that *duo milia hominum*=two thousand men.

NUMERALS.

CARDINALS.	ORDINALS.	DISTRIBUTIVES.	ADVERBS.
1. unus, -a, -um	primus, -a, -um	singuli, -æ, -a	semel
2. duo, -æ, -o	secundus (alter)	bini, -æ, -a	bis
3. tres, -tria	tertius	terni (trini), -æ, -a	ter
4. quattuor	quartus	quaterni, -æ, -a	quater
5. quinque	quintus	quini, -æ, -a	quinquies *
6. sex	sextus	seni, -æ, -a	sexies
7. septem	septimus	septeni, -æ, -a	septies
8. octo	octavus	octoni, -æ, -a	octies
9. novem	nonus	noveni, -æ, -a	novies
10. decem	decimus	deni, -æ, -a	decies
11. undecim	undecimus	undeni, æ, -a	undecies
12. duodecim	duodecimus	duodeni, -æ, -a	duodecies
13. tredecim	tertius decimus	terni deni, -æ, -a	tredecies
14. quattuordecim	quartus decimus	quaterni deni, -æ, -a	quaterdecies
15. quindecim	quintus decimus	quini deni, -æ, -a	quindecies
16. sedecim	sextus decimus	seni deni, -æ, -a	sedecies
17. septemdecim	septimus decimus	septeni deni, -æ, -a	septiesdecies
18. duodeviginti	duodevicesimus	duodeviceni, -æ, -a	duodevicies
19. undeviginti	undevicesimus	undeviceni, -æ, -a	undevicies
20. viginti	vicesimus	viceni, -æ, -a	vicies
21. unus et viginti	primus et vicesimus	" singuli, -æ, -a	semel et vicies
22. duo " "	alter "	" bini, -æ, -a	bis "
23. tres " "	tertius "	" terni, -æ, -a	ter "
24. quattuor "	quartus "	" quaterni, -æ, -a	quater "
25. quinque "	quintus "	" quini, -æ, -a	quinquies "
26. sex "	sextus "	" seni, -æ, -a	sexies "
27. septem "	septimus "	" septeni, -æ, -a	septies "
28. duodetriginta	duodetricesimus	duodetriceni, -æ, -a	duodetricies
29. undetriginta	undetricesimus	undetriceni, -æ, -a	undetricies
30. triginta	tricesimus	triceni, -æ, -a	tricies
40. quadraginta	quadragesimus	quadrageni, -æ, -a	quadragies
50. quinquaginta	quinquagesimus	quinquageni, -æ, -a	quinquagies
60. sexaginta	sexagesimus	sexageni, -æ, -a	sexagies

* It may be noted that another form is quinquiens, sexiens, etc.

	CARDINALS.	ORDINALS.	DISTRIBUTIVES.	ADVERBS.
70.	septuaginta	septuagesimus	septuageni, -æ, -a	septuagies
80.	octoginta	octogesimus	octogeni, -æ, -a	octogies
90.	nonaginta	nonagesimus	nonageni, -æ, -a	nonagies
100.	centum	centesimus	centeni, -æ, -a	centies
101.	" et unus	centesimus primus	centeni singuli,	centies semel
102.	" duo	" secundus	" bini	" bis
103.	" tres	" tertius	" terni	" ter
104.	" quattuor	" quartus	" quaterni	" quater
105.	" quinque	" quintus	" quini	" quinquies
106.	" sex	" sextus	" seni	" sexies
107.	" septem	" septimus	" septeni	" septies
108.	" octo	" octavus	" octoni	" octies
109.	" novem	" nonus	" noveni	" novies
110.	" decem	" decimus	" deni	" decies
111.	" undecim	" undecimus	" undeni	" undecies
112.	" duodecim	" duodecimus	" duodeni	" duodecies
113.	" tredecim	" tertius decimus	" terni deni	" tredecies
114.	" quattuordecim	" quartus decimus	" quaterni deni	" quaterdecies
115.	" quindecim	" quintus decimus	" quini deni	" quindecies
116.	" sedecim	" sextus decimus	" seni deni	" sedecies
117.	" septemdecim	" septimus decimus	" septeni deni	" septiesdecies
118.	" duodeviginti	" duodevicesimus	" duodeviceni	" duodevicies
119.	" undeviginti	" undevicesimus	" undeviceni	" undevicies
120.	" viginti	" vicesimus	" viceni	" vicies
200.	ducenti, -æ, -a	ducentesimus	duceni	ducenties
300.	trecenti, -æ, -a	trecentesimus	treceni	trecenties
400.	quadringenti, -æ, -a	quadringentesimus	quadringeni	quadringenties
500.	quingenti, -æ, -a	quingentesimus	quingeni	quingenties
600.	sexcenti, -æ, -a	sexcentesimus	sexceni	sexcenties
700.	septingenti, -æ, -a	septigentesimus	septingeni	septingenties
800.	octingenti, -æ, -a	octingentesimus	octingeni	octingenties
900.	nongenti, -æ, -a	nongentesimus	nongeni	nongenties
1,000.	mille	millesimus	singula millia	millies
2,000.	duo millia	bis millesimus	bina millia	bis millies
100,000.	centum millia	centies millesimus	centena millia	centies millies
1,000,000.	decies centum millia	decies centies millesimus	decies centena millia	decies centies millies

COMPARISON OF ADJECTIVES.

Adjectives have three degrees of comparison :

1. Positive.   2. Comparative.   3. Superlative.

The comparative and superlative are, ordinarily, both formed from the positive.

The comparative is formed from the positive by changing *i* or *is* of the Gen. Singular into *ior*; as,

| Altus, *high* | Gen. alti | Comp. altior |
| Brevis, *short* | ,, brevis | ,, brevior |

The superlative is formed from the positive by changing *i* or *is* of the Gen. Singular into *issimus*; as,

| Altus, *high* | Gen. alti | Sup. altissimus |
| Brevis, *short* | ,, brevis | ,, brevissimus |

Adjectives however in *er* form their comparative *regularly*, but their superlative by adding *rimus* to the Nom. Singular; as,

| Pulcher, *beautiful* | pulcherrimus |
| Celer, *swift* | celerrimus |

Six Adjectives in *lis*, though they form their comparative *regularly*, form their superlative by changing *is* into *limus*; as, facilis, facilior, facillimus—

| Facilis, *easy.* | Similis, *like.* | Gracilis, *slender.* |
| Difficilis, *difficult.* | Dissimilis, *unlike.* | Humilis, *lowly.* |

But other Adjectives in *lis* are Regular; as,

| Utilis | utilior | utilissimus. |

IRREGULAR COMPARISONS.

Some Adjectives are compared quite irregularly, as in English, the comparative or superlative being obtained from other words long since unused or forgotten.

Bonus, *good*	melĭor	optĭmus
Malus, *bad*	pejor	pessimus
Magnus, *great*	major	maximus
Parvus, *small*	minor	minimus
Multus, *much*	plūs (neuter)	plurimus
Extĕrus, *outward*	exterior	{ extrēmus { extimus
Infĕrus, *low*	inferior	infĭmus and ĭmus
Supĕrus, *high*	superior	{ supremus { summus
Posterus, *next-after*	posterior	{ postrēmus { postŭmus
Nequam, *worthless*	nequior	nequissimus
Vetus, *old*	vetustior	veterrimus
Maturus, *ripe*	maturior	{ maturrimus { maturissimus
Egenus, *needy*	egentior	egentissimus
Providus, *provident*	providentior	providentissimus
Dives, *rich*	divitior or ditior	{ divitissimus or { ditissimus
Senex, *old*	{ senior, { natu major }	natu maximus
Juvenis, *young*	{ junior, { natu minor }	natu minimus

There are a few others.

NOTES ON COMPARISON OF ADJECTIVES.

1. The comparative of *multus* (*plus*) has no masc. or fem. gender in the Singular, but full Plur., though somewhat irregular. Nom. and Acc., *plures, plura;* Gen., *plurium;* Dat. and Abl., *pluribus*

2. Adjectives in *us* pure (i.e. *us* preceded by a vowel) use for comparison *magis* and *maxime;* as, *magis* pius, *maxime* pius; except those in *quus;* as, *antiquus, antiquior, antiquissimus,* and a few others.

3. Adjectives in *dicus, ficus, volus* change *us* of the positive into *entior* and *entissimus;* as, *magnificus,* magnific*entior,* magnificent*issimus.* Ocior, *swifter,* has no positive. Many Adjectives have a positive only.

4. There are some Adjectives which seem to spring from Prepositions.

Preposition.	Positive Adj.	Comparative.	Superlative.
E, ex, *out of*	extĕrŭs, *outside*	extĕrĭŏr	extrēmŭs (extĭmŭs)
Intrā, *within*	—	intĕrĭŏr	intĭmŭs
Sŭpĕr, *above*	sŭpĕrŭs, *high above*	sŭpĕrĭŏr	sŭprēmŭs (summŭs)
Infrā, *below*	infĕrŭs, *deep below*	infĕrĭŏr	infĭmŭs (ĭmŭs)
Præ, *before*	—	prĭŏr	prīmŭs, *first*
Post, *after*	postĕrŭs, *next after*	postĕrĭŏr	postrēmŭs (postŭmŭs)
Cĭtrā, *on near side*	—	cĭtĕrĭŏr	cĭtĭmŭs
Ultrā, *beyond*	—	ultĕrĭŏr	ultĭmŭs, *last*
Prŏpĕ, *near*	—	prŏpĭŏr	proxĭmŭs
Dē, *down from*	—	dētĕrĭŏr, *worse*	dēterrĭmŭs, *worst*

COMPARISON OF ADVERBS.

Adverbs are also compared.

The positive Adverb, when derived from an Adjective, ends chiefly in *e* and *ter;* as, digne, *worthily;* graviter, *heavily;* so also sæpe, *often.*

The comparative Adverb is the same as the neuter of the comparative Adjective; as, dignius, *more worthily;* gravius, *more heavily.*

The superlative Adverb is like the superlative Adjective, only it ends in *e;* as, dignissim*e, most worthily;* gravissime, *most heavily;* sæpis-sime, *most often.*

PRONOUNS.

There are eight kinds of Pronouns.

1. Personal.   5. Definitive.
2. Reflexive.   6. Relative.
3. Possessive.   7. Interrogative.
4. Demonstrative.   8. Indefinite.

1. Personal Pronouns are :
   1. Ego, *I.*
   2. Tu, *thou.*

2. Reflexive :
   Se (sese), *himself, herself, itself, themselves.*

3. Possessive :
   1. Meus, *mine.*   4. Cujus, *whose.*
   2. Tuus, *thine.*   5. Noster, *ours.*
   3. Suus, *his, hers,* etc. 6. Vester, *yours.*

4. Demonstrative :
   1. Is, *that, he, she, it.*   3. Ille, *that (yonder).*
   2. Hic, *this (near me).*   4. Iste, *that (near you).*

5. Definitive :
   Idem, *same.*   Ipse, *self.*

6. Relative :   7. Interrogative :
   Qui, *who* or *which.*   Quis, *who* or *what ?*

8. Indefinite :
   Quis (alïquis) *any one.*

DECLENSION OF PRONOUNS.
PERSONAL PRONOUNS.

S. N. Ego	P. Nos	S. N. Tu	P. Vos
A. Me	Nos	A. Te	Vos
G. Mei	Nostrum *or* ī	G. Tui	Vestrum *or* ī
D. Mihi	Nobis	D. Tibi	Vobis
A. Me	Nobis	A. Te	Vobis

REFLEXIVE PRONOUN.	POSSESSIVE PRONOUNS
N. (none)	are declined like *bonus* or
ı A. Se	*niger*, except that *meus* makes
G. Sui	*mi* in the Voc. Sing. Masc.
D. Sibi	*Tuus* and *suus* have no Voca-
A. Se	tive.

DEMONSTRATIVE PRONOUNS.

1. Is, *that, he, she, it*.
2. Hic, *this (near me)*.

3. Ille, *that (yonder, near him)*.
4. Iste, *that (near you)*.

S. N. Is	eă	id	P.N. Ii (ei)	eæ	ea
A. Eum	eam	id	Eos	eas	ea
G.	Ejus		Eorum	earum	eorum
D.	Ei		Iis *or* eīs		
A. Eo	eā	eo	Iis *or* eīs		
S. N. Hic	hæc	hoc	Hi	hæ	hæc
A. Hunc	hanc	hoc	Hos	has	hæc
G.	Hujus		Horum	harum	horum
D.	Huic		His		
A. Hoc	hac	hoc	His		
S. N. Ille	illă	illud	Illi	illæ	illa
A. Illum	illam	illud	Illos	illas	illa
G.	Illīus		Illōrum	illārum	illōrum
D.	Illi		Illis		
A. Illo	illā	illo	Illis		

Iste is declined like *ille*.

DEFINITIVE PRONOUNS.

Idem, *same*.   Ipse, *self*.

S. N. Īdem	eadem	īdem	P.N. Eīdem	eædem	eădem
A. Eundem	eandem	idem	A. Eosdem	easdem	eadem
G. Ejusdem			G. Eorundem	earundem	eorundem
D. Eidem			D. Iisdem *or* ĕisdem		
A. Eodem	eădem	eodem	A. Iisdem *or* ĕisdem		

Ipse is declined like *ille*, excepting that in the Neut. Nom. and Acc.
Sing. it makes ips*um* instead of ips*ud*.

RELATIVE PRONOUN.
Qui, *who* or *which*.

S. N. Qui	quæ	quod	P.N. Qui	quæ	quæ
A. Quem	quam	quod	A. Quos	quas	quæ
G.	Cujus		G. Quorum	quarum	quorum
D.	Cui		D.	Quibus *or* queis *or* quīs
A. Quo	quā	quo	A.	Quibus *or* queis *or* quīs

The Interrogative Pronoun *quis*, and the Indefinite Pronoun *quis*, are mostly declined like *qui*, with some differences.

INTERROGATIVE.				INDEFINITE.		
Singular.				Singular.		
Nom. Quĭs	(quĭs)	quĭd ⎱		Quĭs	quă	quĭd ⎱
Quī	quæ	quŏd ⎰		Qui	quæ	quŏd ⎰
Acc. Quem	quam	quĭd ⎱		Quem	quam	quĭd ⎱
Quem	quam	quŏd ⎰		Quem	quam	quŏd ⎰
etc.	etc.	etc.		etc.	etc.	etc.
In the other forms as Relative.				In the other forms as Relative.		

who, or what?   *any one.*

Indefinite Plur., Nom., Quī, quæ, quă *or* quæ.

COMPOUNDS OF RELATIVE, INTERROGATIVE, AND INDEFINITE.

1. Quisnam, quidnam ; quīnam, quænam, quodnam, *who, what?*
2. Ecquĭs (*for* en-quĭs), ecquă, ecquĭd? Ecquī, ecquæ, ecquŏd, *any one* (Interrogative.) So numquĭs, sīquĭs, etc.
3. Alĭquĭs, ălĭquă, ălĭquĭd ; Alĭquī, ălĭquă, ălĭquŏd, *some one.*
4. Quispĭam, quæpĭam, quippĭam (quodpĭam), *any one.*
5. Quisquam, quicquam ; Genitive, cŭjusquam, etc., *any one at all.*
6. Quīdam, quædam, quiddam (quoddam), *a certain one.*
7. Quīcumquĕ, quæcumquĕ, quodcumquĕ, *whosoever, whatsoever.*
8. Quisquĭs, *whosoever,* quidquĭd, *whatsoever.*
9. Quīvīs, quævīs, quidvīs (quodvīs), *any you will.*
10. Quīlĭbĕt, quælĭbĕt, quidlĭbĕt (quodlĭbĕt), *any you please.*
11. Quisquĕ, quæquĕ, quicquĕ ; Quisquĕ, quæquĕ, quodquĕ, *each.* So Unusquisquĕ, ūnăquæquĕ, ūnumquicquĕ (-quodquĕ), *each one.*

THE VERB SUM.

Sum, es, esse, fui, futurus, *to be.*

Before other Verbs are given, it is necessary to know the verb SUM, which is called the Auxiliary or *helping* Verb, because it *helps* to conjugate the other verbs ; as Amatus *sum* (p. 40). But when not used as an Auxiliary Verb it is called Copulative, *i.e.* it "couples" the subject to the complement; as, Homo *est* mortalis ; *man is mortal.*

INDICATIVE MOOD.

PRESENT.		IMPERFECT.	
S. Sum	*I am*	Eram	*I was*
Es	*thou art*	Eras	*thou wast*
Est	*he is*	Erat	*he was*
P. Sumus	*we are*	Erāmus	*we were*
Estis	*ye are*	Eratis	*ye were*
Sunt	*they are*	Erant	*they were*

FUTURE SIMPLE.		PERFECT.	
S. Ero	*I shall be*	Fui	*I have been*
Eris	*thou wilt be*	Fuisti	*thou hast been*
Erit	*he will be*	Fuit	*he has been*
P. Erĭmus	*we shall be*	Fuĭmus	*we have been*
Eritis	*ye will be*	Fuistis	*ye have been*
Erunt	*they will be.*	Fuĕrunt	*they have been.*

INDICATIVE MOOD.

FUTURE PERFECT.		PLUPERFECT.	
S. Fuero	*I shall have been*	Fueram	*I had been*
Fueris	*thou wilt have been*	Fueras	*thou hadst been*
Fuerit	*he will have been*	Fuerat	*he had been*
P. Fuerĭmus	*we shall have been*	Fueramus	*we had been*
Fuerĭtis	*ye will have been*	Fueratis	*ye had been*
Fuerint	*they will have been*	Fuerant	*they had been*

CONJUNCTIVE MOOD.

PRESENT.		IMPERFECT.	
S. Sim	*I may be*	Essem *vel* Forem	*I*
Sis	*thou mayest be*	Esses *vel* Fores	*thou*
Sit	*he may be*	Esset *vel* Foret	*he*
P. Simus	*we may be*	Essemus *vel* Foremus	*we*
Sitis	*ye may be*	Essetis *vel* Foretis	*ye*
Sint	*they may be*	Essent *vel* Forent	*they*

might be (bracket for imperfect)

PERFECT.		PLUPERFECT.	
S. Fuerim	*I may*	Fuissem	*I should*
Fueris	*thou mayest*	Fuisses	*thou wouldst*
Fuerit	*he may*	Fuisset	*he would*
P. Fuerimus	*we may*	Fuissemus	*we should*
Fueritus	*ye may*	Fuissetis	*ye would*
Fuerint	*they may*	Fuissent	*they would*

have been (perfect)   *have been* (pluperfect)

IMPERATIVE MOOD.

PRESENT.		FUTURE SIMPLE.	
S. Es	*be thou*	S. Esto	*thou must be*
		Esto	*he must be*
P. Este	*be ye*	Estote	*ye must be*
		Sunto	*they must be*

VERB INFINITE.

Present and Imperfect	Esse	*to be*
Perfect and Pluperfect	Fuisse	*to have been*
Future	Fore *vel* Futurus esse	*to be about to be*
Future Participle	Futurus	*about to be*

No gerunds, supines, or Present Participle.

C

THE VERB.

Verbs are of various forms—

1. **Regular**   as, *Amo, moneo, rego, audio.*

2. **Irregular**   as, *Possum, volo, nolo, malo, etc.*

3. **Deponent**   partly active, partly passive; as, *Loquor,* I speak, p. 48.

4. **Impersonal**   used in 3rd pers. sing. and infinitive mood; as, *Piget me,* it grieves me.

5. **Defective**   not having all their parts; as, *Inquam,* I say.

6. **Quasi-passive, or semi-deponent**—as, *fio,* I am made; *gaudeo, gavisus sum,* I rejoice.

All of which will be mentioned in their proper places.

TRANSITIVE AND INTRANSITIVE VERBS.

Verbs are either—

1. Transitive;   or,   2. Intransitive.

1. Transitive—

The word *transitive* is made up of two Latin words, *trans,* across, and *eo,* to go. For our present purpose it will signify *passing on,* and it means, when spoken of a Verb, that the action of the Verb *passes on* to the case which follows it—

I love the boys.   I hit the table.   I eat an apple.

Here it can be seen at once that *love, hit, eat* are transitive Verbs; that is, that there is an *action* in the Verb which passes on to the case.

2. Intransitive.

A Verb is intransitive, that is, *not* transitive (*in* meaning *not*) when there is no action in the Verb to *pass on;* as—

I stand.   The tree grows.   The bird flies.

Here it can be seen that in *stand, grows, flies* there is no action that will *pass on.*

There are some Verbs which are both transitive and intransitive; as *Doleo,* I grieve, grieve for.

STEM OF THE VERB.

To conjugate a *Verb* a boy must know, not merely the Stem of the Present, but also that of the Perfect and Supine.

The Stem of the Present is found in the Imperative Mood; except (1) in the *Third* Conjugation, where the final " e " must be cut off; and (2) in Deponent Verbs, where *re* or *ere* must be thrown away. Thus the stem of

Amo is *Ama.*	*Venor* is *Vena.*
Moneo is *Mone.*	*Vereor* is *Vere.*
Rego is *Reg-*	*Utor* is *Ut-*
Audio is *Audi.*	*Partior* is *Parti*

The Stem of the Perfect of any Regular (*a*) Verb of

CONJUGATION I. is found by adding *v* to the Stem of the Present; as, *Ama, amav.*

CONJUGATION II. is found by changing *e* of the Stem of the Present into *u*; as, *Mone, monu.*

CONJUGATION IV. is found by adding *v* to the stem of the Present; as, *Audi, audiv.*

The Stem of the Perfect in Conjugation III. is so irregular that it can only be found by consulting a dictionary.

The Stem of the Supine of any Regular (*a*) Verb is found by adding *t* to the Stem of the Present in Conjugations I., IV. ; as, *ama, amat; audi, audit.* In Conjugations II., III., the Stem of the Supine is so irregular that the Verb should be looked out.

We add here the Tenses, etc., formed from the different Stems.

From Stem of Present.	From Stem of Perfect.	From Stem of Supine.
Present Act. and Pass.	Perfect Act.	Supines
Future Simple A. and P.	Future Perfect Act.	Participle Fut. Act.
Imperf. Act. and Pass.	Pluperfect Act.	Infinitive Fut. Pass.
Imperat. Act. and Pass.	Infinitive Perfect Act.	Participle Perf. Pass.
Infin. Pres. Act. and		Perfect Pass.
Pass.		Future Perf. Pass.
Gerund and Gerundive		Pluperfect Pass.
Participle Pres. Act.		Infinitive Perf. Pass.

(*a*) We say *Regular* Verbs, for many are irregular, and it would be beyond the scope of the present manual to enter into the various irregularities.

THE REGULAR VERBS.

Regular Verbs have

4 Conjugations.	2 Numbers.
2 Voices.	6 Persons (generally).
4 Moods.	3 Gerunds.
6 Tenses.	2 Supines.
4 Participles.	

THE FOUR CONJUGATIONS

are known by the ending of the Infinitive Mood.

1. Has *ā* long before *re*; as, amā́re, to love.
2. Has *ē* long before *re*; as, monḗre, to advise.
3. Has *ĕ* short before *re*; as, regĕre, to rule.
4. Has *ī* long before *re*; as, audī́re, to hear.

TWO VOICES.

1. Active. 2. Passive.

FOUR MOODS.

1. Indicative.
2. Conjunctive.
3. Imperative.
4. Infinitive.

SIX TENSES.

1. Present.
2. Future Simple.
3. Imperfect.
4. Perfect.
5. Future Perfect.
6. Pluperfect.

Each tense, in Indicative and Conjunctive Mood, has two Numbers, and three Persons in each Number.

The Imperative has Number and Person, but the latter incomplete.

The Infinitive has neither Number nor Person.

THREE GERUNDS.

1. Nom. or Acc. in *dum*; as, amandum, loving.
2. Genitive in *di*; as, amandi, of loving.
3. Dat. or Abl. in *do*; as, amando, for or by loving.

TWO SUPINES.

1. Supine in *um*; as, amatum, to love.
2. Supine in *u*; as, amatu, to be loved, or in loving.

PARTICIPLES.

There are four Participles:

1. Present in *ans* or *ens;* as, am*ans, loving ;* mon*ens, advising.*
2. Participle in *dus* (known as the Gerundive); as, aman*dus, to be, that is to be,* or *that must be loved.*
3. Perfect in *us;* as, amat*us, loved,* or *having been loved.*
4. Future in *rus ;* as, amat*urus, going to love, about to love.*

These Participles are also classed in another way :

Two Active.	1. Present in *ans* or *ens.*
	2. Future in *rus.*
Two Passive.	1. Perfect in *us.*
	2. Participle in *dus.*

THE REGULAR VERBS CONJUGATED.

	(To love.)	*(To advise.)*	*(To rule.)*	*(To hear.)*
1st Pers. Pres.	Amo	Moneo	Rego	Audio
2nd Pers. Pres.	Amas	Mones	Regis	Audis
Inf. Pres.	Amāre	Monēre	Regĕre	Audīre
Perf.	Amavi	Monui	Rexi	Audivi
Gerund in dum	Amandum ⎞	Monendum ⎞	Regendum ⎞	Audiendum ⎞
,, di	Amandi	Monendi	Regendi	Audiendi
,, do	Amando ⎠	Monendo ⎠	Regendo ⎠	Audiendo ⎠
Supine in um	Amātum ⎞	Monĭtum ⎞	Rectum ⎞	Audītum ⎞
,, u	Amatu ⎠	Monitu ⎠	Rectu ⎠	Auditu ⎠
Part. Pres.	Amans ⎞	Monens ⎞	Regens ⎞	Audiens ⎞
,, Fut.	Amaturus ⎠	Moniturus ⎠	Recturus ⎠	Auditurus ⎠

This long form may be much shortened.

1st Pers. Pres.	Amo	Moneo	Rego	Audio
Inf. Pres.	Amāre	Monēre	Regĕre	Audīre
Perf.	Amavi	Monŭi	Rexi	Audivi
Supine in um	Amātum	Monĭtum	Rectum	Audītum

SHORT FORM FOR PASSIVES.

1st Pers. Pres.	Amor	Monĕor	Regor	Audĭor
Inf. Pres.	Amari	Monĕri	Regi	Audīri
Part. Perf.	Amatus	Monĭtus	Rectus	Audītus
Gerundive	Amandus	Monendus	Regendus	Audiendus

TENSES OF THE REGULAR VERBS—ACTIVE VOICE.

INDICATIVE MOOD.

Present.

S.	Amo	I love
	Amas	thou lovest
	Amat	he loves
P.	Amāmus	we love
	Amatis	ye love
	Amant	they love
S.	Moneo	I advise
	Mones	thou advisest
	Monet	he advises
P.	Monēmus	we advise
	Monetis	ye advise
	Monent	they advise
S.	Rēgo	I rule
	Regis	thou rulest
	Regit	he rules
P.	Regimus	we rule
	Regitis	ye rule
	Regunt	they rule
S.	Audio	I hear
	Audis	thou hearest
	Audit	he hears
P.	Audimus	we hear
	Auditis	ye hear
	Audiunt,	they hear

Imperfect. (loving)

S.	Amābam	I was
	Amabas	thou wast
	Amabat	he was
P.	Amabamus	we were
	Amabatis	ye were
	Amabant	they were
	Monēbam	I was advising
	Regēbam	I was ruling
	Audiēbam	I was hearing
		like Amābam.

Perfect. (loved)

S.	Amāvi	I have
	Amavisti	thou hast
	Amavit	he has
P.	Amavimus	we have
	Amavistis	ye have
	Amavērunt ⎱ Amavēre ⎰	they have
	Monŭi	I have advised
	Rexi	I have ruled
	Audivi	I have heard
		like Amāvi.

CONJUNCTIVE MOOD.

Present. (love)

S.	Amem	I may
	Ames	thou mayest
	Amet	he may
P.	Amēmus	we may
	Ametis	ye may
	Ament	they may

(advise)

S.	Moneam	I may
	Moneas	thou mayest
	Moneas	he may
P.	Moneamus	we may
	Moneatis	ye may
	Moneant	they may
	Regam	I may rule
	Audiam	I may hear
		like Moneam.

Imperfect. (love)

S.	Amarem	I might
	Amares	thou mightest
	Amaret	he might
P.	Amaremus	we might
	Amaretis	ye might
	Amarent	they might
	Monerem	I might advise
	Regerem	I might rule
	Audirem	I might hear
		like Amarem

INDICATIVE MOOD.

Future Simple.

love

S.	Amābo	I shall
	Amabis	thou wilt
	Amabit,	he will
P.	Amabĭmus	we shall
	Amabitis	ye will
	Amabunt	they will

Monebo   I shall advise
     like Amabo.

rule

S.	Regam	I shall,
	Reges	thou wilt
	Reget	he will
P.	Regēmus	we shall
	Regetis	ye will
	Regent	they will

Audiam   I shall hear
     like Regam.

Future Perfect.

have loved

S.	Amavero	I shall
	Amaveris	thou wilt
	Amaverit	he will
P.	Amaverĭmus	we shall
	Amaveritis	ye will
	Amaverint	they will

Monuero   I shall have advised
Rexero   I shall have ruled
Audivero   I shall have heard
     like Amavero.

Pluperfect.

loved

S.	Amaveram	I had
	Amaveras	thou hadst
	Amaverat	he had
P.	Amaverāmus	we had
	Amaveratis	ye had
	Amaverant	they had

Monueram   I had advised
Rexeram   I had ruled
Audiveram   I had heard
     like Amaveram.

CONJUNCTIVE MOOD.

Perfect.

have loved

S.	Amaverim	I may
	Amaveris	thou mayest
	Amaverit	he may
P.	Amaverĭmus	we may
	Amaveritis	ye may
	Amaverint	they may

Monuerim   I may have advised
Rexerim   I may have ruled
Audiverim   I may have heard
     like Amaverim.

Pluperfect.

have loved

S.	Amavissem	I should
	Amavisses	thou wouldest
	Amavisset	he would
P.	Amavissēmus	we should
	Amavissetis	ye would
	Amavissent	they would

Monuissem   I should have advised
Rexissem   I should have ruled
Audivissem   I should have heard
     like Amavissem.

TENSES OF THE REGULAR VERBS—PASSIVE VOICE,

INDICATIVE MOOD.

Present.

loved

S.	Amor	I am
	Amaris (re)	thou art
	Amatur	he is
P.	Amamur	we are
	Amamini	ye are
	Amantur	they are

advised

S.	Moneor	I am
	Moneris (re)	thou art
	Monetur	he is
P.	Monemur	we are
	Monemini	ye are
	Monentur	they are

ruled

S.	Regor	I am
	Regĕris (re)	thou art
	Regitur	he is
P.	Regimur	we are
	Regimini	ye are
	Reguntur	they are

heard

S.	Audior	I am
	Audiris (re)	thou art
	Auditur	he is
P.	Audimur	we are
	Audimini	ye are
	Audiuntur	they are

Imperfect.

being loved

S.	Amabar	I was
	Amabaris	thou wert
	Amabatur	he was
P.	Amabamur	we were
	Amabamini	ye were
	Amabantur	they were

Monebar	I was being, etc.
Regebar	I was being, etc.
Audiebar	I was being, etc.
	like Amabar.

Perfect.

have been loved—was loved

S.	Amatus sum	I
	Amatus es	thou
	Amatus est	he
P.	Amati sumus	we
	Amati estis	ye
	Amati sunt	they

Monitus sum	I have been, etc.
Rectus sum	I have been, etc.
Auditus sum	I have been, etc.

CONJUNCTIVE MOOD.

Present.

be loved

S.	Amer	I may
	Ameris (re)	thou mayest
	Ametur	he may
P.	Amemur	we may
	Amemini	ye may
	Amentur	they may

be advised

S.	Monear	I may
	Monearis (re)	thou mayest
	Moneatur	he may
P.	Moneamur	we may
	Moneamini	ye may
	Moneantur	they may

Regar	I may be, etc.	
Audiar	I may be, etc.	like Monear.

Imperfect.

might be loved.

S.	Amarer	I
	Amareris (re)	thou
	Amaretur	he
	Amaremur	we
	Amaremini	ye
	Amarentur	they

Monērer, Regērer, Audirer, like Amarer.

CONJUNCTIVE MOOD.

Perfect.
may have been loved

S.
Amatus sim	I
Amatus sis	thou
Amatus sit	he

P.
Amati simus	we
Amati sitis	ye
Amati sint	they

Monitus sim	I may, etc.
Rectus sim	I may, etc.
Auditus sim	I may, etc.

like Amatus sim.

Pluperfect.
might have been loved

S.
Amatus essem	I
Amatus esses	thou
Amatus esset	he
Amati essemus	we
Amati essetis	ye
Amati essent	they

Monitus essem	I
Rectus essem	I
Auditus essem	I

like Amatus essem.

INDICATIVE MOOD.

Future Perfect.
shall or will have been loved

S.
Amatus ero	I
Amatus eris	thou
Amatus erit	he

P.
Amati erimus	we
Amati eritis	ye
Amati erunt	they

Monitus ero	I shall, etc.
Rectus ero	I shall, etc.
Auditus ero	I shall, etc.

like Amatus ero.

Pluperfect.
had been loved

S.
Amatus eram	I
Amatus eras	thou
Amatus erat	he

P.
Amati eramus	we
Amati eratis	ye
Amrti erant	they

Monitus eram	I had, etc.
Rectus eram	I had, etc.
Auditur eram	I had, etc.

like Amatus eram.

Future Simple.
shall or will be loved

S.
Amabor	I
Amaberis (re)	thou
Amabitur	he

P.
Amabimur	we
Amabimini	ye
Amabuntur	they

Monebor   *I shall, etc.*
like Amabor.

shall or will be ruled

S.
Regor	I
Regēris (re)	thou
Regetur	he

P.
Regemur	we
Regemini	ye
Regentur	they

Audiar   *I shall be, etc.*
like Regar.

IMPERATIVE MOOD.

PRESENT TENSE.

ACTIVE.		PASSIVE.	
Ama	*love thou*	Amare	*be thou loved*
Amate	*love ye*	Amamini	*be ye loved*
Mone	*advise thou*	Monere	*be thou advised*
Monete	*advise ye*	Monemini	*be ye advised*
Rege	*rule thou*	Regere	*be thou ruled*
Regite	*rule ye*	Regimini	*be ye ruled*
Audi	*hear thou*	Audire	*be thou heard*
Audite	*hear ye*	Audimini	*be ye heard*

FUTURE SIMPLE.

Amato	*thou must love*	Amator	*thou must be loved*
Amato	*he must love*	Amator	*he must be loved*
Amatote	*ye must love*		
Amanto	*they must love*	Amantor	*they must be loved*
Moneto	*thou must advise*	Monetor	*thou must be advised*
Moneto	*he must advise*	Monetor	*he must be advissd*
Monetote	*ye must advise*		
Monento	*they must advise*	Monentor	*they must be advised*
Regito	*thou must rule*	Regitor	*thou must be ruled*
Regito	*he must rule*	Regitor	*he must be ruled*
Regitote	*ye must rule*		
Regunto	*they must rule*	Reguntor	*they must be ruled*
Audito	*they must hear*	Auditor	*thou must be heard*
Audito	*he must hear*	Auditor	*he must be heard*
Auditote	*ye must hear*		
Audiunto	*they must hear.*	Audiuntor	*they must be heard*

INFINITIVE MOOD.

ACTIVE.

Present and Imperfect	Amāre	*to love*
Perfect and Pluperfect	Amavisse	*to have loved*
Future	Amaturus esse	*to be about to love*
Present and Imperfect	Monēre	*to advise*
Perfect and Pluperfect	Monuisse	*to have advised*
Future	Moniturus esse	*to be about to advise*
Present and Imperfect	Regere	*to rule*
Perfect and Pluperfect	Rexisse	*to have ruled*
Future	Recturus esse	*to be about to rule*
Present and Imperfect	Audire	*to hear*
Perfect and Pluperfect	Audivisse	*to have heard*
Future	Auditurus esse	*to be about to hear*

PASSIVE.

Present and Imperfect	Amari	*to be loved*
Perfect and Pluperfect	Amatus esse	*to have been loved*
Future	Amatum iri	*to be about to be loved*
Present and Imperfect	Moneri	*to be advised*
Perfect and Pluperfect	Monitus esse	*to have been advised*
Future	Monitum iri	*to be about to be advised*
Present and Imperfect	Regi	*to be ruled*
Perfect and Pluperfect	Rectus esse	*to have been ruled*
Future	Rectum iri	*to be about to be ruled*
Present and Imperfect	Audiri	*to be heard*
Perfect and Pluperfect	Auditus esse	*to have been heard*
Future	Auditum iri	*to be about to be heard*

GERUNDS, SUPINES, PARTICIPLES.

There are three Gerunds:
1. Ending in *dum*.
2. Ending in *di*.
3. Ending in *do*.

N. A.	Amandum	*loving*
G.	Amandi	*of loving.*
D. A.	Amando	*for* or *by loving*
N. A.	Monendum	*advising*
G.	Monendi	*of advising*
D. A.	Monendo	*for, by, advising*
N. A.	Regendum	*ruling*
G.	Regendi	*of ruling*
D. A.	Regendo	*for* or *by ruling*
N. A.	Audiendum	*hearing*
G.	Audiendi	*of hearing*
D. A.	Audiendo	*for* or *by hear-ing*

There are two Supines :
1. Supine in *um*.
2. Supine in *u*.

Amatum	*to love*
Amatu	*to be loved*
Monitum	*to advise*
Monitu	*to be advised*
Rectum	*to rule*
Rectu	*to be ruled.*
Auditum	*to hear*
Auditu	*to be heard.*

There are four Participles:

ACTIVE.

Present in *ans* or *ens*.
Future in *rus*.

PASSIVE.

Perfect in *us*.
Participle in *dus*,—Gerundive.

ACTIVE.

Amans	*loving*
Amaturus	*about to love*
Monens	*advising*
Moniturus	*about to advise*
Regens	*ruling.*
Recturus	*about to rule*
Audiens	*hearing*
Auditurus	*about to hear*

PASSIVE.

Amatus	*loved*
Amandus	*meet to be loved*
Monitus	*advised.*
Monendus	*meet to be advised*
Rectus	*ruled*
Regendus	*meet to be ruled*
Auditus	*heard*
Audiendus	*meet to be heard.*

IRREGULAR OR ANOMALOUS VERBS.

The following Verbs are called Irregular or Anomalous,

Possum	*I am able.*
Volo	*I am willing.*
Nolo	*I am unwilling.*
Malo	*I am more willing.*
Fero	*I bear.*
Fio	*I am made.*
Eo.	*I go.*

IRREGULAR VERBS CONJUGATED.

1st Pers. Pres.	Possum	Volo	Nolo	Malo
2nd Pers. Pres.	Potes	Vis	Nonvis	Mavis
Inf.	Posse	Velle	Nolle	Malle
Perf.	Potŭi	Volui	Nolui	Malŭi
Gerund in *dum*	—	Volendum	Nolendum	Malendum
,, *di*	—	Volendi	Nolendi	Malendi
,, *do*	—	Volendo	Nolendo	Malendo
Supine in *um*	—	—	—	—
,, *u*	—	—	—	—
Part. Pres.	—	Volens	Nolens	Malens
Fut.	—	—	—	—

1st Pers. Pres.	Fero	Fio	Eo
2nd Pers. Pres.	Fers	Fis	Is
Inf.	Ferre	Fieri	Ire
Perf.	Tuli	Factus sum	Ivi
Gerund in *dum*	Ferendum		Eundum
,, *di*	Ferendi		Eundi
,, *do*	Ferendo		Eundo
Supine in *um*	Latum		Itum
,, *u*	Latu		Itu
Part. Pres.	Ferens		Iens (euntis)
Fut.	Latūrus		Iturus

ANOMALOUS OR IRREGULAR VERBS.

PRESENT.

	Indicative.	Conjunctive.
S.	Possum	Possim
	Potes	Possis
	Potest	Possit
P.	Possumus	Possimus
	Potestis	Possitis
	Possunt	Possint
S.	Volo	Velim
	Vis	Velis
	Vult	Velit
P.	Volumus	Velimus
	Vultis	Velitis
	Volunt	Velint
S.	Nolo	Nolim
	Nonvis	Nolis
	Nonvult	Nolit
P.	Nolumus	Nolimus
	Nonvultis	Nolitis
	Nolunt	Nolint

FUTURE.

	Indicative.	Fut. Perf.
S.	Potero	Potuero
	Poteris	Potueris
	Poterit	Potuerit
P.	Poterimus	Potuerimus
	Poteritis	Potueritis
	Poterunt	Potuerint
S.	Volam	Voluero
	Voles	Volueris
	Volet	Voluerit
P.	Volemus	Voluerimus
	Voletis	Volueritis
	Volent	Voluerint
	Nolam	Noluero
	Malam	Maluero
	Feram	Tulero
	Fiam	Ivero

like Volam and Voluero.

PERFECT.

	Indicative.	Conjunctive.
S.	Potui	Potuerim
	Potuisti	Potueris
	Potuit	Potuerit
P.	Potuimus	Potuerimus
	Potuistis	Potueritis
	Potuērunt or ēre	Potuerint
S.	Volui	Voluerim
	Nolui	Noluerim
	Malui	Maluerim
	Tuli	Tulerim
	Ivi	Iverim

like Potui (Volui, Nolui, Malui)　　*like Potuerim* (Voluerim, Noluerim, Maluerim)

PLUPERFECT.

	Indicative.	
S.	Potueram	Potuissem
	Potueras	Potuisses
	Potuerat	Potuisset
P.	Pótueramus	Potuissemus
	Potueratis	Potuissetis
	Potuerant	Potuissent

N.B.—These tenses of Eo are put out of order to get all the tenses into two pages, and are printed in italics to make them more noticeable.

PLUPERFECT.

Indicative.	Conjunctive.
like Potueram	_like Potuissem_
S. Volueram	Voluissem
Nolueram	Noluissem
Malueram	Maluissem
Tuleram	Tulissem
Iveram	Ivessim

PRESENT OF EO.

Indicative.	Conjunctive.
S. _Eo_	_Eam_
_Is_	_Eas_
_It_	_Eat_
P. _Imus_	_Eamus_
Itis	_Eatis_
Eunt	_Eant_

FUTURE OF EO.

Indicative.	Conjunctive.
S. _Ibo_	_Ivero_
Ibit	_Iveris_
Ibit	_Iverit_
P. _Ibimus_	_Iverimus_
Ibitis	_Iveritis_
Ibunt	_Iverint_

IMPERFECT.

Indicative.	Conjunctive.
S. Poteram	Possem
Poteras	Posses
Poterat	Posset
P. Poteramus	Possemus
Poteratis	Possetis
Poterant	Possent

like Vellem.

Indicative.	Conjunctive.
S. Volebam	Vellem
Volebas	Velles
Volebat ·	Vellet
P. Volebamu	Vellemus
Volebatis	Velletis
Volebant	Vellent

like Volebam

Nolebam	Nollem
Malebam	Mallem
Ferebam	Ferrem
Fiebam	Fierem
Ibam	Irem

PRESENT.

Indicative.	Conjunctive.
S. Malo	Malim
Mavis	Malis
Mavult	Malit
P. Malumus	Malimus
Mavultis	Malitis
Malunt	Malint

Indicative.	Conjunctive.
S. Fio	Fiam
Fis	Fias
Fit	Fiat
P. —	Fiamus
—	Fiatis
Fiunt	Fiant

Indicative.	Conjunctive.
S. Fero	Feram
Fers	Feras
Fert	Ferat
Ferimus	Feramus
Fertis	Feratis
Ferunt	Ferant

IMPERATIVE MOOD.

Present.			*Future.*		
Noli	Nolīte	Nolīto	Nolito	Nolitōte	Nolunto
Fer	Ferte	Ferto	Ferto	Fertote	Ferunto
Fi	Fite				
I	Ite	Īto	Īto	· Ītōte	Eunto

INFINITITE MOOD.

Present and Imperfect.		*Perfect and Pluperfect.*	
Posse	to be able	Potuisse	to have been able
Velle	to be willing	Voluisse	to have been willing
Nolle	to be unwilling	Noluisse	to have been unwilling
Malle	to be more willing	Malluisse	to have been more, etc.
Ferre	to bear	Tulisse	to have borne
Fieri	to be made		
Ire	to go	Ivisse	to have gone

DEPONENT VERBS.

There are some verbs called Deponent—from *de* and *pono*, I *lay aside*, or *lay down*,—which lay aside the Active Form. They may be variously described:

1. They mostly look like a Passive Verb, but are not;
2. They are partly Active, and partly Passive;
3. They have, *chiefly*, a Passive Form and an Active meaning.

Thus *Venor*, to hunt, looks like a Passive Verb, but as the meaning is *I hunt*, and not *I am hunted*, it may be known to be Deponent.

Deponent Verbs take no particular case after them. Some are Active, and are followed by the Accusative case, as *Vereor*, I fear; or by some other case, as *Utor*, I use, which takes an Ablative; *Misereor*, I pity, which takes a Genitive. Some also are Intransitive, and take no case, as *Morior*, I die.

In conjugating a Deponent Verb, it will be seen that they also take of the nature of an Active Verb by having Gerunds and Supines.

They also have four Participles, two (Pres. and Fut.) Active in form and sense; one (Perf.) Passive in form, but *generally* Active in sense; and the Gerundive.

Particular notice must be taken of the meaning of the Perfect Participle of a Deponent Verb, *venatus, veritus, usus, partitus,* the English of which is, *having hunted, having feared, having used, having divided;* whereas if it were the Passive Participle of an Active Verb it would be *hunted, having been hunted,* etc. There is indeed no such convenient Latin Participle as *having loved, having advised,* etc., in Active Verbs.

DEPONENT VERBS CONJUGATED.

	1st Conj. (*To hunt.*)	2nd Conj. (*To fear.*)	3rd Conj. (*To use.*)	4th Conj. (*To divide.*)
1st Pers. Pres.	Venor	Vereor	Utor	Partior
2nd Pers. Pres.	Venāris	Verēris	Utĕris	Partīris
Inf. Pres.	Venāri	Verēri	Uti	Partīri
Perf.	Venātus sum	Verītus sum	Usus sum	Partītus sum
Ger. in dum	Venandum ⎫	Verendum ⎫	Utendum ⎫	Partiendum ⎫
,, di	Venandi ⎬	Verendi ⎬	Utendi ⎬	Partiendi ⎬
,, do	Venando ⎭	Verendo ⎭	Utendo ⎭	Partiendo ⎭
Gerundive	Venandus	Verendus	Utendus	Partiendus
Supine in um	Venātum ⎫	Verītum ⎫	Usum ⎫	Partītum ⎫
,, u	Venatu ⎭	Verītu ⎭	Usu ⎭	Partītu ⎭
Part. Pres.	Venans ⎫	Verens ⎫	Utens ⎫	Partiens ⎫
,, Perf.	Venatus ⎬	Verītus ⎬	Usus ⎬	Partītus ⎬
,, Fut.	Venaturus ⎭	Veriturus ⎭	Usurus ⎭	Partitūrus ⎭

SHORTER FORM.

1st Pers. Pres.	Venor	Vereor	Utor	Partior
Inf. Pres.	Venari	Vereri	Uti	Partiri
Part. Perf.	Venatus	Verītus	Usus	Partītus
Gerundive	Venandus	Verendus	Utendum	Partiendus

D

CONJUGATION OF THE DEPONENT VERB UTOR, *I use* (THIRD).
VERB FINITE.

	INDICATIVE MOOD.		CONJUNCTIVE MOOD.		IMPERATIVE MOOD.	
Present Tense.	S. Utŏr	I use	Utăr	I may	Utĕrĕ	use thou
	Utĕ-rĭs (rē)	thou usest	Ută-rĭs (rē)	thou mayst		
	Utĭtŭr	he uses	Utătŭr	he may	Utĭmĭnĭ	use ye
	Pl. Utĭmŭr	we use	Utămŭr	we may		
	Utĭmĭnĭ	ye use	Utămĭnĭ	ye may	Utĭtŏr } thou	
	Utuntŭr	they use	Utantŭr	they may *use*	Utĭtŏr } he } must use	
					Utuntŏr } they	
Future Simple.	S. Utăr	I shall				
	Utĕ-rĭs (rē)	thou wilt				
	Utĕtŭr	he will				
	Pl. Utēmŭr	we shall				
	Utēmĭnĭ	ye will				
	Utentŭr	they will *use*				
Imperfect.	S. Utēbăr,	I was	Utĕrĕr	I might		
	Utēbā-rĭs (rē)	thou wast	Utĕrĕ-rĭs (rē)	thou mightest		
	Utēbātŭr	he was	Utĕrētŭr	he might		
	Pl. Utēbāmŭr	we were	Utĕrēmŭr	we might		
	Utēbāmĭnĭ	ye were	Utĕrēmĭnĭ	ye might		
	Utēbantŭr	they were *using*	Utĕrentŭr	they might *use*		

VERB INFINITE.

Inf. Pres. Imp.	Uti, to use
Inf. Perf. Plup.	Usus essē, to have used
Inf. Fut. . .	Usūrūs essē, to be about to use
Ger. Nom. Ac.	Utendum, using
Ger. Gen. . .	Utendī, of using
Ger. Dat. Abl.	Utendō, for or by using
Sup. in um .	Usum, to use
Sup. in u . .	Usū, in using, or to be used
Part. Pres. . .	Utens, using
Part. Fut. . .	Usūrūs, about to use
Part. Perf. . .	Usūs, having used
Gerundive .	Utendūs, to be used

Perfect.

have used

S.	Usūs sum	I used	Usus sim	I may
	Usūs ēs	thou usedst	Usus sis	thou mayst
	Usūs est	he used	Usus sit	he may
P.	Usi sūmūs	we used	Usi sīmūs	we may
	Usi estīs,	ye used	Usi sitīs	ye may
	Usi sunt	they used	Usi sint	they may

Future Perfect.

have used

S.	Usus ērō	I shall
	Usus ērīs	thou wilt
	Usus ērit	he will
P.	Usi ērimūs	we shall
	Usi ērītīs	ye will
	Usi ērunt	they will

Pluperfect.

used / *have used*

S.	Usus ēram	I had	Usus essem	I should
	Usus ērās	thou hadst	Usus essēs	thou wouldst
	Usus ērāt	he had	Usus essēt	he would
P.	Usi ērāmus	we had	Usi essēmūs	we should
	Usi ērātīs	ye had	Usi essētīs	ye should
	Usi ērant	they had	Usi essent	they would

IMPERSONAL VERBS.

Impersonal Verbs are those which have no Personal Pronoun as Subject, and are used only in the Third Person Singular (Ind. and Conj.) and in the Infinitive Mood.

It hails, grandinat.   *It vexes me,* me piget.

The greater number of the Impersonal Verbs are of the second conjugation. We give those most commonly used.

CONJUGATION I.

Delectat, *it delights.*   Tonat, *it thunders.*
Juvat, *it delights.*   Fulgurat, *it lightens.*
Constat, *it is evident.*   Grandinat, *it hails.*

CONJUGATION II.

Oportet, *it behoves.*   Pudet, *it shames.*   Licet, *it is lawful.*
Decet, *it becomes.*   Pœnitet, *it repents.*   Liquet, *it is clear.*
Dedecet, *it is unseemly.* Tœdet, *it disgusts.*   Attinet, *it relates.*
Piget, *it irks.*   Miseret, *it moves pity.* Pertinet, *it belongs.*
                           Libet, *it pleases.*

CONJUGATION III.

Accidit, *it happens.*   Pluit, *it rains.*
Contingit, *it befalls.*   Lucescit, *it dawns.*
Ningit, *it snows.*   Vesperascit, *it grows late.*

CONJUGATION IV.

Convenit, *it suits.*   Evenit, *it turns out.*   Expedit, *it is expedient.*

IRREGULAR.

Interest, *it imports.*   Refert, *it concerns.*

The Impersonal Verbs may be arranged also according to the case they are constructed with. The following are used with the Accusative Case—

Decet.	Oportet.
Dedecet.	Piget.
Delectat.	Pœnitet.
Juvat.	Pudet.
Miseret.	Tœdet.

The following are used with the Dative Case—

Libet.	Accidit.	Convenit.
Licet.	Contingit.	Expedit.
	Evenit.	

Some of these Impersonal Verbs, however, are constructed with *ad* and the Accusative, *e.g.* attinet and pertinet, while others, *in addition to an Accusative of the person, have a Genitive as well*, as piget, pudet, etc. So we may sum up the case-construction of these Impersonal Verbs thus:—

Those which require

    a. Accusative of Object: oportet, decet, etc.

    b. Dative of the Object: libet, licet, etc.

    c. Ad with Accusative: attinet, pertinet, etc.

    d. A Genitive with an Accusative, piget, pudet, etc.

To these we may add *interest* and *refert*, which admit a Genitive unless it is necessary to use a pronoun ; when, *in place of the Genitive*, we use meâ, tuâ, suâ, nostrâ, vestrâ, agreeing with *re.* 129 (III. *a*).

The Impersonals—

Fulgurat, *it lightens,*	Pluit, *it rains,*	Vesperascit, *it gets late,*
Tonat, *it thunders,*	Grandinat, *it hails,*	Ningit, *it snows,*
	Luscescit, *it dawns,*	

are of course not used with any Personal or other Object.

DEFECTIVE VERBS.

Irregular or *Anomalous Verbs* (see pp. 45–48) are those which have for the most part the usual tenses, but are irregular as regards the formation of some of these tenses ; as—

> Possum, *I am able.*
> Volo, *I am willing.*
> Nolo, *I am unwilling.*
> Malo, *I prefer.*
> Fero, *I bear.*
> Fio, *I am made.*
> Eo, *I go.*
> Queo, *I am able.*

But *Defective Verbs* are those which want some of the usual parts of a Verb, and may be divided into—

1. Those which have no Tenses derived from the Present stem, though they have the English of the Present ; as—

> Cœpi, *I have begun* (Present-Past)
> Odi, *I hate.*
> Memini, *I remember.*

2. Those which have Perfect without Supine, and those which have neither Perfect nor Supine ; as, Tremo, *I tremble*, which has no Supine, and Mitesco, *I grow mild*, which has no Perfect or Supine.

3. Verbs defective in various forms ; as—

> Aio, *I say.*   Inquam, *I say.*
> Quæso, *I entreat.* Fari, *to speak.*

Imperatives: Apage, *begone;* cedo, *give here;* have, salve, *hail;* age, *come ;* vale, *farewell.*

QUASI-PASSIVE AND SEMI-DEPONENT VERBS.

Quasi-Passive Verbs are those which unite an Active form with a Passive meaning; as—

> Exulo, *I am banished.*
> Fio, *I am made.*
> Liceo, *I am put to auction.*
> Vapulo, *I am beaten.*
> Veneo, *I am on sale.*

SEMI-DEPONENT VERBS

(1) are, first, those which have an Active Present but a Perfect of Passive form (Active meaning); as—

Audeo, *I dare.*	Perfect, Ausus sum, *I dared.*
Fido, *I trust.*	„ Fisus sum, *I trusted.*
Gaudeo, *I rejoice.*	„ Gavisus sum, *I rejoiced.*
Soleo, *I am wont.*	„ Solitus sum, *I was wont.*

(2) Those which have an Active Perfect with Deponent Perfect Principle; as—

Present.	Perfect.	Perfect Participle.
Juro, *I swear.*	Juravi, *I swore.*	Juratus, *having sworn.*
Ceno, *I sup.*	Cenavi, *I supped.*	Cenatus, *having supped.*
Prandeo, *I dine.*	Prandi, *I dined.*	Pransus, *having dined.*

So nupta, *wedded;* potus, *having drunk,* and some others.

DERIVED VERBS.

Derived Verbs are divided into—

1. Frequentative.   2. Inceptive.   3. Desiderative.

1. *Frequentative* Verbs express repeated or intenser action, and are of the *First* Conjugation, and end in *to* or *so*, or *ĭto, ĭtor*.

The principal Frequentative Verbs are:

Canto	*sing.*	Hæsito	*stick fast.*
Capto	*catch up.*	Lectĭto	*gather often.*
†Curso	*run hither & thither.*	Merso	*dip in.*
Cursĭto	*run hither & thither.*	Minitor	*threaten.*
Clamĭto	*cry aloud.*	Pulso	*strike.*
Dicto	*say often.*	†Rogito	*ask often.*
Dictito	*say often.*	Salto	*dance.*
Gesto	*bear*	†Ventito	*come often.*

These are all conjugated regularly; *-āre, -avi, -atum*, except those marked†, which have no perfect or supine; but
Minitor, -āri, -atus sum, is deponent.

2. *Inceptive* Verbs (sometimes called Inchoative) express beginning of action, and are of the *Third* Conjugation, and end in *asco* or *esco;* as—

Labasco, *I begin to totter.*
Pallesco, *I turn pale.*
Puerasco, *I become a boy.*
Mitesco, *I become mild.*

3. *Desiderative* Verbs express desire of action, and are of the *Fourth* Conjugation, and end in *urio ;* as—

Esurio, *I am hungry, wish to eat.*
Parturio, *I am in labour, wish to produce.*

ADVERBS.

There are four kinds of Adverbs—

1. Adverbs of place.
2. Adverbs of time.
3. Adverbs of number.
4. Adverbs of description.

1. Adverbs of place answer the questions—

1. Ubi, *where ?*   4. Unde, *whence ?*
2. Quo, *whither ?*   5. Qua, *which way ?*
3. Quorsum, *whitherward ?* 6. Quatĕnus, quousque, *how far ?*

2. Adverbs of time answer the questions—

1. Quando, ubi, *when ?*   2. Quamdĭu, *how long ?*

3. Adverbs of number answer the question—

Quotĭes, *how often ?*

4. Adverbs of description express

manner   quality   quantity.

Many Adverbs are derived from Adjectives, and end in ē, *ter ;* as—

Pulchrē, *finely.*   Fortĭtēr, *bravely.*
Misĕrē, *wretchedly.*   Sapientēr, *wisely.*

N.B.—Adverbs of negation are non, haud, *not.*

PREPOSITIONS.

There are three classes of Prepositions—

1. Those which are followed by the Accusative Case.
2. Those which are followed by the Ablative.
3. Those which are followed by the Acc. and Abl.

1. Prepositions followed by the Accusative Case—

Ad, *to, at*
Adversus } *toward, against*
Adversum }
Ante, *before*
Apud, *at, in, among*
Circum, *around*
Circa, circiter, *about*
Cis, citra, *on the near side of*
Contra, *against, over against*
Erga, *towards* (of the feelings)
Extra, *outside of, out of*
Infra, *below*
Inter, *between, among, amid*
Intra, *within*

Juxta, *adjoining to, beside*
Ob, *over against, by reason of*
Penes, *in the power of*
Per, *through*
Pone, *behind*
Post, *after, behind*
Præter, *beside*
Prope, *near ;* propius, proxime
Propter, *nigh, on account of*
Secundum, *next, along, according*
Supra, *above* [*to*
Trans, *across*
Ultra, *beyond*
Versus, versum, *towards*

2. Prepositions followed by the Ablative Case—

A, ab, abs, *by* or *from*
Absque, *without*
Clam, *without the knowledge of*
Coram, *in the presence of*
Cum, *with*
De, *down from, from, concerning*

Ex, e, *out of, from*
Palam, *in sight of* [*with*
Præ, *before, owing to, compared*
Pro, *before, for, instead of*
Sine, *without*
Tenus, *reaching to, as far as*

3. Prepositions followed by the Accusative or Ablative—

In, *into, against* (Acc.)
In, *in, upon, among* (Abl.)
Sub, *up to, under* (Acc.)
Sub, *under* (Abl.)
Super, *over, upon*
Subter, *under*

In and *sub*, with Accusative, imply *motion;* with Ablative, *rest.*

CONJUNCTIONS.

There are two kinds of Conjunctions—

1. Co-ordinative.   2. Sub-ordinative.

1. Co-ordinative are those which join words and sentences together, but do not affect mood ; as—

Et, que, ac, atque, *and.*
Aut, vel, ve, *either, or.*
Sed, autem, *but.*
Nam, enim, *for,* etc., etc.

2 Sub-ordinative are those which join sentences, influencing mood ; as—

Ut, *that.*   Quum, *when, since.*
Ne, *lest.*   Si, *if.*
Quod } *because.*   Nisi, *unless.*
Quia }

INTERJECTIONS.

An interjection is used to express pleasure, pain, astonishment, etc., and is used with different cases.

O, O ! *oh !*
A, ah, *alas !*   May be used with a Nominative,
Eheu, heu, *alas !*   Vocative, or Accusative Case.
Pro, proh, *forbid it !*

En   } *lo ! behold !*   { May be used with Nominative or
Ecce }   { Accusative.

Hei, *alas !* } May be used with a Dative.
Væ, *woe !* }

PROSODY.

GENERAL RULES FOR THE QUANTITIES OF LATIN WORDS.

I.

The following are **LONG** :—

1. A vowel before two consonants; as, *jăctántes*.
2. A vowel before a double consonant or a *j* in same word; as, *felĭx, Amázon, Ājăx.*
3. Diphthongs; as, *mensæ, paūca, pænæ, Teūcri, hŭī.*
4. Datives and ablatives singular and plural when they end in *a, æ, i, o, u, is* (and *e* of the 5th declension); as, *mensā, mensæ, lapidī, graduī, meliorī, dominō, bonō, gradū, mensīs, dominīs, faciē.*
5. Accusatives plural, unless they end in *a.*

SHORT.

1. One vowel before another vowel in the same word is *short*, as *vĭa;* but *diĕi, fĭo* are long, and *fidĕi, illius* are common.
2. All cases in *a* except ablative of the first declension and its corresponding adjectives; as, *mensă, bonă.*

COMMON.

Syllables are sometimes common (*i.e.* long or short) when a vowel in the same word stands before two consonants, of which the first is a mute and the second is a liquid (*l, r*); as *dŭplex, latĕbra.*

The last syllable but one (penultimate) of a three-syllable or four-syllable word may be marked *long* or *short* (‒ ◡) as the pupil hears his tutor pronounce it, or as he himself may know; as, *lapĭde, operĭbus, domĭnus, amābam.*

N.B.—This is a very useful rule for all common words which the pupil is familiar with. He marks the penultimate *long* or *short* directly he hears it pronounced in dictation, or because, having heard it again and again, he is quite sure of the quantity.

To see how these few general rules work we subjoin a couplet marked according to these rules—and these rules only—and we find that we have the quantities of considerably more than half the syllables.

Quāscūnque ăspicĭes, lăcrўmæ fecere, litūrās;
Sĕd tamen ĕt lăcrўmæ pŏndĕră vocis habĕnt.

II.

THE LONG AND SHORT *TERMINATIONS* WITH PRINCIPAL EXCEPTIONS.

LONG.

a, i, o, u—c—as, es, os.

a

ā is long, as *frustrā* ; but—
1. Pută, ită, quiă, ejă are short.
2. All cases in *a* are short—as *mensă, operă*—except the ablative of the first declension, as *mensā.*

i is long, as *dominī;* but—
1. Nisĭ, quasĭ are short.
2. Some dative and vocative cases of Greek nouns are short, as Chlorĭ.
3. Mihĭ, tibĭ, sibĭ, ubĭ, ibĭ, have the *i* common.

o

ŏ is long, as dominŏ; but—
egŏ, modŏ, citŏ, duŏ, sciŏ, nesciŏ, are short—putŏ, common.

u

ŭ is long, as tū, genŭ.

c

c is long, as āc, hīc (here); but—
1. Nĕc, donĕc, făc, are short.
2. Hīc (he, this) is common.

as

ăs is long, as musăs; but—
Greek cases in as of third declension, as

Pallăs, lampadăs (acc.), are short, and anăs (a duck).

es

ĕs is long, as hostĕs; but—
1. Some words in es increasing short in the gen. are short—comĕs, comĭtis; but though increasing short —abiēs, ariēs, Cerēs, pēs, are long.
2. Ĕs from sum and its compounds are short, and penĕs and some Greek plurals, as Troadĕs.

os

ŏs is long, as gladiŏs; but some Greek words are short, as Argŏs, Delŏs, and ŏs, ossis (a bone), and compŏs.

SHORT.

e, y—b, d, t, l, r, n—is, ys, us.

e

e is short, as regĕ; but—
1. Imperatives of second conjugation; as, monē;
2. Ablatives of the fifth declension, as diē;
3. Adverbs derived from adjectives in us, as operosē,—are long. Benĕ and malĕ are however short.
4. Monosyllables in e (except the enclitics quĕ, nĕ, vĕ) are long; as, mē, tē, sē, dē, ē, nē.
5. Quarē, hodiē, ferē, fermē, ohē, are long.
6. Cavĕ and cavē are both used.
7. Famē, abl. of fames, is long.

b, d, t, y

are short, as ăb, sĕd, ĕt, amăt, chelȳ.

l

is short, as Hannibăl; but nīl, sāl, sōl, are long—nihĭl, common.

r

r is short, as vĭr; but—
1. Lăr, Năr, vĕr, fūr, cūr.
2. Păr with its compounds dispăr, etc.

3. æthĕr, aĕr, because derived from
αἰθήρ, ἀήρ, are long.

n

n is short, as tegmĕn; but in many Greek words, such as Hymēn, it is long.

Is, ys

ĭs is short, as dulcĭs; but—
1. Datives and ablatives in īs, as domīnīs;
2. Sīs, from sum, and its compound possīs,
3. Vīs, from volo, and its compound, vīs, strength;
4. Second per. sing. of the pres. of the fourth conjugation, as audīs, also malīs, nolīs, velīs, are long. ȳs is short, as chelȳs.

us

ŭs is short, as dominŭs; but—
1. Words increasing long in the genitive, as juventūs, salūs, senectūs;
2. The monosyllables crūs, thūs;
3. The ūs of the fourth declension, except Nom. and Voc. Singular, are long.

Syllables that cannot be marked by the help of this Table and by the General Rules already given must be looked out in Dictionary or Gradus; as for instance the first syllable of words such as quoque, genĕrĕ, gradus, etc.

EPITOME.

There are

8 Parts of Speech.	6 Tenses.
2 Numbers.	3 Persons.
3 Genders.	Singular. I, thou, he.
6 Cases.	Plural. Them, you, they.
5 Declensions (Substantives).	3 Gerunds.
3 Classes of Adjectives.	2 Supines.
8 Kinds of Pronouns.	4 Participles.
4 Conjugations of Verbs.	4 Kinds of Adverbs.
2 Voices.	3 Classes of Prepositions.
4 Moods.	2 Kinds of Conjunctions.

EIGHT PARTS OF SPEECH:

1. Substantive ⎫
2. Adjective ⎬ declined.
3. Pronoun   ⎪
4. Verb   ⎭

5. Adverb   ⎫
6. Preposition ⎬ undeclined.
7. Conjunction ⎪
8. Interjection ⎭

SIX CASES,

with their signs in English.

1. Nominative, No sign.
2. Vocative,   O.
3. Accusative, No sign.
4. Genitive,   Of.
5. Dative,   To or for.
6. Ablative,   In, with, from, by.

FIVE DECLENSIONS OF SUB-STANTIVES.

1. æ. Gen.   3. is.
2. i.   4. ūs.
    5. ei.

TWO NUMBERS:

1. Singular, as mensa, *a table.*
2. Plural, as mensæ, *tables.*

THREE GENDERS:

1. Masculine.
2. Feminine.
3. Neuter.

THREE CLASSES OF ADJECTIVES

1. Those which have in the Nominative *three* termina-tions:

us, a, um, as Bon*us, a, um.*
er, a, um, as Ten*er,* tene*ra,* tene*rum.*
er, is, e, as Ac*er,* ac*ris,* ac*re.*

2. Those which have *two.*
is, e, as Trist*is,* trist*e.*
or, us, as Meli*or,* meli*us.*

3. Those which have *one.*
Feli*x,* ingens, præstans.

PRONOUNS.

There are 8 Kinds of Pronouns:
1. Personal.
2. Reflexive.
3. Possessive.
4. Demonstrative.
5. Definitive.
6. Relative.
7. Interrogative.
8. Indefinite.

1. PERSONAL PRONOUNS :

1. Ego, *I*.
2. Tu, *thou (you)*.

Plur.
3. Nos, *we*.
4. Vos, *you, ye*.

2. REFLEXIVE :

Se (sese), *himself, herself, itself, themselves*.

3. POSSESSIVE :

1. Meus, *mine*.
2. Tuus, *thine, your*.
3. Suus, *his, hers*, etc.
4. Cujus, *whose*.
5. Noster, *ours*.
6. Vester, *yours*.

4. DEMONSTRATIVE :

1. Is, *that, he, she, it*.
2. Hic, *this (near me)*.
3. Ille, *that (yonder)*.
4. Iste, *that (near you)*.

5. DEFINITIVE :

1. Idem, *same*. 2. Ipse, *self*.

6. RELATIVE :

Qui, *who* or *which*.

7. INTERROGATIVE :

Quis, *who* or *what?*

8. INDEFINITE :

Quis (aliquis), *any one*.

VERBS.

Verbs have
4 Conjugations.
2 Voices.
4 Moods.
6 Tenses.
6 Persons.
   3 Singular.
   3 Plural.
3 Gerunds.
2 Supines.
4 Participles.

FOUR CONJUGATIONS
Known by the endings of the Infinitive Mood :

1. Has $\bar{a}$ long before *re*.
2. Has $\bar{e}$ long before *re*.
3. Has $\breve{e}$ short before *re*.
4. Has i long before *re*.

TWO VOICES :
1. Active. 2. Passive.

FOUR MOODS :
1. Indicative.
2. Conjunctive.
3. Imperative.
4. Infinitive.

SIX TENSES:

1. Present.
2. Future Simple.
3. Imperfect.
4. Perfect.
5. Future Perfect.
6. Pluperfect.

THREE PERSONS:

Singular.   I, thou (you), he.
Plural   We, ye (you), they.

THREE GERUNDS:
1. Ending in *dum*.
2. Ending in *di*.
3. Ending in *do*.

TWO SUPINES:
1. Supine in *um*.
2. Supine in *u*.

FOUR PARTICIPLES:
1. Present in *ans* or *ens*.
2. Participle in *dus*.
3. Perfect in *us*.
4. Future in *rus*.

PARTICLES.

The four Parts of Speech which are *undeclined* are:

1. Adverb.   2. Conjunction.
3. Preposition.   4. Interjection.

4 KINDS OF ADVERBS:

1. Adverbs of Place.   2. Adverbs of Time.
3. Adverbs of Number.   4. Adverbs of Description.

3 CLASSES OF PREPOSITIONS:

1. Those which are followed by the Accusative case.
2. Those which are followed by the Ablative.
3. Those which are followed by the Accusative and Ablative.

2 KINDS OF CONJUNCTIONS:

1. Co-ordinative.   2. Sub-ordinative.

INTERJECTIONS

are particles of exclamation, and are not classed or divided except
as regards the cases they are used with.

END OF PART I.

PART II. SYNTAX.

PART II. SYNTAX.

CONTENTS.

PART II. SYNTAX.

A SIMPLE SENTENCE.

THE simplest sentence that can be framed contains a single thought only ; as

Puer amat.   Puer amatur.
The boy loves.   *The boy is loved.*

That of which or of whom something is said is called the *subject*, as, " the boy "; and that which is said of the subject is called the *predicate* (from *prædĭco*, to assert), as " loves," " is loved."

We cannot indeed speak without having a *subject* to speak about, and we cannot frame a sentence without *saying something* concerning that subject.

The *subject* in the simplest sentence is always the Nominative Case, and that which is said about the subject—called the *predicate*—is the Verb.

Now this Subject or Nominative case may be either
    1. A Substantive.
    2. An Adjective used as a Substantive.
    3. A Pronoun.
    4. An Infinitive Mood.
    5. A Clause.

1. Puer amat.   *The boy loves.*
2. Omnes amant vitam.   *All men love life.*
3. Nos amamus.   *We love.*
4. Amare est jucundum.   *To love is pleasant.*
5. Amare patriam est decorum.   *To love one's country is honourable.*

A simple sentence may, however, consist of a single word only—because if a *Pronoun* is the *subject* the latter is implied in the ending of the Verb, as *amamus*, "*we* love," not necessarily *nos amamus*.

But a simple sentence, though not the simplest sentence, may consist of more than a *subject* and *verb* by the introduction of what is called an *object;* as for example in our simplest sentence, " The boy loves," if we wish to say *whom* or *what* the boy loves, we must add an *object*, which will generally be in the Accusative, as

> Puer amat *matrem.*
> *The boy loves* his mother.

Thus we see that a simple sentence may consist of (1) a Subject, (2) a Verb, or Predicate, (3) an Object.

Of course any of these three elements may be extended; *e.g.* we may add

1. An Adjective (say *bonus*) to puer;
2. An Adverb (say *valde*) to amat;
3. An Adjective (say *caram*) to matrem : as

> *Bonus* puer *valde* amat *caram* matrem.
> *The good boy greatly loves his dear mother.*

These Adjectives *bonus* and *caram* are called *epithets* (from two Greek words, ἐπι τίθημι, " epi," *on to,* and "tithēmi," *I place*), and qualify (or *attribute* some *quality to*) each of the Substantives, and hence are said to be *in attribution to* them.

Valde is an Adverb (*i.e.* something added to the Verb) and qualifies the Verb *amat.* The Adverb frequently increases or lessens the force of the Verb. Instead, however, of *valde* we might have had an *adverbial expression,* as *magno studio* (with great affection) :

> Bonus puer amat magno studio caram matrem.

Note that the Object is so generally in the Accusative case that we speak of the *Accusative* or *Object.*

We have already learned that most Verbs take the Accusative after them, but we have also learned that some take other cases; as

> (a) Puer potītur pecuniæ (gen.).
> *The boy gains possession of money.*

> (b) Puer paret matri (dat.).
> *The boy obeys his mother.*

(c) Puer utitur cultro (abl.).
The boy uses his knife.

We can extend a sentence also by putting in some other Substantives which refer to the Substantives we already have, and these second Substantives are then said to be in *apposition*.

Æneas dux amat Achaten comitem.
Æneas the leader loves Achates his attendant.

Here *dux* is in *apposition* to *Æneas*, and *comitem* in *apposition* to *Achaten*.

Again : instead of a *single* we sometimes have a *double* object. One is then called the *nearer object*, and is put in the Accusative case, the other the *remoter object*, and is put in the Dative ; as

Puer dat librum matri.
The boy gives a book to his mother.

These remarks do not apply to the Verbs which are called *Copulative* from *copula*, a link, as

Puer est bonus.   *The boy is good.*
Puer fit vir.   *The boy becomes a man.*
Vir nascitur poeta.   *The man is born a poet.*

For in these sentences the word *linked* or *joined to* the subject and *completing* the sense, is called the *complement* (or completion), both *copula* and *complement* forming the *predicate*.

	PREDICATE.	
Subject.	Copula.	Complement.
Vir.	Nascitur.	Poeta.

Of course the ways of enlarging a simple sentence might be multiplied in a greater degree.

*** Reference is made in the following pages to the *Public School Latin Primer* Rules. This is the meaning of the figures that follow each rule. The more important of these rules are also given in full in Latin and English in parallel columns on pp. 192–206.

FOUR GENERAL RULES.

A.

A FINITE Verb agrees with its Nominative Case in Number and Person. 88.

Rex *pugnat.*	Nos *pugnamus.*
Reges *pugnant.*	Etc., etc., etc.

B.

An Adjective agrees with its Substantive in Gender, Number, and Case. 89.

Fortis rex habet *peritum* ducem.

C.

A Substantive is put in the same Case as that with which it is in apposition. 90.

Rex, *fortis vir,* pugnat.   Rex vincit ducem, *fortem virum.*
Filius regis, *sapientis viri,* pugnat.

D.

A Relative agrees with its Antecedent in everything but in *Case; i.e.* in Gender, Number, and Person. 91.

Rex, *quem* regina amavit, ibat, etc.
Regina, *quam* rex amavit, ibat, etc.
Vidi regem *qui* ibat, etc.
Rex amabit te, O femina, *quæ* amas reginam.

72

THE VERB AND ITS NOMINATIVE OR SUBJECT.

I.

Every finite Verb must have a Nominative Case as its Subject. 93.

Rex pugnat.   *Reges* pugnant.

II.

This Nominative Case or Subject need not always be put in, but is understood.

Pugnat (understand *ille.*)
Pugnant (understand *illi.*)

III.

The Verb must agree with its Nom. Case or Subject in Number (Sing. or Pl.) and in Person (First, Second, Third). 88.

Ego pugno.   Nos pugn*amus.*
Tu pugn*as.*   Vos pugn*atis.*
Ille pugn*at.*   Illi pugn*ant.*

IV.

When a Pronoun (*ego, tu, ille, nos, vos, illi*) is the Nominative Case or Subject, it is only put in for the sake of emphasis or distinction.

Ego pugno, *tu* fugis.
Nos pugnamus, *vos* fugitis.

But " I fight," " we flee," without any distinction between "*I*" and "*we*," would be simply *pugno, fugimus.*

V.

Two or more Substantives of the Singular Number will have a Verb in the Plural Number. 92.

Rex et dux pugnant.

VI.

If the Nominative Case or Subjects are of different Persons (as *Ego tu ille*), the Verb (in the Plural Number of course) will agree with the *First* Person rather than with the *Second*, and with the *Second* rather than with the *Third.* 92, 1.

Ego et tu pugnamus.
Tu et ille pugnatis.

VII.

Sometimes an Infinitive Mood is the Nominative Case or Subject to a Verb, which Infinitive Mood is then considered a Substantive in the Neuter Gender. 140, I. 26, 4.

Mentiri est improbum.

VIII.

Sometimes a clause is the Nominative Case or Subject; and this is also looked upon as a Neuter Substantive. 156, 3.

Celare suas culpas mentiendo est improbum.

IX.

Though it has been stated that all Verbs have a Nominative Case or Subject, yet there are *Impersonal Verbs,* of which more will be said (see page 106, 107)

THE ADJECTIVE AND SUBSTANTIVE.

I.

The use of the Adjective is to describe the nature of the Sub·
stantive with which it goes, *i.e.*, it " qualifies the Substantive."

II.

The Adjective (including the Participle and   Adjective Pronoun,
which partake of the nature of the Adjective) agrees with the
Substantive in Gender, Number, and Case—*i.e.*, if the Substantive
be of the Masculine Gender, the Adjective must be Masculine ;
if the Substantive be of the Singular Number, the Adjective
must be Singular ; if the Substantive be in the Nominative Case,
the Adjective must be in the Nominative, &c.

Bonus rex regit cives.   Rex laudat *fortem* ducem.
Doni reges regunt cives.   Rex laudat *fortes* duces.

Bonus rex regit cives.
rex being Masculine, *bonus* is Masculine
rex being Singular, *bonus* is Singular
rex being Nominative, *bonus* is Nominative

Doni reges regunt cives.
reges being Masculine, *boni* is Masculine
reges being Plural, *boni* is Plural
reges being Nominative, *boni* is Nominative.

Rex laudat fortem ducem
ducem being Masculine, *fortem* is Masculine
ducem being Singular, *fortem* is Singular
ducem being Accusative, *fortem* is Accusative.

III.

If the Adjective, however, has to go with Substantives, which are
of different Genders, it agrees with the Masculine rather than
the Feminine ; but in things without life it will often be put in
the Neuter Gender. 92, 2.   92 (*a.*)

Rex et regina sunt boni.
Labor (m) et ignavia (f.) sunt dissimillima (n.)

IV.

Adjectives are often used by themselves as Substantives to re·
present either persons or things, 156, as

Multi, *many men.*
Multa, *many things.*
Vera dicere est honestum.

APPOSITION.

When two Substantives come together representing the same thing, they are put in the same Case. 90.

Reges, *fortes viri*, pugnant.
Rex amat reginam, *bonam feminam.*
Filius regis, *fortis viri*, pugnat.
Rex dat ensem duci, *bono viro*.
Rex utitur ense, *acuto telo*.

But the two Substantives need not necessarily be of the same Number or Gender.

Vixit Thebis *magno oppido*.
Dedit regi ensem, *donum reginæ*.

This is called Apposition—from *appono, to place beside*—

a Substantive placed (*in meaning*) by the side of another Substantive.

To explain this—

Reges, fortes viri, pugnant

As *reges* and *viri* are both of them evidently the same persons referred to—put in *apposition*, or placed *by the side of each other*—they are both of them in the same Case, the Nominative.

Rex dat ensem duci, bono viro.

Here *viro*, referring to *duci*, is put in the same Case as *duci* (Dative). In the last sentence (*Rex utitur ense*, &c.) it is very plain that *telo* refers to *ense;* it is therefore put in the same Case as *ense* (Ablative).

THE RELATIVE AND ANTECEDENT.

I.

The *Relative* means the Relative Pronoun "qui," which *relates* or *refers* to some person or thing mentioned before.

The *Antecedent* means the person or thing mentioned before—from *ante*, before, and *cedo*, to go.

The *Relative* and *Antecedent* are doubtless most difficult for young boys to understand, chiefly because, in whatever Case the Relative Pronoun is, it must, according to the English language, come before its Verb to make sense, and because it has to be taken as near

I.

to its Antecedent as possible. Many boys will parse

Puer fecit hoc,
The boy did this,

who will not be able to parse

Quod puer fecit,
Which the boy did,

though both contain simply a Nominative Case, a Verb, and an Accusative Case. They will stumble at the latter because they have to take the Accusative Case first.

II.

This Relative Pronoun agrees (see p. 31), with its Antecedent (*i. e.,* the word to which it refers) in everything but *Case*.

91

Rex, *qui* amavit reginam, ibat, &c.
Regina, *quæ* amavit regem, ibat, &c.
Reges, *quos* regina amavit, ibant, &c.
Regina, *quam* rex amavit, ibat, &c.
Rex amavit te, O femina, quæ amas reginam.

Taking the first sentence—

Rex, qui amavit reginam, ibat, &c.

rex being Sing., *qui* is also Sing.
rex being Mas., *qui* is also Mas.
rex being 3rd Per., *qui* is also 3rd Per.

But though *rex* is Nom. and *qui* is Nom., *qui* is not the Nom. because *rex* is, for *rex* is the Nom. to the Verb *ibat*, and *qui* is the Nom. to *amavit*.

Taking the fourth sentence—

Regina, quam rex amavit, ibat, &c.

Regina being Fem., *quam* is also Fem.
Regina being Sing., *quam* is also Sing.

But *regina* is Nom. and *quam* is Acc., because *regina* is the Nom. to the Verb *ibat* and *quam* is the Acc. after the Verb *amavit*.

III.

The *Case* of the Relative Pronoun may be *any Case* which the Verb governs, as—

Ensis, *quem* dux habet, est acutus

Pauperes, *quorum* boni miserentur, sunt grati (thankful).
Morbus, *cui* medicus medetur, est gravis.
Ensis, *quo* rex utitur, est acutus.

Again—

Rex, *cui* dux dat ensem, est fortis.
Rex, *cujus* ensis est acutus, est fortis.
Rex, *a quo* civitas gubernator, est fortis.
Milites, *quibuscum* dux ibat, sunt fortes.

In the sentences given above it will be seen that in turning them into English the Relative Pronoun, in whatever case it is, is taken before its Verb, that it may come as near to its Antecedent—the word to which it refers—as possible, as—

The sword, *which* the leader has, &c.
    which Acc. after *has*.
The poor, *whom* the good pity, &c.
    whom Gen. after *pity*.
The disease, *which* the physician, &c.
    which Dat. after *heal*.
The sword, *which* the king uses, &c.
    which Abl. after *uses*.

Again—

The king, *to whom* the leader gives, &c. *to whom* Dat. after *gives*.
The king, *whose* sword is sharp, &c.
    whose Gen. of the possessor.
The king, *by whom* the state is, &c.
    whom Abl. after *a*.
The soldiers, *with whom* the general, &c.
    whom Abl. after *cum*.

THE VERB AND ITS ACCUSATIVE OR OBJECT.

I.

All ordinary Transitive Verbs take an Accusative case after them, which Accusative Case is called the nearer object. 95, 96.

Rex laudat *ducem.*

The word *Transitive* is made up of two Latin words, *trans*, across, and *eo*, to go. To our present purpose it will signify *passing over*, and it means, when spoken of a Verb, that the action of the Verb *passes over* to the Noun which governs it.

By an ordinary Transitive Verb, then, is meant a Verb after which you can place some Common Substantive to complete the sense, as—

I touch.

This will take any such common word, as *table, chair, pen, ink, book, cat, dog, house,* &c.

In other words, there is an action in *touch* which passes on to *table, chair, pen, ink,* &c.

II.

A Verb is call *Intransitive*—that is, *not* Transitive (*in*

II.

implying *not*)—when there is no action in the Verb to pass over

Sto, *I stand.*
Arbor crescit, *the tree grows.*
Avis volat, *the bird flies.*

Here it can be seen that *stand, grows, flies* are *Intransitive*, for there is no action to *pass over.* We need put no Substantive after them to make sense.

Intransitive Verbs then (as a rule) take no Case.

Intransitive Verbs are also called *Neuter.*

The following are some common *Neuter* or *Intransitive* Verbs—

Cado, *I fall.*   Sedeo, *I sit.*
Cubo, *I lie down.*   Sto, *I stand.*
Curro, *I run.*   Vivo, *I live.*

III.

Some Neuter Verbs, however, *do* take an Accusative after them, but only an Accusative of some particular word which is of like meaning with the Verb.

Servio *servitutem.*   Ludo *aleam.*
                    Vivo *vitam.*

This Accusative is called the Accusative of *kindred meaning.*

97

THE NOMINATIVE AFTER THE VERB.

Although most verbs take after them an *Accusative* Case, after some a *Nominative* appears, a full list of which will be found on p. 156 of P.S.L.P.

They are—

1. Copulative Verbs.
2. The Passive of those Verbs which in the Active are called Factitive Verbs.

N.B.—These words—Copulative, Factitive, &c.—are explained, see P.S.L.P. p. 176, and p. 75.

I.

The Copulative Verbs are—

Sum, *I am.*
Fio, *I become.*
Appareo, *I appear.*
Existo, *I stand forth.*
Audio, *I am called.*
Maneo, *I remain.*
Nascor, *I am born.*
Videor, *I seem.*
Evado, *I turn out.*

II.

The following are the passive of some of the principal Factitive Verbs—

Habeor, *I am esteemed.*
Existimor. *I am thought.*
Nominor, *I am named.*
Appellor, *I am called.*
Dicor, *I am said.*
Creor, *I am created.*

It will be seen that after these Verbs a Nominative appears, which must be regarded as a *Complement*, or that which *completes* the sense.

Examples—

$$\text{Rex} \begin{cases} \text{est} \\ \text{fit} \\ \text{videtur} \\ \text{habetur} \\ \text{appellatur} \\ \text{vocatur} \end{cases} \text{dux.}$$

Nemo nascitur *sapiens.*
Poeta evadit *orător.*

III.

When, however, the Copulative Verb is in the Infinitive, and is preceded by an Accusative, its Complement will also be in the Accusative.

$$\text{Dicunt } \textit{regem} \begin{cases} \text{esse} \\ \text{fieri} \\ \text{vocari} \end{cases} \textit{ducem.}$$

Dicunt *poetam* evadére *oratórem.*

The Latin Primer Rule for this is : "*Copulative Verbs. whether finite or infinite, generally have a Complement agreeing with the Subject,*" but this requires some such explanation as we have given above.

THE GENITIVE AFTER THE VERB.

I.

Some Verbs are followed by the Genitive—*Sum* when it signifies—127 (*b*)

Nature Function Token Dùty

Hom*inis* est (*it is the nature*) errare.
Reg*is* est (*it is the duty*) imperare recte

II.

Interest, *it imports.* Refert, it *concerns.* 129.

Reg*is* interest regere recte.
Reg*is* refert regere recte.

III.

Verbs of Accusing, Acquitting, Condemning, Warning, &c. 133.

These, as well as a Genitive case of the charge, take an Accusative of the Object (see p. 12).

Rex
{ accusat ducem *ignaviæ.*
condemnat ducem mult*orum* scel*erum.*
absolvit ducem *ignaviæ.*
admonet ducem pristi*næ fortunæ.*

IV.

Many Verbs of Abounding, Wanting, Enriching, Depriving (and also Potior). 119 (*b*)

Rex { eget *pecuniæ.*
potitur *urbis.*
liberat ducem *culpæ.*

These also take an Ablat., see p.

V.

Misereor and miseresco, *I pity.* 135.

Misereor
Miseresco } pauper*um.*

Miseror, commiseror, take an Accusative

VI.

Memini, reminiscor, recordor, *I remember*; obliviscor, *I forget* 133 (*a*).

Rex {
meminit
reminiscitur
recordatur
obliviscitur
} suarum cul-parum.

These also take an Acc. (see p.83).

VII.

Piget, *it irks;* Pudet, *it shames;* Pœnitet, *it repents;* Tædet, *it disgusts;* Miseret, *it moves pity*—take a Genitive with an Accusative (see p. 82). 134.

Regem {
piget
pudet
pœnitet
tædet
} scelerum (crimes.)

Regem miseret pauperum.

These sentences literally rendered, are—

It irks, it shames, it repents, the king,

but in construing, the Accusative should be taken first, as if it were a Nominative.—

The king repents, &c., of his crimes.

THE DATIVE AFTER THE VERB.

I.

Some Verbs are followed by the Dative. Many of these may be remembered if learned in the following rhyme (See Henry's " First Latin Book," (pp. 62, 63) :

A Dative put, remember pray,
After *envy, spare, obey,*
Persuade,believe, command; to these
Add *pardon, succour,* and *displease;*
With *vacare* " to have leisure,"
And *placēre* " to have pleasure,"
With *nubere* (of the female said),
The English of it is " to wed ;"
Servire add, and add *studere,*
Heal, *favour, hurt,resist,* and *indul-
gere.*

104, 105, 106.

N.B.—Juvo *I please,* lædo *I hurt,* govern an Acc. Jubeo *I order* governs an Acc. (or Dative).

> invidet (envies)
> parcit spares)
> paret (obeys)
> persuadet (per-
>   suades)
> credit (believes)
> imperat (commands)
> Rex   ignoscit (pardons)   *duci.*
> succurrit (succours)
> displicet (displeases)
> placet (pleases)
> favet (favours)
> nocet (hurts)
> resistit (opposes)

Rex vacat (has leisure for) *philo-
sophiæ.*
Regina nubit (marries) *regi.*
Rex servit (is the slave of) *duci.*

I

Rex studet (is eager after) *literis.*
Medicus medetur (heals) *morbo.*
Rex indulget (indulges in) *dolori.*

II.

Verbs compounded with the following Particles—106 (*a.*)

bene, male, satis, re,
ad, ante, con, in, inter, de,
ob, sub, super, post *et* præ.

> benefacit (does good to)
> maledicit   (speaks ill
>   of)
> satisfacit (satisfies)
> resistit (resists)
> adhæret (keeps close
>   to)
> antecellit (surpasses)
> confidit (trusts in)
> infert bellum (wages
> Rex   war on)   *duci.*
> interdicit (forbids) bel-
>   lum
> detrahit (takes away
>   from) pecuniam
> obstat (opposes)
> subvenit (assists)
> superfuit (has out-
>   lived)
> præstat (is superior
>   to)

Rex postfert (sacrifices) suas opes *libertati.*

*Many Verbs, however, so com-
pounded are construed with the Accusative or with the Case of their
own Preposition — the Preposition
being of course repeated.*

III.

Sum, with its compounds except *possum*. 107 (*b*).

Absum, *I am absent.*
Adsum, *I am present, stand by.*
Desum, *I am wanting.*
Insum, *I am in*, or *upon.*
Intersum, *I take part in.*
Obsum, *I am against, injure.*
Præsum, *I am at the head of.*
Prosum, *I am serviceable.*
Subsum, *I am under.*
Supersum, *I survive.*

Rex {
  est causa doloris *duci.*
  abest reginæ.
  adest duci.
  interfuit prœliis.
  obfuit duci.
  præfuit exercitui.
  prodest multis.
  superfuit reginæ.
}

III.

Virtus *deest* (is wanting to) *regi.*
Magna fortitudo *inerat duci.*
Dux *subest arbori.*

IV.

Est, sunt, when used for *habeo*, take a Dative. 107 (*c*.)

Est mihi pater—There is a father to me; i.e., *I have a father.*

V.

Sum and other Verbs are sometimes followed by two Datives, one being used as a Complement, the other being the Dative of the Recipient. 108.

Mare est *exitio nautis*—The sea is *a destruction to sailors.* (See p.   .)

THE ABLATIVE AFTER THE VERB.

I.

Some Verbs are followed by the Ablative. 119 (IX. *a.*)

Fungor, *to perform.*
Fruor, *to enjoy.*
Utor, *to use.*
Vescor, *to eat (feed upon.)*
Potior, *to get possession of.*
Dignor, *to deem worthy.*

Rex {
  fungitur *munere* ducis.
  fruitur *victoriâ.*
  utitur *pecuniâ.*
  vescitur *carne.*
  potitur *urbe.*
  dignatur se *honore.*
}

Potior takes also a Gen. (see p.79).

II.

Verbs of Abounding, Wanting, Enriching, Depriving. 119 (*b.*)

Rex {
  abundat (abounds) *divitiis.*
  eget (is in need of) *pecuniâ.*
  locupletavit (enriched) ducem *auro.*
  fraudat (defrauds) me *pecuniâ.*
}

These also take a Gen. (p.79.).

III.

Verbs when compounded with Prepositions, *ab, de, ex.* 122 (*a.*)

Consul *magistratu* abiit (retired from office.)
Rex se dejecit (threw himself down *equo.*
Dux exiit (went out of) *domo.*

F

VERBS WHICH TAKE TWO CASES.

ACCUSATIVE AND GENITIVE.

I.

Verbs of Accusing, Acquitting, Condemning, Warning.

Rex
{
accusat duc*em* ignavi*æ* (cowardice.)
condemnat duc*em* mult*orum* sceler*um.*
absolvit (acquits) duc*em* ignavi*æ.*
admonet duc*em* pristin*æ* fortun*æ.*
}

II.

Piget, *it irks.*	Pœnitet, *it repents.*
Pudet, *it shames.*	Tædet, *it disgusts.*
	Miseret, *it moves pity.*

Regem
{
piget
pudet
pœnitet
tædet
}
scelerum

Regem miseret pauper*um.*

ACCUSATIVE AND DATIVE.

Verbs of Comparing, Giving, Restoring, Promising, Owing, Paying, Telling, Threatening, Withdrawing.

Rex confert magn*a* parv*is.*

Rex
{
dat præmi*um*
reddit præmi*um*
promittit præni*um*
debet pecuni*am*
solvit pecuni*am*
narrabat h*æc*
minatur mort*em*
detrahit pecuni*am*
}
duci

In all these sentences the Accusative is the Case of the *nearer Object.* and the Dative the Case of the *remoter Object.*

VERBS WHICH TAKE EITHER OF TWO CASES.

GENITIVE OR ACCUSATIVE.

Memini, *I remember.*
Recordor, *I remember.*
Reminiscor, *I remember*
Obliviscor, *I forget.*

Rex $\left\{\begin{array}{l}\text{meminit}\\\text{reminiscitur}\\\text{recordatur}\\\text{obliviscitur}\end{array}\right\}$ $\left\{\begin{array}{l}\text{su}\textit{arum} \text{ culp-}\\\textit{arum} \quad (\text{or}\\\text{euas culp}\textit{as}.)\end{array}\right.$

GENITIVE OR ABLATIVE.

See pp.79.81.

Verbs of Abounding or Wanting,
Enriching or Depriving, as also
potior.

Rex eget pecuni*æ* (or pecnni*â*).
Rex potitur urb*is* (or nrb*e*).
Rex liberat ducem culp*æ* (or culp*â*).

VERBS WHICH TAKE A DOUBLE CASE.

TWO ACCUSATIVES—PERSON AND THING.

Verbs of Asking, Teaching, Entreating, Demanding, Admonishing, Concealing.

Rex $\left\{\begin{array}{l}\text{rogavit } \textit{hoc} \text{ duc}\textit{em.}\\\text{docuit fili}\textit{um} \text{ liter}\textit{as.}\\\text{orat } \textit{te hoc.}\\\text{poscit ducem pac}\textit{em.}\\\text{monuit ducem } \textit{ea.}\\\text{celavit } \textit{ea} \text{ duc}\textit{em.}\end{array}\right.$

TWO ACCUSATIVES—OBJECT AND COMPLEMENT.

Verbs of making, Calling, Thinking, &c.

Rex $\left\{\begin{array}{l}\text{fecit milit}\textit{em} \text{ duc}\textit{em.}\\\text{vocavit urb}\textit{em} \text{ Rom}\textit{am}\\\text{putat duc}\textit{em} \text{ stult}\textit{um}\end{array}\right.$

TWO DATIVES.

Sum with other words.

Filius est dedecor*i* matr*i*—*The son is a disgrace to his mother.*
Vertis id vitio mih*i*—*You impute it as a fault to me.*

ADJECTIVES AND THEIR CASES.

It should be noted here, that although logically the construction of Cases
with Verbs and Adjectives ought to be considered under one head, it has been
found convenient in this very elementary work to treat the Verbs and
Adjectives apart.

Adjectives, like Verbs, take certain Cases after them. We
will give them in the following order.

1. Those which take the Genitive.
2. Those which take the Dative.
3. Those which take the Ablative.
4. Those which take the Genitive or Ablative.

THE GENITIVE AFTER THE ADJECTIVE.

I

The Genitive of the Thing Measured follows words denoting
quantity, such as *satis, parum,* &c., and Neuter Adjectives, such
as *aliquid, multum,* &c.   131.

Rex habet *satis sapientiæ (sufficient wisdom.)*
Rex habet *multum pecuniæ (much money.)*

II.

Adjectives which signify—

skill,   knowledge,   desire,   fear,
care,   memory,   power,   innocence,

and their contraries —132 (I.), 133 (II.)—

take a Genitive after them—

Rex est
{
peritus *belli.*
negligens *(regardless of) officii.*
cupidus *laudis.*
potens *(master of) sui*
conscius *recti.*
memor *beneficii.*
timidus *mortis.*
insons *mendacii (falsehood)*
}

THE DATIVE AFTER THE ADJECTIVE.

Adjectives which signify—

advantage,	pleasure,
disadvantage,	displeasure,
likeness,	submission,
unlikeness,	nearness, &c., &c.

take a Dative after them. 105, 106.

Rex est
$\begin{cases} \text{utilis } patriæ, \text{ inutilis } exercitui. \\ \text{similis } deo, \text{ dissimilis } patri. \\ \text{gratus } omnibus. \\ \text{supplex } reginæ. \\ \text{finitimus } (near\ akin\ to)\ pootæ \end{cases}$

THE ABLATIVE AFTER THE ADJECTIVE.

I.

The following Adjectives take an Ablative—119 (IX. *a*)—

dignus, *worthy;*
indignus, *unworthy;*
contentus, *contented;*
fretus, *relying;*
præditus, *endued.*

ex est
$\begin{cases} \text{dignus } culpâ. \\ \text{indignus } laude. \\ \text{contentus } parvo, \\ \text{præditus } virtute. \end{cases}$

Rex fretus *divitiis* abiit

II.

As also the Substantives *opus* and *usus*—119 (IX. *a*).

Opus est mihi *pecuniâ.*
Usus est mihi *pecuniâ.*

III.

Adjectives which take a Geni tive or Ablative. 119 (IX. *b*.)

abounding,
wanting,
enriching,
depriving.

Terra est dives *equorum* (or *equis*).
Rex est expers *metus* (or *metu*).

DIFFERENT USES OF CASES.

We have given the Cases as they come after Verb or Adjective. We proceed now to consider some of the different uses of the different Cases, and to give examples.

NOMINATIVE.

I.

The Nominative as Subject. 93.

Rex pugnat.

II.

Nominative put in Apposition. 90.

Rex, filius ducis, pugnat.

III.

Nominative used in exclamations with or without an Interjection. 138.

Infandum !—Unutterable !
Ecce nova turba !—Lo ! a new disturbance !

IV.

Nominative, with *quam*, after Comparative. 124, xiv. (I.)

Ferrum est durius quam cera.

Nominative after certain Verbs (see p.78).

VOCATIVE.

The Vocative is said to stand out of the sentence, as it never depends on any word. 137.

O Rex, pugnas.

ACCUSATIVE.

I.

Accusative as Subject of the Infinitive. 93 (2).

Scio regem pugnare.

N.B.—This will be fully explained in another place (see p.100).

II.

Accusative put in Apposition. 90.

Rex laudat ducem, fortem virum.

III.

Accusative of Respect. 100.

Rex tremit artus.
Rex est nudus lacertos.

IV.

Accusatives used in Exclamations with or without an Interjection. 138.

Me miserum, wretched me !
En quatuor aras ! Lo, four altars !

V.

Accusative, Duration of Time 102 (1).

Rex regnavit duos annos.

VI.

Accusative, Measure of Space. 102 (2).

Muri erant *duos pedes* alti.
See Ablative of Measure, p.

VII.

Accusative, after certain Prepositions (see list, p.58).

Rex dixit *contra spem.*

VIII.

Accusative of Place *Whither.* 101.

Rex ivit *Romam.*

IX.

Accusative, with *quam*, after Comparative. 124 (xiv. 2)

Puto mortem leviorem *quam dedecus.*

Accusative after Transitive Verbs, as already mentioned.

GENITIVE.

I.

Genitive of the Author and Possessor. 127.

Rex est filius *ducis.*

II.

Genitive put in Apposition. 90.

Rex est filius ducis, *fortis viri.*

III.

Genitive of Quality (with Epithet. 128 (II.)

Rex est vir *magnæ fortitudinis.*

III.

Ablative may be also used (see p. 88.)

IV.

Elliptic Genitives. (128) (*a.*)

Parvi, *of little value.*
Minoris, *of less value.*
Minimi, *of very little value.*
Magni, *of great value.*
Pluris, *of more value.*
Plurimi, *of high value.*
Tanti, *of so great value or price.*
Quanti, *of what price.*
Maximi. *of very great price.*

Rex emit fundum *magni, at a great price.*

Genitive after certain Verbs (see p.79.) and Adjectives.

DATIVE.

I.

Dative in Apposition. 90.

Rex dat librum *duci, forti viro*

II.

With the exclamations, hei, alas! væ, *woe!* 139.

He *mihi!* Væ *regi!*

III.

Dative after certain Verbs (see p.80). 104, 105, 106.

ABLATIVE.

I.

Ablative in Apposition.   90.

Rex utitur *ense, telo acuto.*

II.

Ablative after the Comparative degree.   124 (XIV.)

Rex est *fortior duce.*

III.

Ablative after certain Prepositions (see list).   122 (XII.)

Dux dicebat *coram rege.*

After some when compounded.

Rex abiit *magistratu.*

IV.

Ablative of the Agent takes the Preposition, *a*, *ab.*   122 (XII. *b*).

Rex culpatur *a reginâ.*

V.

Ablative of Cause (*a.*)

Rex est bonus *amore* virtutis.

VI.

Ablative of the Instrument. (*b.*)

Rex defendit se *manibus.*

VII.

Ablative of Manner (*c*)

Rex vicit ducem *fraude.*

Excepting in a few phrases Ablative of Manner without Epithet requires *cum.*

VIII.

Ablative of Condition.   (*d.*)

Rex est fortis *mea sententia.*

IX.

Ablative of Quality with Epithet.   (*e.*)

Rex est *benigno vultu.*

X.

Ablative of Respect.   (*f.*)

Rex augitur (*is distressed*) *animo.*

XI.

Ablative of Price.   (*g.*)

Rex emit fundum *magna pecunia.*

XII.

Ablative of Measure.   (*h.*)

Murus erat latus *pede* (*a foot broad.*)

XIII.

Ablative of Matter.   (*i.*)

Cibus ducis constat *carne,* &c.

XIV.

Ablative of Time *When?* 120 (X.)

Rex pugnavit *hieme.*
Rex veniet *biduo* (*in two days*).
Romulus vixit *paucis annis* ante
Numam, *multis annis* post Home-
rum.

XV.

Ablative of Place *Where?*   121 (XI. *B.*)

See Locative Case, below.

Rex vixit *Neapoli* et postea *Thebis.*
Templa patent (*are open*) *tota urbe.*

XVI.

Ablative of a Town when the question is *Whence?* 121 (XI.*C.*)

Rex fugit *Roma.*
So also with *domo* and *rure.*

XVII.

The Ablative of Place is put without a Preposition, when the question is *By what road?*
121 (XI. *A.*)

Rex ibat præcipiti via.

XVIII.

Ablative Absolute.   (125)

Urbe condita, Romulus factus est rex.

This Ablative Absolute, how-ever, we must explain at greater length.

LOCATIVE CASE.

I.

See Latin Primer.   121 (B, *a.*)

"Place Where" is put in a Case resembling the Genitive Singular if the word be of the First or Second Declension, *Singular Number;* if not, in a Case resembling the Ablative.

II.

Like to the above are used.   121 (B, *b*).

humi, *on the ground.*	belli	} *at the*
domi, *at home.*	militiæ	} *wars*

ruri, *in the country.*

Rex est fortis *domi* et *militiæ.*

ABLATIVE ABSOLUTE.*

The Latin Primer Rule is as follows :

A Substantive combines with a Participle in the Ablative which is called Absolute.

Now this requires some explanation which a teacher will always supply when possible *vivâ voce* to his pupil or class. But some people take up the study of Latin without any help but that derived from Books. Hence many explanations in the Author's Books will, of course, be passed over by those who, in a much better way, will make the explanation by word of mouth.

In turning Latin into English, the rule for construing is this :

Take the Ablative Case of the Substantive as if it were a *Nominative* —by which I mean, take it without putting any sign before it—and then take the Participle either *directly*, or *as soon after* as you can.

It must be noted, however, that it is not always a *Substantive* that is used ; but sometimes it may be an *Adjective* (used

as a Substantive), and sometimes the Relative Pronoun.

EXAMPLE 1.—"In eodem quondam prato pascebantur anseres et grues. *Adveniente domino* prati, grues,' &c., &c.

The Latin words in italics form an Ablative Absolute. Follow the Rule given. Take the Ablative Case of the Substantive, *domino*, but put no sign to it— saying, *Domino*, " the master ;" *prati*, " of the field ; " and then the Participle (which you will find in the Ablative Case, *ad veniente*, " coming up." " The master of the field coming up, the cranes (easily flew away)."

EXAMPLE 2.—" Mures aliquando habuerunt consilium quomodo a fele caverent. *Multis aliis propositis*, omnibus placuit," &c.

Multis aliis propositis is an Ablative Absolute in the Plural Number. There is no Substantive to take, but there are two Adjectives. So we take *multis aliis*, putting no sign before it, and say, *Multis aliis*, "many other things;" *propositis*, having been proposed *placuit*, "it pleased," &c.,&c.,&c.

* N.B.--Absolute, *i.e.* released (absolutus) so to speak from government.

Example 3.—" Agricola senex quum mortem sibi propinquare sentiret, filios convocavit, quos, ut fieri solet, interdum discordare noverat, et fascem virgultorum afferri jussit. *Quibus allatis*, filios hortabatur, &c. &c.

Quibus allatis is an Ablative Absolute, the Relative Pronoun being used. We take *quibus* (agreeing with *virgultis*, understood), putting no sign before it, and say, *Quibus*, " which ; " *allatis*, " having been brought ;" *hortabatur*, " he exhorted," &c.

Sometimes instead of a *Participle* another Substantive (or an Adjective) is used.

Cæsare duce vincemus.

Cæsar, being our leader, we shall conquer.

There will be still more difficulty in knowing when to use an Ablative Absolute in turning English into Latin.

The King, when he has conquered his enemies, will return home.

Here it is said that the King will do a certain thing after another thing has been done— that he will return home when he has conquered his enemies ; *when he has conquered his enemies*

may therefore be put into an Ablative Absolute, as—

Rex, *hostibus victis*, red bit domum.

If you are my leader, I shall conquer.

If you are my leader may be an Ablative Absolute.

Te duce, vincam.

Care must be taken not to put in the Ablative Case a Substantive having a participle agreeing with it when it forms the *subject of the Verb.*

Cæsar, being made consul, departed

We must not put the words *Cæsar being made Consul* as an Ablative Absolute ; if we did, we should leave " departed" without any Nominative Case.

Cæsar factus consul, (not *Cæsare facto consule)* abiit.

If, however, we say ;

Cæsar, his enemies being conquered, departed.

we can put *his enemies being conquered* into an Ablative Absolute (victis hostibus), as it does not form the Nominative Case or Subject to the Verb.

QUAM AFTER THE COMPARATIVE DEGREE.

There are two ways of expressing the word "than" in Latin aft.r a comparative degree (124 xiv.).

I. By the word *quam*, which is followed by *any* case, the things compared being in the *same* case.

Iron is harder than wax.
Ferrum est durius quam *cera.*

They say that iron is harder than wax.
Dicunt *ferrum* esse *duriorem* quam *ceram.*

Sooner forget injuries than kindnesses.
Citius obliviscere *injuriarum* quam *beneficiorum.*

II. By the Ablative case, *quam* being left out.

Iron is harder than wax.
Ferrum est durius *cerâ* (Abl.).

I think that death is lighter than disgrace.
Puto mortem esse leviorem *dedecore.*

But in comparison with cases other than the Nominative or Accusative *quam* must be used, as also where its omission would cause any ambiguity.

This is more useful to me than to you.
Hoc est utilius *mihi* quam *tibi.*

I have lost more money than you (have).
Ego amisi plus pecuniæ quam *tu.*

He is richer in lands than in servants.
Est ditior *agris* quam *ministris.*

SEQUENCE OF TENSES.

One very important thing for a boy to remember is the proper Sequence of Tenses.

The Present, Future, and Perfect (with " have"), are followed by *Present or Perfect Subjunctive, or Future Participle in* rus *with* Sim.

The Imperfect, Pluperfect, and Perfect are followed by *Imperfect or Pluperfect Subjunctive, or Future Participle in* rus *with* Essem.

Quæro, *1 ask.*	Quid agas, *what you are doing.*
Quæram, *1 will ask.*	Quid egeris, *what you did or have done.*
Quæsivi, *1 have asked.*	Quid acturus sis, *what you are going to do.*

Quærebam, *I was asking.*	Quid ageres, *what you were doing.*
Quæsivi, *1 asked.*	Quid egisses, *what you had done.*
Quæsiveram, *1 had asked.*	Quid acturus esses, *what you were about to do.*

Let these points also be noted.

Dicit se amare, *he says that he is loving.*
Dixit se amare, *he said that he was loving.* .

Dicit se amavisse, *he says that he has loved, or loved.*
Dixit se amavisse, *he said that he had loved.*

Pollicetur se amaturum esse, *he promises that he will love.*
Pollicitus est se amaturum esse, *he promised that he would love.*

INFINITIVE MOOD.

I.

The Verb Infinite consists of Verb-Nouns.

(1.) The Infinitive.

(2.) The Gerunds } which supply
(3.) The Supines } cases to Infinitive.

(4.) Participles.

See Latin Primer, 45 (II.)

II.

The Infinitive with the Gerunds, Participles, and Supine in *um*, governs the same cases as the Verb Finite. 142 (III.)

Dux vult obedire *magistro.*
Dux cupidus est obediendi *magistro.*

III.

The Infinitive is often used as a Substantive for the Nominative or Accusative Case. 140 (I.)

Discere (Nom) est difficile.
Puer dicit (calls it) miserum *mori*
(Acc.)

IV

It is used Obliquely (or in what is known as Enuntiatio Obliqua) with Accusative of Subject. 140 (3); 93 (2).

Aiunt terram *esse* rotundam.

V.

It is used in narration for a Finite Verb. 140 (2).

Fors omnia *regere.*
Chance governed all things.

VI.

It is used to carry on the construction of a Verb or Adjective. 140 (4).

Puir voluit *discere* multa
Puer paratus (ready) *discere* multa

GERUNDS.

I.

There are three Gerunds ending in *dum*, *di*, *do*, reckoned as part of the Verb Infinite, and, as mentioned above, forming as it were cases when the Infinitive is declined as a Verbal Substantive.

II.

These Gerunds are called

1. Accusative in *dum*, Amand*um*, *loving.*
2. Genitive in *di*, Amand*i*, *of loving.*
3. Dative or Ablative in *do*, Amand*o*, *to* or *for* or *by loving.*

III.

The *Accusative* Gerund is joined to Prepositions. 141 (1.)

Puer natus est *ad agendum.*

IV.

The *Genitive* Gerund is joined to Substantives and Adjectives. 141 (2).

Rex didicit artem *scribendi.*
Rex est cupidus bene *scribendi.*

V.

The *Dative* Gerund is joined to Nouns and Verbs 141 (3.)

Puer dat operam *discendo.*

VI.

The *Ablative* Gerund is of cause or manner, or is used with a Preposition. 141 (4.)

Puer discit *docendo.*
Puer vincit *pugnando.*
Reges rixantur (quarrel) *de spoliando.*

SUPINES.

I.

There are two Supines called—
1. Supine in *um*, Amat*um*, *to love.*
3. Supine in *u*, Amat*u*, *to be loved.*

II.

The Supine in *um* is an Accusative after Verbs of motion; it is thus equivalent to " ut" with the Subjunctive. 141 (5.)

Puer it (goes) *dormitum.*

This Supine, used with *iri*, which is the Present Infini-

II.

tive Passive of eo, *to go*, forms the Infinitive of the Future Passive. 141 (5 *a.*)

Dux sperat proelia non *pugnatum iri!*

III.

The Supine in *u* follows the indeclinable Substantives *fas*, *nefas* *opus* & certain Adjectives, & is an Abl. of Respect. 141 (6.)

Difficile est dictu.
It is difficult to say, or *to be said*, or *in saying.*

PARTICIPLES.

I.

There are Four Participles.

1. Present in *ans* or *ens*, as—
Amans, monens.

2. Participle in *dus* (the Gerundive), as—
Amandus.

3. Perfect in *us*, as—
Amatus.

4. Future in *rus*, as—
Amaturus.

They are arranged in this order for the sake of their being more easily formed, as follows :

1. *The Present Participle* is formed from the present tense by changing *o* into *ans* or *ens*, as amo, amans; rego, regens.

N.B.—In the Second Congngation it will be by changing *eo* into *ens*, as moneo, monens.

2. *The Participle in dus* (Gerundive) is formed from the present Participle by throwing away *s* and adding *dus*, as amans, amandus; regens, regendus.

2. *The Perfect Participle* is formed from the Supine in *um* by changing *um* into *us*, as amatum, amatus; rectum, rectus.

4. *The Future Participle* is formed from the Supine in *u* by adding *rus*, as amatu, amaturus; rectu, recturus.

N.B.—*It will be seen that before the Participles can be formed in this way the Supines must be known.*

II.

These Participles are also classed in another way :

Two Active—

1. Present in *ans* or *ens*.
2. Future in *rus*.

Two Passive.

1. Perfect in *us*.
2. Participle in *dus*.

THE PRESENT PARTICIPLE.

I.

The *Present Participle* is used in Latin Prose to express continuous action, as—

The boy went, carrying his books with him.
Puer ibat gerens suos libros secum.

That is, he was carrying his books *all the time* he was going.

II.

It must not be used to express a single instantaneous action, as—

Drawing his sword (—really, " having drawn his sword"), the king attacked the enemy.
Ense stricto (or) quum ensem strinxisset (*not ensem stringens*) rex inpetum fecit in hostes.

III.

The pupil will hardly require to be reminded that though *ing* is the ending of the Present Participle, yet that a word may end in *"ing"* and yet not be translated by a *Present Participle* in Latin, as—

1. *Learning is useful. Learning* here will be translated by the Infinitive Mood, *discere.*

2. *The love of hunting. Of hunting* will be the Genitive Gerund, *Venandi;* or the Substantive *Venationis.*

3. *We learn by teaching. By teaching* will, of course be the Ablative Gerund.

PARTICIPLE IN DUS.

This has been fully explained as *The Gerundive,* pp. 98, 99.

THE PERFECT PARTICIPLE PASSIVE.

I.

The *Perfect Participle Passive* is the one most frequently found in Latin, as Amatus *loved, having been loved.* It is also the Participle generally used in the Ablative Absolute.

Cæsar having been made consul departed.

Cæsar factus consul abiit.

Cæsar, Brutus having been made consul, departed.

Cæsar, Bruto facto consule, abiit.

II.

We must remember that Intrasitive Verbs have no *Perf. Part. Pass.,* such as "ventus" from "venio," and that the Perf. Part. of a Deponent Verb, means *having* (and not *having been*), as *usus,* having used from *utor.*

FUTURE PARTICIPLE.

I.

The *Future Part:* always ends in *urus* and the English is "about to," "going to," "intending to," and also simply "to"

Amaturus, *"about to love," "going to love," "intending to love,"* or simply, *"to love,"* with, of course, a future meaning.

II.

This *Future Part:* is used with the Infinitive of the Verb

II.

sum to form the *Future Infinitive Active.*

The boy said that he would come.

Puer dixit se *venturum esse.*

III.

This *Future Part:* is sometimes used to *express a purpose* instead of *ut* with the *Subjunctive.*

The boy goes away to consult *his father.*

Puer abit *consulturus* patrem.

G

THE GERUNDIVE.

I.

The Gerundive is another name, and no doubt a more correct one, for the old-fashioned *Participle in dus*. It is of like form with the *Gerund*, hence the name *Gerundive*. It is sometimes used in place of the Gerund—

Puer est studiosus *audiendi* patrem.
The boy is very desirous of hearing *his father.*

Here we have the *Genitive Gerund* with the Accusative Case after it, but instead of this the *Gerundive* may be used. We put our Substantive in the case we want it to be (here *his father* will be the Genitive) and make our Gerundive agree with it. 143.

Puer est studiosus *patris audiendi.*
Rex interfectus est in *liberandâ urbe.*

This is called the *Gerundive Attraction*, and should only be used when the Verb governs the Accusative.

II.

The English of the Gerundive with *sum* is "is to be," "is meet to be," "must be."

Amandus est, *He is to be loved, must be loved, is meet to be loved.*

III.

When the word *must* has to be turned into Latin we must generally use the *Gerundive* in agreement with the Substantive, provided the Verb *governs an Accusative*. 144 (IV. 2.)

The gate must be shut.
Porta claudenda est.

The food must be taken.
Cibus sumendus est.

The state must be ruled.
Respublica regenda est

IV.

When the Gerundive of *neuter* or *intransitive* Verbs, as "live," "die," has to be used, it must be used Impersonally in the neuter Gender with "est," and what might be supposed to be the Nominative Case is to be turned into the Dative. 144 (IV, I. a.)

We *must live well.*
Bene vivendum est *nobis.*

I must live well.
Bene vivendum est *mihi.*

He *must live well.*
Bene vivendum est *illi.*

The boy *must live well*
Puero bene vivendum est.

V.

When the English Nominative means "*we*," or "*people in general*," it is generally left out.

We must live well.
Bene vivendum est (nobis).
We must die.
Moriendum est (nobis).

VI.

If this Gerundive comes from a Verb which governs the Dative Case (as *credo*), the sentence is a little more puzzling, as there will then be two Datives in the sentence — the Dative after the Gerundive (Agent) and the Dative of the Object after the Verb. 144 (IV. 1, *b*).

We *must believe* good people.

i.e.,

Good people *must be believed* by us.
Credendum est *nobis bonis hominibus.*

But in instances of this kind, where the sense would be doubtful, the agent is sometimes expressed by *a* or *ab* with the Ablative, as—

A nobis credendum est *bonis hominibus.*

Sometimes, however, the agent may be left out (see v.) where its omission can cause no ambiguity, and the sentence stand,

Credendum est *bonis hominibus.*

VII.

Let the pupil study well these sentences, of which we give both the Latin and the English.

We must labour.
Laborandum est (nobis).
The wicked must die.
Improbis moriendum est.
We must believe.
Credendum est (nobis).
We must believe the wise.
Credendum est sapientibus.
(Dat. of Object).
We must read the book.
Liber legendus est nobis,
We must fear the wicked
Improbi nobis timendi sunt.
The wicked must fear.
Improbis metuendum est.
We must pardon the boys.
Ignoscendum est pueris
(Dat. of Object.)

VIII.

"Must" and "ought," are to be expressed in Latin, however, sometimes by the Impersonal Verb *oportet*—

We ought to—*we* must—*believe you*
Oportet nos credere vobis.

Or by *necesse est*, it is necessary,

We must *obey our parents.*
Necesse est nobis parere parentibus.

IX.

There are yet, however, other senses in which *must* is used, and the Latin will therefore be altogether different—

You must *hear me,* i.e., nothing shall prevent *your hearing me.*
Nihil obstabit quominus audias me.

ACCUSATIVE CASE AND INFINITIVE MOOD.

This foim of expression, like that of the *Ablative Absolute*, is also one which beginners are very slow to learn, but a few words of explanation and example should make it plain.

This *Accusative and Infinitive* is called *Enuntiatio (bliqua* or *Oblique (Indirect) Enuncia-tion*, or *statement*.

The Latin Primer Rule is—

"The Subject of an Infinitive is put in the Accusative."

It having been just previously stated that

" The Subject of a Finite Verb is a Nominative."

And the two examples it gives are—

Anni fugiunt. *Years flee.*
Constat *annos* fugere. *It is evident that years flee.*
(Latin Primer, 98. 1, 2.)

In the first example we have a Finite Verb (*fugiunt*) with the Nominative (*anni*) ; and in the second example we have the Infinitive Verb (Verb in the Infinitive Mood) with the Accusative *annos*.

As with the *Ablative Absolute* it will be well to take this as found in Latin, that the Pupil may first learn how to con-strue it when he sees it in a Latin Sentence. This will enable him also to know how to turn the *Oblique Enuncia-tion* into Latin, though here again the more difficult thing will be to know when to use the Accusative and Infinitive, and when to use *ut* with the Subjunctive Mood.

Let us look carefully at the following sentence, and see how we ought to construe it.

Videmus aves auctumno in alias terras migrare.
We see that birds migrate into other lands in autumn.

Here we have an Accusative Case (*aves*), and an Infinitive Mood (*migrare*). We take *vide-mus*, according to the old, but never-to-be-forgotten, rule— "*Take the Nominative Case, first, and, if there is not one, take the Verb, and put in a Nominative;*"—then we will take *aves*, as the Accusative Case, and Subject of the Infinitive Mood *migrare*; before the Accusative. Case, we will put in the most important word "THAT"; and, as *migrare* is the Present Infinitive, we will construe it as if it were the Third Person Plural of the Present Indicative—videmus, *we see* aves *that birds* migrare *migrate.*

In turning such a Sentence into Latin — *We see that birds migrate,* we leave out the word "*that,*" turn what might be the Nominative into the Accusative, and put the Verb in the Infinitive Mood; instead of, as learners might think they were to do, using "*ut*" with the Subjunctive.

But here sometimes is the difficulty—the knowing when to use the Accusative and Infinitive, and when to use "*ut*" with the *Subjunctive.* The explanation however that seems most satisfactory is—

When before the word "that" in English you can insert the words "as a matter of fact,"

then in Latin the *Accusative with Infinitive* is used, as—

1. They say (as a matter of fact that the earth is round.
Aiunt TERRAM ESSE *rotundam.*

3. It is certain (as a matter of fact) that the earth moves round the sun.
Constat TERRAM MOVERI *circum solem.*

3. We believe (as a matter of fact) that God is the Creator of all things.
Credimus DEUM ESSE *Creatorem omnium rerum.*

But we enter more particularly into this in the following pages, which we head with the word "THAT."

Reverting, however, for a moment to the mode of construing such sentences as we have given, we see that in all these we have first to put in the word "*that,*" take the Accusative Case as if it were a Nominative, then take the Infinitive Mood and construe it, as if it were the Indicative Mood. And as in the *first* and *third* sentences the Accusative comes before *esse* (as the Subject), we take care to have the Accusative after *esse* (as the Complement).

"THAT" AND "UT."

There are two common ways of expressing "THAT" in Latin—

1. Accusative and Infinitive.

We hear that the boy is sick.
Audimus *puerum esse ægrum.*

2. "Ut" with the Subj.

The boy is so idle that *he has learned nothing.*
Puer est tam ignavus *ut* didicerit nibil.

But when to express "*that*" by the Accusative and Infinitive, and when by "ut" with the Subjunctive, is no doubt very puzzling. We give here some very simple rules and explanations.

I.

Use the Acc. and Infin. after Verbs of saying, thinking, knowing, hearing, perceiving, &c., and with such words as *constat, manifestum est, fama est,* &c., &c.

The boy says } that he has learned
The boy thinks } many things well.

It is certain } that the boy has learned
It is evident } many things well.

Puer dicit } *Se didicisse* multa bene.
Puer putat }

Constat *puerum didicisse* multa bene.

II.

"*Ut*" with the Subjunctive however, is used generally after

Accidit, *it happens.*
Reliquum est, *it remains.*
Sequitur, *it follows.*

And many other like words.

Accidit *ut* puer *puniatur.*
Reliquum est *ut* puer *eat* domum.
Sequitur *ut* puer *sit* domi.

III.

When "to," the ordinary sign of the Infinitive, can be turned into "that," "in order that," it expresses a *purpose* and must be rendered by "*ut*" with the *Subjunctive*, as—

The boy was sent to school to learn (*i.e.,* that, in order that, he might learn, *i.e.,* for the purpose of learning).
Puer missus est ad ludum *ut disceret.*

IV.

After "so" and "such," "*ut*" with the *Subjunctive* is used to express a *consequence.*

The boy is so idle that he has learned *nothing.*
Puer est tam ignavus *ut didiceri* nibil

V.

The word "*that*" is also used after Verbs of *doubting*, if preceded by a negative or a question, &c., in which case it must be translated by "quin," and "quin" takes the Subjunctive ;

There is no doubt
Who doubts
{ that *the boy loves his mother very much*.

Non est dubium
Quis dubitat
{ quin (=qui non) puer *amet* matrem valde.

VI.

When "that not" can be turned into "lest,' it is called a *negative* PURPOSE, and must be translated by "ne."

The boy is sent to school that *he may not be ignorant of letters*. -

Puer mittitur ad ludum ne (*that not*, lest) sit ignarus literarum.

But when "that not" is used to express a *negative* CONSEQUENCE, "ut non" must be used.

He was so idle as not to learn *many things*.

Erat tam ignavus *ut non disceret* multa

VII.

When there is a comparative in the dependent clause, the word "that" must be translated by "quo," and requires the Subjunctive, as—

The boy is punished that he may be *the more industrious*.

Puer punitur quo sit diligentior.

VIII.

With words of fearing, "ne" and "ut" seem to exchange places; "*that*" must be translated by "*ne*" "*that not*" by "*ut*," as—

I fear that *the boy* will not *come*.
Vereor ut puer veniat.

I fear that *the boy* will *come*, i.e., I am afraid lest he come.
Vereor ne puer veniat.

IX.

After words expressing *hindrance* use *quominus* with the Subjunctive,

What prevents *the boy* from going home ?

Quid obstat quominus puer eat domum ?

X.

It has been said that when "that" introduces a *purpose*, it must be translated by "*ut*" with the Subjunctive; but sometimes the idea of *purpose* is not clearly brought out in the English sentence, as, e.g., after the Verbs—

Advise, ask, command (not *jubeo*), Exhort, beg, strive (not *conor*),

where, nevertheless, a *purpose* is implied, and therefore "*ut*" with the *Subjunctive* is used, as—

Moneo te *ut* bene *vivas*.
I advise you to live *well*.
Impero tibi *ut* bene *vivas*.
I command you to live *well*.

OBLIQUE STATEMENT.

An Oblique Statement is ordinarily formed by the Infinitive Clause (Accusative with Infinitive) and depends on an Impersonal Verb, or a Verb of *declaring, thinking, perceiving*, &c.

In Oblique Statement all the *principal* Verbs will stand in the Infinitive Mood, whereas all the *Subordinate* Verbs, *i.e.*, the Verbs in the Subordinate Clauses (provided they express the words and opinions of the original speaker) will be in the Subjunctive.

Cæsar "Plura sunt" inquit "quæ volo dicere tibi." (Direct.)
Cæsar said, " There are more things which I wish to mention to you."

Here *Sunt* is the principal Verb and *Volo* the Subordinate Verb ; therefore in Oratio Obliqua the sentence will run thus—

Cæsar dixit plura *esse* quæ *vellet* dicere ei.   (Oblique.)
Cæsar said, that there were more things which he wished to mention to him.

QUI.

Qui requires the Subjunctive when there is implied—

(1.) *In order that*, Litteras scripsi quibus (= tu iis) puerum. monerem.

(2.) *Since*, Pudet me tui qui (= quum tu) tam ignavus sis.

(3.) *Such that*, Sunt qui (= ejusmodi ut) discant multa.

(4.) *Although*, Ego, qui (= quamvis ego) senex sim, disco multa.

SUBJUNCTIVE MOOD.

Many pages might here be written on the Subjunctive Mood, but we will be content with giving the principal conjunctions which are followed by the Subjunctive Mood.

I.

CONSECUTIVE—ut, *so that;* quin, *but that.*

The boy is so foolish that he knows nothing.
Puer est ita stultus *ut* nihil *sciat.*
There is no doubt but that these things are true.
Non est dubium *quin* (=ut non) hæc vera *sint.*
Who is there who does not weep ?
Quis est *quin* (=qui non) *fleat ?*

II.

FINAL—ut, *in order that.*   Quo, *in order that.*
ne, *lest, that not.*   Quominus, *but that.*

I will strive to conquer, i.e. in order that I may conquer.
Enitar *ut vincam.*
I will strive that you may not conquer (i.e. lest you should).
Enitar *ne vincas.*
I will strive in order that I may conquer *the more easily.*
Enitar *quo* facilius *vincam.*
What hinders me from conquering (i.e. but that I may conquer)?
Quid obstat *quominus* (=ut eo minus) *vincam ?*

III.

CAUSAL—quum, *since.*
Since *these things* are *so, I will go.*
Quæ *quum* ita *sint,* ibo.

IV.

CONDITIONAL—Dum, modo, dummodo, *provided that.*
The general will conquer provided that he fears *nothing.*
Dux vincet *dum* nihil *metuat.*

V.

CONCESSIVE—Licet, quamvis, ut, *although.*
Although *those things* are *true, I will not go.*
Ut ea vera *sint* non ibo.

VI.

COMPARATIVE—Tanquam, ceu, velut, quasi, *as if.*
You talk as if I were *foolish.*
Loqueris *tanquam* stultus *sim.*

IMPERSONAL VERBS.

I.

Impersonal Verbs are those which have no Personal Pronoun as Subject, and are used only in the Third Person Singular (Ind. and Conj.) and in the Infinitive Mood.

It hails, grandinat.
It vexes me, me piget.

For the Conjugation of Impersonal Verbs see pp. 61, 62, of the *Latin Primer*.

II.

The greater number of the Impersonal Verbs are of the second conjugation. We give those that are most commonly used.

I. Conjugation.

Delectat, *it delights.*
Juvat, *it delights.*
Constat, *it is evident.*
Tonat, *it thunders.*
Fulgurat, *it lightens.*
Grandinat, *it hails.*

II.—Conjugation.

Oportet, *it behoves.*
Decet, *it becomes.*
Dedecet, *it is unseemly.*
Piget, *it irks.*
Pudet, *it shames.*
Pœnitet, *it repents.*
Tædet, *it disgusts.*
Miseret, *it moves pity.*
Libet, *it pleases.*
Licet, *it is lawful.*
Liquet, *it is clear.*
Attinet, *it relates.*
Pertinet, *it belongs.*

III. Conjugation.

Accidit, *it happens.*
Contingit, *it befalls*
Ningit, *it snows.*
Pluit, *it rains.*
Lucescit, *it dawns.*
Vesperascit, *it grows late.*

IV. Conjugation.

Convenit, *it suits.*
Evenit, *it turns out.*
Expedit, *it is expedient.*

Irregular.

Interest, *it imports.*
Refert, *it concerns.*

III.

Intransitive Verbs also, and Verbs which take a Dative Case after them if used in the Passive Voice, are used impersonally

There is playing by me, or I play.
Luditur a me.
I am believed. Creditur mihi.

IV.

The Neuter of the Gerundive is often used impersonally.

I must play.—There must be playing by me. Ludendum est mihi.

V.

In using Impersonal Verbs the different persons, *I, thou, he,* &c., are expressed by the different cases the Verbs take after them.

The following are used with the Accusative Case—

Decet.	Juvat.	Piget.
Dedecet.	Oportet.	Pœnitet.
Delectat.	Miseret.	Pudet.
	Tædet.	

as

Oportet me ire, *it behoves me to go,* or *I ought to go.*
Oportet te ire   „   *you* „   *you* „
Oportet eum ire   „   *him* „   *he* „
   &c.   &c.   &c.   &c.

VI.

The following are used with the Dative Case—

Libet.   Licet.   Accidit.   Contingit.   Evenit.   Convenit.   Expedit.

as

Licet mihi ire, *it is allowed me to go,* or *I may go.*
Licet tibi ire   „   *you* „   *you* „
Licet ei ire   „   *him* „   *he* „
   &c.   &c.   &c.   &c.

VII.

Intransitive Verbs when used impersonally in the Passive Voice sometimes have the Ablative and Preposition, to express the person, as—

Luditur a me, *there is playing by me,* or *I play.*
Luditur a te   „   *you* „ *you play.*
Luditur ab eo   „   *him* „ *he plays.*
   &c.   &c.   &c.   &c.

But this Ablative is often left out.

VIII.

Interest, refert, are used with the Genitive as also with the Possessive Cases, meā, tuā, suā, nostrā, vestrā. 129 (III. *a*).

Regis interest facere recte,
Regis refert facere recte,
It imports (it concerns) the king to act rightly.

See also p. II.

Et *tuā* et *meā* interest te valere,
It is both to your interest and mine that you should be well.

IX.

The Impersonals—

Fulgurat, *it lightens.*   Pluit, *it rains.*   Luscescit, *it dawns.*
Tonat, *it thunders.*   Grandinat, *it hails.*   Vesperascit, *it gets late*
                Ningit, *it snows*

are of course not used with any Personal or other Object.

MODE OF ASKING QUESTIONS.

The Interrogative Pronoun "quis" asks a question, as—

>   Quis homo est? *Who is the man ?*
>   Quæ sunt illæ puellæ? *Who are those girls ?*
>   Quid agis? *What are you doing ?*
>   Quid est nomen tibi? *What is your name ?*
>   Cujus est hic liber? *Whose is this book ?*

Such words also, as—

<table>
<tr><td>Quando, when ?</td><td>Quo, whither ?</td></tr>
<tr><td>Ubi, When ?</td><td>Quorsum, whitherward ?</td></tr>
<tr><td>Quamdiu, how long ?</td><td>Unde, whence ?</td></tr>
<tr><td>Quoties, how often ?</td><td>Qua, which way ?</td></tr>
<tr><td>Ubi, where ?</td><td>Quatenus, how far ?</td></tr>
<tr><td colspan="2" align="center">Quousque, how far ?</td></tr>
</table>

are all of them Interrogatives, but they can ask only particular questions, as—

>   Quo curris? *Whither do you run?*
>   Quando redibis? *When will you return?*
>   Quoties dixisti hoc? *How often have you said this ?*
>   &c., &c., &c.

1.

But in asking questions in Latin the word *ne* is frequently
used, in much the same way that we use the note of Interro-
gation in (?) English ; no English is to be given to it, as—·

>   Videsne, puer?
>   *Do you see, boy ?*

II.

If there is a *non* in the sentence *ne* will come at the end of *non*, and will thus make non*ne*, as—

Nonne est puer diligens ?
Is not *the boy industrious ?*

From the very wording of the sentence, it will be seen that the answer "yes" is expected —*nonne* therefore is said to be a sign of a question when the answer "yes" is expected.

III.

Num is put when the answer "no" is expected, and, like *ne*, must not be translated, as—

Num est puer diligens?
Is *the boy industrious ?*

Here, however, the answer "no" being expected, the question may be turned so as to show this—and the words rendered not simply—

Is the boy industrious?

to which "yes" or "no" is applicable, but—

The boy is not *industrious, is he?*

to which it is clearly seen that the answer "no" is expected.

IV.

When there is a double question asked, *Utrum*, "whether," (or *num* or *ne*), is used, followed by *an*, " or," as—

Utrum est puer *an* puella diligentior ?
Whether *is the boy or the girl more industrious ?*

Utrum need not, however, be translated, as it is quite enough to say—

Is the boy or girl more industrious ?

Neither, indeed, need *Utrum* be put in in Latin, but it may be left out in the same way as "whether" is left out in English, for it matters not whether we say—

Utrum est puer *an* puella diligentior ?

or

Est puer *an* puella diligentior ?

V.

In *indirect questions* the Verb is put in the Subj. Mood—

He asks who you are.
Rogat quis *sis*.
He asks whether the boy or girl is more industrious.
Rogat utrum puer an puella *sit* diligentior

PRONOUNS.

There are Eight kinds of Pronouns—

1. Personal.
2. Reflexive.
3. Possessive.
4. Demonstrative.
5. Definitive.
6. Relative.
7. Interrogative.
8. Indefinite.

1. Personal Pronouns are—

1. Ego, *I.*
2. Tu, *Thou.*
3. Nos, *We.*
4. Vos, *Ye.*

2. Reflexive—

Se (sese), *himself, herself, itself, themselves.*

8. Possessive—

1. Meus, *my, mine.*
2. Tuus, *thy, thine, your.*
3. Suus, *his own, her own,* &c.
4. Cujus, a, um, *whose.*
5. Noster, *our.*
6. Vester, *your.*

4. Demonstrative—

1. Is, *that (he, she, it).*
2. Hic, *this (near me).*
3. Ille, *that (yonder).*
4. Iste, *that (near you).*

5. Definitive—

Idem, *same.*   Ipse, *self.*

6. Relative—

Qui, *who or which.*

7. Interrogative—

Quis, *who or what?*

8. Indefinite—

Quis, *any one.*

N.B.   2 D's, 2 I's, 2 R's, 2 P's,
Will give the Pronouns eight
with ease.

PERSONAL PRONOUNS.

I.

The Personal Pronouns, *ego, tu, nos, vos,* and the Demonstrative Pronouns, *ille, illi,* are sometimes used as the Nominative Case to the Verb where no other Nominative is expressed or evidently understood.

Amo means *Ego amo, I love.*
Amas   „   *Tu amas, Thou lovest.*
Amat   „   *Ille amat, He loves.*
Amamus „   *Nos amamus, We love.*
Amatis „   *Vos amatis, Ye love.*
Amaut „   *Illi amant, They love.*

II.

But this Personal Pronoun is not generally expressed, except for the purpose of emphasis.

I am walking in the garden,
Ambulo (not *ego* ambulo) in horto.

III.

But if I wish to show some distinction between what *I* am doing and what *somebody else* is doing, I must use *ego.*

I am walking in the garden, you are sitting in the house.
Ego ambulo in horto, *tu* sedes in domo.

REFLEXIVE PRONOUNS.

The Reflexive Pronoun *se* is often misunderstood, and therefore misplaced.

The master said "that he" was writing.

The master praised the boy and said "that he" was good.

In the first sentence the man is speaking of himself, so we must use "se." In the second sentence the man is speaking of the boy, so we must use "eum."

Magister dixit *se* scribere.

Magister laudavit puerum et dixit *eum* esse bonum.

POSSESSIVE PRONOUNS.

I.

The Possessive Pronouns, like Adjectives, agree with their Substantives, and THAT ALONE.

He was reading his book.
She was reading her book.
They were reading their book.

Must be all turned into *suum librum.*

II.

Notice the difference between *ejus,* and *suus.*

The boy was reading his (own) book.
Puer legebat *suum* librum.
The boy was sitting near his brother and reading his book.
Puer sedebat prope fratrem et legebat *ejus (i.e.,* his brother's) librum.

III.

Note that "you" in English is both singular and plural *tu* and *vos*; and "your" is both "*tuus*" "and *vester,*"—be careful whether you are speaking to, or of one person or more than one.

What are you doing, my boy?
Quid *agis,* puer?
What are you doing, my boys?
Quid *agitis,* pueri?
Soldier, hasten your flight.
Miles, matura *tuam* fugam.
Soldiers, hasten your flight.
Milites, maturate *vestram* fugam.

DEMONSTRATIVE PRONOUNS.

The distinction between *hic, ille* and *iste* must be remembered : *hic* means "this near me," *ille* "that yonder,"pointing at something at some distance, and *iste,* "that of yours, or that by you."

Boy, do you see this book?
Videsne *hunc* librum, puer?

Boy, give me that book (yonder).
Da mihi *illum* librum, puer.

Boy, give me that book of yours (near you).
Da mihi *istum* librum puer

PREPOSITIONS.

I.

The Preposition must stand—

1. Either immediately before the word that it governs.
2. Or before the Adjective agreeing with that word.
3. Or before a Genitive depending on that word.

Milites ibant *trans agros* hostium.

Milites ibant *trans fertiles* agros hostium.

Milites ibant *trans hostium* fertiles agros.

Tenus, however, *follows* its case, which is sometimes a Genitive. So also do *versus* and *versum.*

II.

A, ab for *by* is used of an Agent, but not to express the instrument.

The man was killed by me.
Vir occisus est *a me* (agent).
The man was killed by a stone.
Vir occisus est *lapide* (instrument).

Ad is used after Verbs of motion, but not before names of Towns, etc.

He was going to the city.
Ibat *ad* urbem.

He was going to Rome.
Ibat *Romam.*

III.

Cum is not used ordinarily for " with," unless it may be turned into " together with," " along with,"—

The king went with (together with) *his legions.*
Rex ivit *cum legionibus.*

The king fought with *his sword.*
Rex pugnavit *gladio.*

In (in) is used before ordinary words, but not before a *name of a Town,* or a Noun denoting *Time when,* as—

The king was sitting in the garden.
Rex sedebat *in* horto.

The king was fighting in *Italy.*
Rex pugnabat *in* Italia.

The king was living in *Carthage* (i.e. *at Carthage*).
Rex vivebat *Carthagine.*

In *winter the cold is intense.*
Hieme frigus est magnum.

In, when it is followed by the Abl. signifies *rest in*

Sedeo *in* domo.

In, when it is followed by the Acc., signifies *motion into,* or *on to* or *to,*

Festino *in* domum.

For list of Prepositions, see p. 58.

END OF PART II.

PART III.   IRREGULAR VERBS.

PART III. IRREGULAR VERBS.

CONTENTS.

PART III. IRREGULAR VERBS.

It is to be noted throughout that forms thus marked * occur only in compounds.

———◆———

Irregular Verbs—Conjugation I.

Crepo	crepui	crepitum	*creak.*
Cubo	cubui	cubitum	*lie.*
Domo	domui	domitum	*tame.*
Mico	micui	—	*glitter.*
Plico	*plicui	*plicitum	*fold.*
Sono	sonui	sonitum	*sound.*
Tono	tonui	tonitum	*thunder,*
Veto	vetui	vetitum	*forbid.*
Seco	secui	sectum	*cut.*
Do	dĕdi	dătum	*give.*
Sto	stĕti	statum	*stand.*
Jŭvo	jūvi	jutum	*help.*
Làvo	lāvi ·	lotum	*wash.*

Irregular Verbs—Conjugation II.

Deleo	delēvi	delētum	*blot out.*
Fleo	flēvi	fletum	*weep.*
*Pleo	*plēvi	*pletum	*fill.*
Neo	nevi	netum	*spin.*
Ardeo	arsi	arsum	*take fire.*
Fulgeo	fulsi ·	—	*glitter.*
Hœreo	hœsi	hœsum	*stick.*
Jubeo	jussi	jussum	*command.*

Maneo	mansi	mansum	*remain.*
Mulceo	mulsi	mulsum	*soothe.*
Rideo	risi	risum	*laugh.*
Suadeo	suasi	suasum	*advise.*
Urgeo	ursi	—	*press.*

Lugeo	luxi	—	*mourn.*
Luceo	luxi	—	*shine.*

Mordeo	momordi	morsum	*bite.*
Pendeo	pependi	pensum	*hang.* (intr.)
Spondeo	spopondi	sponsum	*pledge.*
Tondeo	totondi	tonsum	*shear.*

Prandeo	prandi	pransum	*lunch.*
Sĕdeo	sēdi	sessum	*sit.*
Vĭdeo	vīdi	visum	*see.*

Fŏveo	fōvi	fōtum	*cherish.*
Mŏveo	mōvi	mōtum	*move.*
Vŏveo	vōvi	vōtum	*vow.*

Căveo	cāvi	cautum	*beware.*
Făveo	fāvi	fautum	*favour.*

Doceo	docui	doctum	*teach.*
Misceo	miscui	{ mistum mixtum }	*mix.*
Torreo	torrui	tostum	*roast*
Teneo	tenui	tentum	*hold.*

Augeo	auxi	auctum	*increase.* (trans.)
Indulgeo	indulsi	indultum	*be indulgent.*
Torqueo	torsi	tortum	*twist.*

Audeo	ausus sum	} semi-deponent.	{ *dare.*
Gaudeo	gavisus sum		*rejoice.*
Soleo	solitus sum		*be wont.*

CONJUGATION III.

All the Verbs of the Third Conjugation are of themselves so irregular that they require to be classed in some such way as the following.

I. PERFECT *xi*, SUPINE *tum*.

Cingo	cinxi	cinctum	*surround.*
Coquo	coxi	coctum	*cook.*
Dico	dixi	dictum	*say.*
Duco	duxi	ductum	*lead.*
Fingo	finxi	fictum	*fashion.*
Juugo	junxi	junctum	*join.*
Pingo	pinxi	pictum	*paint.*
Rego	rexi	rectum	*rule.*
*Stinguo	*stinxi	*stinctum	*quench.*
Struo	struxi	structum	*pile.*
Tego	texi	tectum	*cover.*
Tinguo	tinxi	tinctum	*dye.*
Traho	traxi	tractum	*draw.*
Unguo	unxi	unctum	*anoint.*
Veho	vexi	vectum	*carry.*
Vivo	vixi	victum	*live.*

II. PERFECT *xi*, SUPINE *xum*.

Figo	fixi	fixum	*fix.*
Flecto	flexi	flexum	*bend.*
Fluo	fluxi	fluxum	*flow.*
Necto	nexi (nexui)	nexum	*bind.*

III. PERFECT *si*, SUPINE *sum*.

Cedo	cessi	cessum	*yield.*
Claudo	clausi	clausum	*shut.*
Divido	divisi	divisum	*divide.*

Lædo	læsi	læsum	*hurt.*
Ludo	lusi	lusum	*play.*
Mergo	mersi	mersum	*drown.*
Mitto	misi	missum	*send.*
Plaudo	plausi	plausum	*applaud.*
Premo	pressi	pressum	*press.*
Rado	rasi	rasum	*scrape.*
Rodo	rosi	rosum	*gnaw.*
Spargo	sparsi	sparsum	*sprinkle.*
Tergo	tersi	tersum	*wipe.*
Trudo	trusi	trusum	*thrust.*
Vado	*vasi	*vasum	*go.*
Vello	vulsi (velli)	vulsum	*pluck.*

IV. PERFECT *si*, SUPINE *tum*.

| Gero | gessi | gestum | *carry on.* |
| Uro | ussi | ustum | *burn.* |

V. PERFECT *psi*, SUPINE *ptum*.

Carpo	carpsi	carptum	*pluck.*
Como	compsi	comptum	*adorn.*
Demo	dempsi	demptum	*take away.*
Nubo	nupsi	nuptum	*be married.*
Promo	prompsi	promptum	*take forth.*
Repo	repsi	reptum	*creep.*
Scalpo	scalpsi	scalptum	*scratch.*
Scribo	scripsi	scriptum	*write.*
Serpo	serpsi	serptum	*crawl.*
Sumo	sumpsi	sumptum	*take.*
Temno	tempsi	temptum	*despise.*

VI. PERFECT *ui*, SUPINE *tum*.

Acuo	acui	acūtum	*sharpen.*
Alo	alui	altum (alĭtum)	*nourish.*
Arguo	argui	argutum	*prove.*

Colo	colui	cultum	*till.*
Consulo	consului	consultum	*consult.*
*Cumbo	*cubui	*cubitum	*lie down.*
Exuo	exui	exutum	*put off.*
Fremo	fremui	fremitum	*murmur.*
Gemo	gemui	gemitum	*groan.*
Gigno	genui	genitum	*produce.*
Imbuo	imbui	imbūtum	*tinge.*
Induo	indui	indutum	*put on.*
Luo	lui	luïtum	*wash, atone.*
Minuo	minui	minūtum	*lessen.*
Occulo	occului	occultum	*hide.*
Pono	posui	positum	*place.*
Ruo	rui	† rutum	*rush, fall.*
Sero	serui	sertum	*join.*
Statuo	statui	statūtum	*set up.*
Strepo	strepui	strepitum	*roar.*
Texo	texui	textum	*weave.*
Tribuo	tribui	tributum	*assign.*
Vomo	vomui	vomitum	*vomit.*

† The Primer gives ruitum as supine, and ruiturum occurs in *Ovid,* Met. iv. 460; but Andrews gives rutum. Cf. obrutus.

VII. PERFECT *ui*, NO SUPINE.

Metuo	metui	—	*fear.*
Nuo	nui	—	*nod.*
Tremo	tremui	• —	*tremble.*
Volo	volui	—	*wish.*

VIII. PERFECT *vi*, SUPINE *tum.*

Arcesso	arcessivi	arcessitum	*send for.*
Cerno	crevi	cretum	*sift.*
Cresco	crevi	cretum	*grow.*
Lacesso	lacessivi	lacessitum	*provoke.*
Lino	levi	lïtum	*smear.*
Nosco	novi (*I know*)	notum	*become acquainted with.*

Pasco	pavi	pastum	*feed.*
Peto	petivi	petitum	*ask.*
Quæro	quæsivi	quæsitum	*seek.*
Quiesco	quievi	quietum	*rest.*
Sero	sevi	sătum	*sow.*
Sino	sīvi	sĭtum	*allow.*
Sperno	sprevi	spretum	*despise.*
Sterno	stravi	stratum	*strew.*
Suesco	suevi	suetum	*be wont.*
Tero	trivi	tritum	*rub.*

IX. PERFECT WITH REDUPLICATION : SUPINE *tum, sum.*

Cado	cecĭdi	casum	*fall.*
Cœdo	cecīdi	cæsum	*cut, beat, kill.*
Cano	cecĭni	cantum	*sing.*
Curro	cucurri	cursum	*run.*
Fallo	fefelli	falsum	*deceive.*
Parco	peperci	parsum	*spare.*
Pango	pepigi	pactum	*fasten.*
Pario	peperi	partum	*bring forth.*
Pello	pepuli	pulsum	*drive.*
Pendo	pependi	pensum	*weigh.*
Pungo	pupugi	punctum	*prick.*
Tango	tetigi	tactum	*touch.*
Tendo	tetendi	tensum & tentum	*stretch.*
Tollo	sustuli	sublatum	*take up.*
Tundo	tutudi	tunsum	*thump.*

PERFECT WITH REDUPLICATION, NO SUPINE.

Disco	didici	—	*learn.*
Posco	poposci	—	*demand.*

X. Perfect *di*, Supine *sum*.

*Cando	*cendi	*censum	*set on fire.*
Ĕdo	ēdi	esum	*eat.*
*Fendo	*fendi	*fensum	*strike.*
Findo	fĭdi	fissum	*cleave.*
Fundo	fudi	fusum	*pour.*
Pando	pandi	pansum (passum)	*spread.*
Prehendo	prehendi	prehensum	*grasp.*
Scando	scandi	scansum	*climb.*
Scindo	scĭdi	scissum	*tear.*

XI. Compounds of *do*: Perfect *didi*, Supine *ditum*.

Abdo	abdĭdi	abditum	*hide.*
Addo			*add.*
Condo			*found, hide.*
Credo			*believe.*
Dedo			*give up.*
Edo			*give forth.*
Perdo	-didi	-ditum	*lose.*
Prodo			*betray.*
Reddo			*restore.*
Subdo			*substitute.*
Trado			*deliver.*
Vendo			*sell.*

XII. Verbs that cannot be arranged under Previous Headings.

Ago	egi	actum	*do.*
Bibo	bibi	bibitum	*drink.*
Emo	ēmi	emptum	*buy, take.*
Frango	fregi	fractum	*break.*
Lego	legi	lectum	*choose, read.*
Linquo	liqui	*lictum	*leave.*
Meto	messui	messum	*to mow.*
Rumpo	rupi	ruptum	*break.*
Sisto	*stiti	*statum	*make to stand.*

Solvo[1]	solvi	solūtum	*loosen.*
Vello[2]	velli & vulsi	vulsum	*pull.*
Verto	verti	versum	*turn.*
Vinco	vici	victum	*conquer.*
Volvo[1]	volvi	volūtum	*roll.*

[1] These might have been included in those making Perfect *vi*, Supine *tum*, but they only make *vi* because there is a *v* in the present.

[2] This because it also makes *vulsi* has been included in those making Perfect *si*, Supine *sum* (see p. 4).

VERBS IN io OF THE THIRD CONJUGATION.

Allicio	allexi	allectum	*allure.*
Capio	cēpi	captum	*take.*
Cupio	cupīvi	cupĭtum	*desire.*
Elicio	elicui	elicĭtum	*entice forth.*
Facio	feci	factum	*make.*
Fodio	fōdi	fossum	*dig.*
Fugio	fūgi	fugĭtum	*flee*
Jacio	jeci	jactum	*throw.*
Pario	peperi	partum	*bring forth.*
Quatio	quassi	quassum	*shake.*
Rapio	rapui	raptum	*seize.*
*Specio	*spexi	*spectum	*espy.*
Sapio	sapi(v)i	—	{ *to taste of, be wise.*

PECULIARITIES OF SOME COMPOUND VERBS.

REGO.

Surgo (sub-rego)	surrexi	surrectum	*arise.*
Pergo (per-rego)	perrexi	perrectum	*go on.*

LEGO.

Most of its compounds make -legi, -lectum. But diligo, intelligo, negligo, -lexi, -lectum.

The Compounds of Reduplicated Verbs seldom retain the reduplication, *e.g.*, occīdo (ob-cædo), occīdi, except disco, posco, curro, do, sto.

IRREGULAR VERBS—CONJUGATION IV.

Aperio	aperui	apertum	*open.*
Operio	operui	opertum	*cover.*
Salio	salui	saltum	*leap.*
Sepelio	sepelivi	sepultum	*bury.*
Sancio	sanxi	sanctum	*consecrate.*
Vincio	vinxi	vinctum	*bind.*
Fulcio	fulsi	fultum	*prop.*
Haurio	hausi	haustum	*drain.*
Sarcio	sarsi	sartum	*mend.*
Sæpio	sæpsi	sæptum	*hedge in.*
Sentio	sensi	sensum	*feel.*
Comperio	comperi	compertum	*find.*
Reperio	repperi	repertum	*discover.*
Věnio	vēni	ventum	*come.*

PRINCIPAL NEUTER VERBS.

Neuter Verbs indicate a *state* or an *action not* exercised *upon an object :* they take an accusative of kindred meaning, *e.g.* "Duram servit servitutem." There are exceptional uses in the poets, *e.g.*, "Ire vias." Prop. I. i. 18. "Currimus æquor." Virg. Æn. III. 191. Many of them too are followed by the accusative of part affected, *e.g.* tremit artus, dolet caput, etc.

Algeo	algēre	alsi	—	*be cold.*
Ambulo	ambulare	ambulavi	ambulatum	*walk.*
Ardeo	ardēre	arsi	arsum	*take fire.*
Caleo	calēre	calui	—	*be warm.*
Clango	clangĕre	—	—	*resound.*

Conniveo	connivēre	{ connīvi / connixi }	—	*shut the eyes.*
Curro	currĕre	cucurri	cursum	*run.*
Cubo	cubare	cubui	cubitum	*lie.*
Eo	īre	īvi, ii	ĭtum	*go.*
Ferveo	{ fervēre / fervĕre }	{ ferbui / fervi }	—	*boil.*
Floreo	florēre	florui	—	*flourish.*
Frigeo	frigēre	—	—	*be cold.*
Jaceo	jacēre	jacui	jacĭtum	*lie.*
No	nare	navi	—	*swim.*
Pendeo	pendēre	pependi	pensum	*hang.*
Salio	salire	salui	saltum	*leap.*
Sĕdeo	sedēre	sēdi	sessum	*sit.*
Servio	servīre	servīvi(ii)	servītum	*serve.*
Sto	stare	stĕti	statum	*stand.*
Vĕnio	venire	vēni	ventum	*come.*
Vigeo	vigēre	—	—	*flourish.*
Vireo	virēre	—	—	*be green.*
Vivo	vivĕre	vixi	victum	*live.*

PRINCIPAL VERBS WHICH ARE BOTH ACTIVE AND NEUTER.

Doleo	dolēre	dolui	dolitum	{ *feel pain, grieve for.* }
Fleo	flēre	flevi	fletum	*weep, weep for.*
Gemo	gemĕre	gemui	gemitum	*groan, sigh over.*
Horreo	horrēre	—	—	{ *stand on end, shudder at.* }
Incipio	incipĕre	incepi	inceptum	*begin.*
Lugeo	lugēre	luxi	—	*mourn, lament.*
Maneo	manēre	mansi	mansum	*remain, await*

Ruo	rnĕre	ruī	rutum	*rush, cast down or up.*
Sapio	sapĕre	sapivi(ii)	—	*be wise, know.*
Sitio	sitire	sitivi(ii)	—	*be thirsty, thirst for.*
Tremo	tremĕre	tremui	—	*tremble, tremble at.*
Verto	vertĕre	verti	versum	*turn.*
Vigilo	vigĭlare	vigilavi	vigilatum	*watch, watch through.*

COMMON DEPONENT VERBS.

A. Regular.

Conj. I.	Arbitror	arbitrari	arbitratus sum	*think.*
	Miror	mirari	miratus sum	*wonder at.*
	Moror	,,	,,	*delay.*
	Spatior	,,	,,	*walk.*
	Testor	,,	,,	*bear witness.*
	Vagor	,,	,,	*wander.*
	Venor	,,	,,	*hunt.*

Conj. II.	Mereor	mereri	meritus sum	*deserve.*
	Misereor	,,	,,	*pity.*
	Polliceor	,,	,,	*promise.*
	Vereor	,,	,,	*fear.*

Conj. III.	Utor	uti	usus sum	*use.*

Mostly classed with the irregular verbs.

Conj. IV.	Partior	partiri	partitus sum	*divide.*

PRINCIPAL DEPONENT VERBS.

B. Irregular.

Conjugation II.

Fateor	fatēri	fassus sum	confess.
Medeor	mederi	————	heal.
Reor	reri	ratus sum	think.

Conjugation III.

Amplector	amplecti	amplexus sum	embrace.
Apiscor	apisci	aptus sum	obtain.
Comminiscor	comminisci	commentus sum	devise.
Expergiscor	expergisci	experrectus sum	wake up.
Fatiscor	fatisci	fessus sum	grow weary.
Fruor	frui	fruitus sum	enjoy.
Fungor	fungi	functus sum	discharge.
Gradior	gradi	gressus sum	step.
Irascor	irasci	iratus sum	be angry.
Labor	labi	lapsus sum	glide.
Loquor	loqui	locutus sum	speak.
Morior	mori	mortuus sum	die.
Nanciscor	nancisci	nactus sum	obtain.
Nascor	nasci	natus sum	be born.
Nitor	niti	$\left\{ \begin{array}{l} \text{nisus} \\ \text{nixus} \end{array} \right\}$ sum	strive.
Obliviscor	oblivisci	oblītus sum	forget.
Paciscor	pacisci	pactus sum	bargain.
Patior	pati	passus sum	suffer.
Proficiscor	proficisci	profectus sum	set out.
Queror	queri	questus sum	complain.
Sequor	sequi	secūtus sum	follow.
Ulciscor	ulcisci	ultus sum	avenge.
Utor	uti	usus sum	use.

Conjuqation IV.

Assentior	assentīri	assensus sum	*agree to.*
Experior	experīri	expertus sum	*try.*
Metior	metīri	mensus sum	*measure.*
Opperior	opperīri	· oppertus sum	*wait for.*
Ordior	ordīri	orsus sum	*begin.*
Orior	orīri	ortus sum	*rise.*

QUASI PASSIVES AND SEMI-DEPONENT.

I. ACTIVE FORM WITH PASSIVE MEANING.

Exulo	exulare	exulavi	exulạtum	*be banished.*
Fio [1]	fieri	factus sum		*be made.*
Liceo	licēre	licui	licitum	{ *be put up to auction.*
Vapulo [2]	vapulare	vapulavi		*be beaten.*
Vēneo [3]	venire	venii	venĭtum	*be on sale.*

II. ACTIVE PRESENT WITH PERFECT OF PASSIVE FORM.

Audeo	audēre	ausus sum	*dare.*
Fido	fidēre	fisus sum	*trust.*
Gaudeo	gaudēre	gavisus sum	*rejoice.*
Soleo	solēre	solitus sum	*be wont.*

III. ACTIVE PERFECT WITH DEPONENT PERFECT PARTICIPLE.

Ceno	cenavi	cenatus	*sup.*
Juro	juravi	juratus	*swear.*
Prandeo	prandi_	pransus	*dine.*
Also	Nupta		*wedded.*
	Potus		*having drunk.*

---

[1] *Fio*, pass. of *facio.*   [2] *Vapulo*, pass. of *verbero.*   [3] *Veneo*, pass. of *vendo.*

I

COMPOUNDS OF SUM.

Absum	abesse	$\left\{\begin{array}{l}\text{abfui}\\\text{afui}\end{array}\right\}$	*be absent.*
Adsum	adesse	affui	— *present.*
Desum	deesse	defui	— *wanting.*
Insum	inesse	infui	— *in.*
Intersum	interesse	interfui	— *among.*
Obsum	obesse	obfui	— *in the way of.*
Præsum	præesse	præfui	— *before.*
Prosum	prodesse	profui	— *useful.*
Subsum	subesse	—	— *under.*
Supersum	superesse	superfui	— *over, remain.*

COMPOUNDS OF EO.

Abeo	abire	abīvi	abĭtum	*go away.*
Adeo	adire	adīvi	adĭtum	*go to.*
Anteo	anteire	anteivi	—	*go before.*
Circumeo	circumire	circumivi	circuitum	*go round.*
Coeo	coire	coivi	coitum	*go together.*
Exeo	exire	exivi	exitum	*go out.*
Ineo	inire	inivi	initum	*go into*
Intereo	interire	interi(v)i	interitum	*perish.*
Obeo	obire	obivi	obitum	*encounter.*
Pereo	perire	peri(v)i	peritum	*perish.*
Præeo	præire	præivi	præitum	*go before*
Prætereo	præterire	præterivi	præteritum	*go by.*
Prodeo	prodire	prodi(v)i	proditum	*go forth.*
Redeo	redire	redī(v)i	reditum	*return.*
Subeo	subire	subī(v)i	subitum	$\left\{\begin{array}{l}\textit{go under,}\\\textit{undergo.}\end{array}\right.$
Transeo	transire	transi(v)i	transitum	*go over.*

The Perfects of all these verbs have also the *v* left out; as, *obivi, obii,* etc., etc., which is, indeed, the more usual form. Where the *v* is bracketed the long form is not given.

VERBS SIMILAR IN SPELLING,*

THOUGH THEY HAVE TOTALLY DISTINCT MEANINGS.

Appello	appellare	appellavi	appellatum	call.
Appello	appellĕre	appuli	appulsum	land.
Compello	compellare	compellavi	compellatum	address.
Compello	compellĕre	compuli	compulsum	compel.
Colligo	colligāre	colligavi	colligatum	bind.
Colligo	colligĕre	collegi	collectum	collect.
Dĭco	dicare	dicavi	dicatum	devote.
Dĭco	dicere	dixi	dictum	say.
Ēdo	edere	edĭdi	edĭtum	give forth.
Ĕdo	ĕdĕre (esse)	ēdi	esum	eat.
Edŭco	educāre	educavi	educatum	educate.
Edūco	edūcĕre	eduxi	eductum	lead out.
Lēgō	legāre	legavi	legatum	depute.
Lĕgo	legĕre	lēgi	lectum	gather.
Occĭdo	occĭdĕre	occĭdi	occāsum	fall.
Occīdo	occīdĕre	occīdi	occīsum	slay.
Sĕro	serĕre	serui	sertum	join.
Sĕro	serĕre	sēvi	sātum	sow.
Vŏlo	volare	volavi	volatum	fly.
Vŏlo	velle	volui	—	wish.

Est	3rd sing. pres. indic. of sum	I am.
Est	„ „ „ „ edo	I eat.
Nĭtēre	inf. pres. of niteo	shine.
Nĭtĕre	2nd sing. imperat. pres. of nitor	strive.
Oblĭtus	part. pass. pf. of oblĭno	smear.
Oblītus	part. pf. of obliviscor	forget.
Părĕre	inf. pres. act. of pario	bring forth.
Pārēre	„ „ pareo	obey.
Vĕnit ⎫ Vēnit ⎭	⎰ 3rd. sing. pres. ind. of venio ⎱ ⎱ 3rd. sing. perf. ind. of „ ⎰	come.
Vĕnit	3rd. sing. pres. ind. of veneo	be sold.

* Notice that the quantities differ in many cases.

Cases in which the same Verb has different Meanings.

These will often be found to be reducible to one idea—thus,

Lĕgo means (1) To *gather, select.*
"Illa legit calthas."

    (2) To *read.*
"Plurimus orbe legor."

    (3) To *coast along, skim.*
"Inarimen Prochytamque legit."

These come under the one idea of "gathering:" (1) to gather literally; (2) to pick out the letters and words; (3) to skim lightly over or pass along. All these involve a notion of moving lightly along from one thing to another as one does in gathering flowers.

Ruo means (1) To *fall.*
"Ruit alto e culmine Troja."—Virg. *Æn.* ii.

    (2) To *rush.*
"Quoquo scelesti ruitis ? "—*Hor.*

    (3) To *throw up.*
"Et ruit atram
Ad cœlum picea crassus caligine nubem."

These all fall under the idea of "violent motion." "To be in violent motion" (intransitive); "to put in violent motion" (transitive). The motion may be in any direction—up or down.

Verbs which have no Perfect.

Antecello	*surpass.*	Furo	*rage.*
Ambigo	*waver.*	Glubo	*bark, peel.*
Frendo	*gnash.*	Labasco	*resound.*
	Plecto	*punish.*	

Verbs that have no Supine.

Algco	*be cold.*	Niteo	*shine.*
Ango	*vex.*	Nolo	*be unwilling.*
Antecello	*surpass.*	Nuo	*nod.*
Audeo	*dare.*		
		Pateo	*lie open.*
Compesco	*restrain.*	Paveo	*fear.*
Conniveo	*wink.*	Plecto	*punish.*
		Posco	*demand.*
Dego	*live.*	Possum	*be able.*
Disco	*learn.*	Psallo	*play on harp.*
Ferveo, fervo	*boil.*	Sapio	*be wise.*
Fido	*trust.*	Scabo	*scratch.*
Fio	*become.*	Sileo	*be silent.*
Frigeo	*be cold.*	Soleo	*be wont.*
Fulgeo	*glitter.*	Sterto	*snore.*
		Strideo, strido	*creak.*
Gaudeo	*rejoice.*		
Incesso	*assail.*	Timeo	*fear.*
		Tremo	*tremble.*
Lateo	*lie hid.*	Tumeo	*swell.*
Luceo	*shine.*	Turgeo	*swell.*
Lugeo	*mourn.*		
		Vergo	*bend.*
Malo	*prefer.*	Vigeo	*flourish.*
Metuo	*fear.*	Vireo	*be green.*
Mico	*glitter.*	Volo	*wish.*

Also following Inceptives :—

conticesco	horresco	pallesco
crebresco	languesco	tumesco
delitesco	maturesco	vanesco
extimesco	obmutesco	vesperasco

With many others.

Verbs which have neither Perfect nor Supine.

Ambigo	*waver.*	Furo	*rage.*
Antecello	*surpass.*	Plecto	*punish.*
Dignosco	*distinguish.*	Præcello	*excel.*

Also following Inceptives :—

hebesco   labasco   mitesco   puerasco

And many others.

Verbs which have two Supines.

Alo	alitum, altum	*feed.*
Applico	applicitum, applicatum	*join.*
Eneco	enectum, enecatum	*kill.*
Frendo	fressum, fresum	*gnash*
Frico	frictum, fricatum	*rub.*
Frigo	frictum, frixum	*parch.*
Lavo	lavatum, lautum, lotum	*wash.*
Misceo	mistum, mixtum	*mix.*
Pando	passum, pansum	*expand.*
Pango	panctum, pactum	*fix.*
Plico	*plicitum, plicatum	*fold.*
Poto	potatum, potum	*drink.*
Sancio	sanctum, sancitum	*consecrate.*
Tendo	tentum, tensum	*stretch.*
Tundo	tunsum, tusum	*thump.*

Two or more Supines from the Same Verb.

Alitum Altum }	Alo	*feed.*
Applicitum Applicatum }	Applico	*join*
Enectum Enecatum }	Eneco	*kill.*
Fressum Fresum }	Frendo	*gnash.*
Frictum Fricatum }	Frico	*rub.*
Frictum Frixum }	Frigo	*parch.*
Lavatum Lautum Lotum }	Lavo	*wash.*
Mistum Mixtum }	Misceo	*mix.*
Passum Pansum }	Pando	*expand.*
Panctum Pactum }	Pango	*fix.*
*Plicitum Plicatum }	Plico	*fold.*
Potatum Potum }	Poto	*drink.*
Sanctum Sancitum }	Sancio	*consecrate.*
Tentum Tensum }	Tendo	*stretch.*
Tunsum Tusum }	Tundo	*thump.*

SUPINES SOMEWHAT SIMILAR THAT COME FROM DIFFERENT VERBS.

captum	capio	*take.*
carptum	carpo	*pluck.*
casum	cado	*fall.*
cæsum	cædo	*cut.*
censum	censeo	*vote.*
sensum	sentio	*feel.*
scītum	scisco	*decree.*
scītum	scio	*know.*
sĭtum	sino	*allow.*
cĭtum	cieo	*put in motion.*
cessum	cedo	*yield.*
sessum	sedeo	*sit.*
cretum	cerno	*sift.*
cretum	cresco	*grow.*
fixum	figo	*fix.*
fictum	fingo	*fashion.*
frictum	frico	*rub.*
frictum	frigo	*parch.*
genitum	gigno	*beget.*
gemitum	gemo	*groan.*
mansum	maneo	*remain.*
mansum	mando	*chew.*
messum	meto	*mow.*
missum	mitto	*send.*
mulsum	mulceo	*soothe.*
mulsum	mulgeo	*milk.*
parsum	parco	*spare.*
partum	pario	*bring forth.*

scssum	sedere	*sit.*
sensum	sentire	*feel.*
tensum(tum)	tendo	*stretch.*
tentum	teneo	*hold.*
textum	texo	*weave.*
tectum	tego	*cover.*
versum	verro	*sweep.*
versum	verto	*turn.*
visum	viso	*visit.*
visum	video	*see.*
vinctum	vincio	*bind.*
victum	vinco	*conquer.*
victum	vivo	*live.*
vectum	veho	*carry.*

PERFECTS SOMEWHAT SIMILAR THAT COME FROM DIFFERENT VERBS.

cecĭdi }	cado	*fall.*
cecīdi }	cœdo	*cut.*
crevi }	cerno	*sift.*
crevi }	cresco	*grow.*
scivi }	scisco	*seek to know, decree.*
scivi }	scio	*know.*
ēdi }	ĕdo	*eat.*
ēdĭdi }	ēdo	*publish.*
fixi }	figo	*fix.*
finxi }	fingo	*fashion.*
frixi }	frigesco	*grow cold.*
frixi }	frigo	*parch.*
fulsi }	fulcio	*prop.*
fulsi }	fulgeo	*glitter.*

luxi	}	luceo	*shine.*
luxi		lugeo	*mourn.*
mandi	}	mando	*chew.*
mansi		maneo	*remain.*
messui	}	meto	*reap.*
metui		metuo	*fear.*
mulsi	}	mulceo	*soothe.*
mulsi		mulgeo	*milk.*
nactus	}	nanciscor	*obtain.*
natus		nascor	*be born.*
orsus		ordior	*begin.*
ausus	}	audeo	*dare.*
ortus		orior	*rise.*
pavi	}	pasco	*feed.*
pavi		paveo	*fear.*
peperci	}	parco	*spare.*
peperi		pario	*bring forth.*
pependi	}	pendeo	*hang.*
pependi		pendo	*cause to hang, weigh.*
pinxi	}	pingo	*paint.*
pinsi (pinsui)		pinso	*pound.*
quivi	}	queo	*be able.*
quievi		quiesco	*rest.*
scivi	}	scio	*know*
civi		cieo	*put in motion.*
vici		vinco	*conquer*
vinxi	}	vincio	*bind*
vixi		vivo	*live*

PRINCIPAL INCEPTIVE VERBS.

These, which are also called Inchoative Verbs, express the
beginning of action, and are of the 3rd Conjugation.

(a) THOSE WITH PERFECT AND SUPINE.

Abolesco	-ere	abolevi	abolitum	*pass away.*
Adolesco	-ere	adolevi	adultum	*grow up.*
Coalesco	-ere	coalui	coalitum	*grow together.*
Concupisco	-ere	concupivi	concupitum	*desire.*
Consuesco	-ere	consuevi	consuetum	*get accustomed.*
Convalesco	-ere	convalui	convalitum	*get well.*
Exardesco	-ere	exarsi	exarsum	*blaze forth.*
Inveterasco	-ere	inveteravi	inveteratum	*become old.*
Obdormisco	-ere	obdormivi	obdormitum	*fall asleep.*
Scisco	-ere	scivi	scitum	*decree.*
Mansuesco	-ere	mansuevi	mansuetum	*grow tame.*
Revivisco	-ere	revixi	revictum	*come to life again.*

(β) THOSE WITH PERFECT ONLY :—

Consenesco	ere	consenui	*grow old.*
Conticesco	-ere	conticui	*become silent.*
Delitesco	-ere	delitui	*lie hid.*
Duresco	-ere	durui	*grow hard.*
Effloresco	-ere	efflorui	*bloom.*
Expavesco	-ere	expavi	*grow alarmed.*
Horresco	-ere	horrui	*shudder.*
Incalesco	-ere	incalui	*get warm.*
Incandesco	-ere	incandui	*glow.*
Incanesco	-ere	incanui	*become white.*
Increbresco	-ere	increbrui	*become frequent.*
Ingemisco	-ere	ingemui	*groan over.*
Illucesco	-ere	illuxi	*grow light.*
Languesco	-ere	langui	*grow languid.*
Maturesco	-ere	maturui	*grow ripe.*

Obmutesco	-ere	obmutui	*become mute.*
Obstupesco	-ere	obstupui	*become amazed.*
Pallesco	-ere	pallui	*grow pale.*
Patesco	-ere	patui	*become open.*
Rubesco	-ere	rubui	*become red.*
Tepesco	-ere	tepui	*become warm.*
Viresco	-ere	virui	*become green.*

(γ) WITHOUT PERFECT OR SUPINE.

Hebesco	-ere	*grow blunt.*	Labasco	*begin to totter.*
Ingravesco	-ere	*grow heavy.*	Mitesco	*grow ripe.*
		Puerasco	*become a boy*	

PRINCIPAL FREQUENTATIVE VERBS.

These signify repeated or intenser action, and are of the 1st Conjugation. Such are :—

Canto	*sing.*	Hæsito	*stick fast.*
Capto	*catch up.*	Lectito	*gather often.*
†Curso	*run hither and thither*	Merso	*dip in.*
Cursito	*run hither and thither*	Minitor	*threaten.*
Clamito	*cry aloud.*	Pulso	*strike.*
Dicto	*say often.*	†Rogito	*ask often.*
Dictito	*say often.*	Salto	*dance.*
Gesto	*bear.*	†Ventito	*come often.*

These are all conjugated regularly, *-are*, *-avi*, *-atum*, except those marked †, which have no perfect or supine.
Minitor, *-ari*, *-atus sum*, deponent.

DESIDERATIVE VERBS.

These signify "desire to do a thing," and are of the 4th Conjugation.

Esurio, esurire, — esuritum	*wish to eat.*
Parturio, parturire, parturivi & -ii, —	*am in labour, wish to produce.*

PRINCIPAL IMPERSONAL VERBS.

These are mostly of the 2nd Conjugation, and are con-jugated as such only in 3rd Person Singular of Finite Verb and in the Infinitive.

CONJUGATION 1.—INFINITIVES REGULAR IN *āre.*

Constat	constitit	*it is acknowledged.*
Delectat		*it delights.*
Juvat	juvit	*it pleases.*

CONJUGATION 2.—INFINITIVES REGULAR IN *ēre.*

Attinet	attinuit	*it relates..*
Dedecet	dedecuit	*it misbecomes.*
Decet	decuit	*it becomes.*
Libet	libuit & libitum est	*it pleases.*
Licet	licuit & licitum est	*it is lawful.*
Liquet	liquit & licuit	*it is clear.*
Miseret	miseruit & miseritum est	*it pities.*
Oportet	oportuit	*it behoves.*
Pertinet	pertinuit	*it belongs.*
Piget	piguit & pigitum est	*it irks.*
Pœnitet	pœnituit	*it repents.*
Pudet	puduit & puditum est	*it shames.*
Tædet	tæduit & pertæsum est	*it disgusts.*

CONJUGATION 3.—INFINITIVES REGULAR IN *ĕre.*

Accidit	accidit	*it happens.*
Contingit	contigit	*it befalls*

CONJUGATION 4.—INFINITIVES REGULAR IN *īre.*

Convĕnit	convĕnit	*it suits.*
Evĕnit	evĕnit	*it turns out.*

Interest	interfuit	interesse	*it imports.*
Rēfert	rētulit	rēferre	*it concerns.*

IMPERSONALS RELATING TO THE WEATHER, ETC.

Advesperascit	advesperascĕre	-avit	*it approaches evening.*
Fulgurat	fulgurare		*it lightens.*
Illucescit	illucescĕre	illuxit	*it grows light.*
Lucescit	lucescĕre		*it dawns.*
Ningit	ningĕre	ninxit	*it snows.*
Pluit	pluĕre	pluit (pluvit)	*it rains.*
Tonat	tonare	tonuit	*it thunders.*
Vesperascit	vesperascĕre	vesperavit	*it becomes evening.*

SPECIMEN OF AN IMPERSONAL VERB IN FULL.

	Indic. Mood.	*Conj. Mood.*	*Inf. Mood.*
Pres.	Oportet	oporteat	oportere.
Fut.	Oportebit		
Imperfect.	Oportebat	oporteret	
Perfect.	Oportuit	oportuerit	oportuisse.
Fut. Perf.	Oportuerit		
P. Perf.	Oportuerat	oportuisset.	

ANOMALOUS VERBS,

I.e., Verbs which do not form their parts according to Rule.

Eo	ire	ivi (ii), ĭtum	*go.*
Fero	ferre	tuli, latum	*bear.*
Fio	fieri	factus sum	*am made.*
Malo	malle	malui	*had rather.*
Nolo	nolle	nolui	*am unwilling.*
Possum	posse	potui	*am able.*
Queo	quire	quivi	*am able.*
Volo	velle	volui	*wish.*

THE IRREGULARITIES IN ĔDO (*to Eat*) ARE :—

Indicative Present.

Act.   Edis *or* es   edit *or* est   editis *or* estis.
Pass.   3 sing.   Editur *or* estur.

Imperative Present.

Act.   Ede *or* es,   edite *or* este.

Imperative Future.

Act.   Edito *or* esto, editote *or* estote.

Conjunctive Present.
Act.   Edam *or* edim.

Conjunctive Imperfect.
Act.   Ederem *or* essem.
Pass.   Ederetur *or* essetur.

Infinitive.
Edere *or* esse.

DEFECTIVE VERBS.

INQUAM, *I Say.*

Ind. Pres.	Inquam	inquis	inquit.
	inquimus		inquiunt.
Fut. Simple.		inquies	inquiet.
Imperf.			inquiebat.
			inquiebant.
Perf.		inquisti	inquit.
Imperative Pres.		inque, inquite.	
Imperative Fut.		inquito.	

AIO, *I Say.*

Ind. Pres.	Aio	ais	ait, aiunt.
Ind. Imp.	Aiebam, etc., regular, sing. and plural.		
Conj. Pres.		aias	aiat, aiant.

DEFECTIVE VERBS (continued).

The following have no present stem, and therefore no
tenses derived from that stem.

Cœpi,   *I have begun or began.*
. Odi,   *I hate.*
Memini,   *I remember.*

Indicative Mood.

Perf.	{ Cœp- Od- Memin-	} i, isti, it, } imus, istis, erunt.
Pluperf.	{ Cœp- Od- Memin-	} eram, eras, erat, } eramus, eratis, erant.
Fut. Perf.	{ Cœp- Od- Memin-	} ero, eris, erit, } erimus, eritis, erint.

Conjunctive Mood.

Perf.	{ Cœp- Od- Memin-	} erim, eris, erit, } erimus, eritis, erint.
Pluperf.	{ Cœp- Od- Memin-	} issem, isses, isset, } issemus, issetis, issent.

Imperative Mood.   memento, mementote.

Verb Infinite.

Infinitive. Perf.	Cœpisse	odisse	meminisse.
Part. Perf. Pass.	Cœptus	osus.	
Part. Fut. Act.	Cœpturus	osurus.	

N.B. Perf. Memini   *I remember.*   Odi   *I hate.*
  P.P. Memineram { *I was remembering,* Oderam { *I was hating,*
        { *remembered.*   { *hated.*
  F.P. Meminero *I shall remember.*   Odero   *I shall hate.*

FARI, *to Speak.*

The forms in brackets only found in compounds,
e.g. affari, effari, prŏfari, prœfari.

Ind. Pres.	Fatur, (famur), (famini).	
Fut.	Fabor, (faberi), fabitur, (fabimur).	
Imperf.	(Fabar).	
Perf.	Fatus sum, etc.	
Pluperf.	Fatus eram, etc.	
Conj. Imperf.	(Farer).	
Perf.	Fatus sim, etc.	
Pluperf.	Fatus, essem, etc.	

Imperative Present. Fare.

Infinitive. Fari. *Ger.* Fandi, fando. *Supine.* Fatu.

Part. Pres. Fantem, fantis, etc. *Part. Perf.* Fatus, a, um.

Gerundive. Fandus.

AGE, AVE, ETC.

Age, agite, *come.*

Apage, *begone.*

Ave (sometimes spelt *have*), avete, aveto, avēre (*Infin.*) *hail!*

Salve, salvete, salveto, salvebis (*fut.*), salvēre (*Infin.*), *hail!*

Cĕdo, cedite *or* cette, *give here.*

Quæso, *pl.* quæsumus, *entreat.*

Vale, valete, valeto, valebis (*fut.*), valēre (*Infin.*), *farewell.*

Infit, *he begins.* (*Only in this form.*)

K

IRREGULAR VERBS,

ALPHABETICALLY ARRANGED.

NOTE.—*Those marked with an asterisk are only used in compounds.*

Abolesco, -levi, abolitum, 3. *to pass away.*

Accendo, -di, -sum, 3. *to set on fire.*

Acuo, acui, acûtum, 3. *to sharpen.*

Adolesco, -levi, adultum, 3. *to grow up.*

Agnosco, -novi, -nītum, 3. *to recognise.*

Ago, egi, actum, 3. *to do.*

Aio, ais, ait, *I say,* defect.

Algeo, alsi, 2. *to be cold.*

Allicio, allexi, allectum, 3. *to allure.*

Alo, alui, alītum or altum, 3. *to nourish.*

Ambigo, 3. *to waver.*

Amicio, amicui, amictum, 4. *to clothe.*

Ango, anxi, 3. *to squeeze.*

Antecello, 3. *to surpass.*

Aperio, aperui, apertum, 4. *to open.*

Appello, appuli, appulsum, 3. *to land.*

Applico, applicui applicavi, applicītum applicatum, 1. *to apply.*

Arcesso, -ivi, -ītum, 3. *to send for.*

Ardeo, arsi, arsum, 2. *to take fire.*

Arguo, argui, argûtum, 3. *to prove.*

Audeo, ausus sum, 2. *to dare.*

Augeo, auxi, auctum, 2. *to increase.*

Bibo, bībi, bibitum, 3. *to drink.*

Cado, cecīdi, câsum, 3. *to fall.*

Cædo, cecīdi, cæsum, 3. *to cut, beat, kill.*

Caleo, calui, 2. *to be warm.*

*Cando, *cendi, *censum, 3. *to set on fire.*

Cano, cěcīni, cantum, 3 *to sing.*

Capesso, -sivi, -sītum, 3. *to seize.*

Capio, cepi, captum, 3. *to take.*

Carpo, carpsi, carptum, 3. *to pluck.*

Caveo, cavi, cautum, 2. *to beware.*

Cedo, cessi, cessum, 3. *to yield.*

Censeo, censui, censum, 2. *to vote.*

Cerno, crevi, cretum, 3. *to sift.*

Cieo, civi, cītum, 2. *to stir up.*

Cingo, cinxi, cinctum, 3. *to surround.*

Clango, 3. *to resound.*

Claudo, clausi, clausum, 3. *to shut.*

Coalesco, coalui, coalitum, 3. *to grow together.*

Cognosco, -novi, -nītum, 3. *know.*

Cogo, coěgi, coactum, 3. *to compel.*

Colligo, collegi, collectum, 3. *to collect.*

Colo, colui, cultum, 3. *to till.*

Como, compsi, comptum, 3. *to adorn.*

Compello, -puli, -pulsum, 3. *to compel.*

Comperio, -pěri, -pertum, 4. *ascertain.*

Compesco, compescui, 3. *to restrain.*

Concupisco, -ivi, -itum, 3. *to desire.*

Conniveo, -nivi and -nixi, 2. *to wink.*

Consenesco, consenui, 3. *to grow old.*

Consuesco, consuevi, consuetum, 3. *to get accustomed.*

Consŭlo, -sŭlui, -sultum, 3. *to consult.*

Conticesco, conticui, 3. *to become silent.*

Convalesco, -valui, -valitum, 3. *to get well.*

Coquo, coxi, coctum, 3. *to cook.*

Crepo, crĕpui, crepĭtum, 1. *to creak.*
Cresco, crēvi, crētum, 3. *to grow.*
*Cŭbo, *cubui, *cubĭtum, 1. *to lie down.*
Cŭdo, cudi, cūsum, 3. *to fashion.*
Cumbo, cubui, cubĭtum, 3. *to lie down.*
Cupio, cupĭvi, cupĭtum, 3. *to desire.*
Curro, cŭcurri, cursum, 3. *to run.*

Defendo, defendi, defensum, 3. *to defend.*
Dēgo, 3. *to live.*
Deleo, dēlēvi, delctum, 2. *to blot out.*
Delitesco, delitui, 3. *to lie hid.*
Demo, dempsi, demptum, 3. *to take away.*
Depso, -sui, -stum, 3. *to knead.*
Dico, dixi, dictum, 3. *to say.*
Dignosco, 3. *to distinguish.*
Diligo, dilexi, dīlectum, 3. *to lore.*
Dimico, -avi and -ui, -atum, 1. *to fight.*
Disco, dĭdĭci, 3. *to learn.*
Divĭdo, divīsi, divisum, 3. *to divide.*
Do, dĕdi, dătum, 1. *to give.*

  Abdo, abdidi, abditum, 3. *to hide.*

Addo		*to add.*
Condo		*to found, hide.*
Credo		*to believe.*
Dedo		*to give up.*
Edo		*to give forth.*
Perdo	-didi, -ditum, 3.	*to lose.*
Prodo		*to betray.*
Reddo		*to restore.*
Subdo		*to substitute.*
Trado		*to deliver.*
Vendo		*to sell.*

Doceo, docui, doctum, 2. *to teach.*
Doleo, dolui, dolitum, 2. *to feel pain.*
Dŏmo, dŏmui, dŏmĭtum, 1. *to tame.*
Duco, duxi, ductum, 3. *to lead.*
Duresco, durui, 3. *to grow hard.*

Edo, ĕdi, ĕsum, 3. *to eat.*
Effloresco, efflorui, 3. *to bloom.*
Elicio, elicui, elicitum, 3. *to entice forth.*

Emo, emi, emptum, 3. *to buy, take.*
Eneco, -cui & -avi, -ctum & -ātum, 1. *kill.*

Eo, -ivi, -ĭtum, *to go.*
  Abeo, -ivi and -ii, -ĭtum, *to go away.*
  Adeo, -ivi and -ii, -ĭtum, *to go to.*
  Ante-eo, ante-ivi, *to go before.*
  Circu(m)eo, -ivi, -itum, *to go round.*
  Coeo, coivi, coitum, *to go together.*
  Exeo, exivi, exitum, *to go out.*
  Ineo, inivi, initum, *to go into.*
  Intereo, -i(v)i, -ĭtum, *to perish.*

  Obeo, obivi, obĭtum, *to encounter.*
  Pereo, peri(v)i, peritum, *to perish.*
  Præeo, -ivi, -itum, *to go before.*
  Prætereo, -ivi, -itum, *to go by.*
  Prodeo, -i(v)i, -itum, *to go forth.*
  Redeo, redi(v)i, reditum, *to return.*
  Subeo, subi(v)i, subitum { *to go under, undergo.*
  Transeo, -i(v)i, -ĭtum, *to go over.*

Exardesco, -arsi, -arsum, 3. *to blaze forth.*
Excello, excellui, 3. *to excel.*
Expavesco, expavi, 3. *to grow alarmed.*

Facesso, -si, -sĭtum, 3. *to accomplish.*
Facio, fēci, factum, 3. *to do, make.*
Fallo, fĕfelli, falsum, 3. *to deceive.*
Farcio, farsi, fartum, 4. *to stuff.*
Faveo, favi, fautum, 2. *to favour.*
*Fendo, *fendi, *fensum, 3. *to strike.*
Fero, inf. ferre, tŭli, latum, *to bear.*
Ferveo and -vo, -bui and -vi, 2, 3. *to boil.*
Fīdo, fīsus sum, 3. *to trust.*
Fīgo, fixi, fixum, 3. *to fix.*

Findo, fīdi, fissum, 3. *to cleave.*
Fingo, finxi, fictum, 3. *to fashion.*
Fio, inf. fĭĕri, factus sum, *to become.*
Flecto, flexi, flexum, 3. *to bend.*
Fleo, flevi, flētum, 2. *to weep.*
Floreo, florui, 2. *to flourish.*
Fluo, fluxi, fluxum, 3. *to flow.*

Fodio, fŏdi, fossum, 3. *to dig.*
Foveo, fovi, fotum, 2. *to cherish.*
Frango, fregi, fractum, 3. *to break.*

Fremo, -ui, -itum, 3. *to murmur.*
Frendo, fressum & frēsum, 3. *to gnash.*
Frico, frĭcui, frictum & -atum, 1. *to rub.*
Frigeo, 2. *to be cold.*
Frigo, -xi, -ctum or -xum, 3. *to parch.*
Fugio, fugi, fugitum, 3. *to flee.*
Fulcio, fulsi, fultum, 4. *to prop.*
Fulgeo, fulsi, 2, *to glitter.*
Fundo, fūdi, fusum, 3. *to pour, rout.*
Furo, furui, 3. *to rage.*

Gaudeo, gavīsus sum, 2. *to rejoice.*
Gemo, gemui, gĕmĭtum, 3. *to groan.*
Gero, gessi, gestum, 3. *to carry on.*
Gigno, genui, genitum, 3. *to produce.*
Glubo, 3. *to bark, peel.*

Hœreo, hæsi, hæsum, 2. *to stick.*
Haurio, hausi, haustum, 4. *to drain.*
Horresco, horrui, 3. *to shudder.*

Ico, ici, ictum, 3. *to strike.*
Ignosco, ignŏvi, ignōtum, 3. *to pardon.*
Illucesco, illuxi, 3. *to grow light.*
Imbuo, imbui, imbutum, 3. *to tinge.*
Incalesco, incalui, 3. *to get warm.*
Incandesco, incandui, 3. *to glow.*
Incanesco, incanui, 3. *to become white.*
Incendo, -cendi, -censum, 3. *to set on fire*
Incesso, -cessĭvi, or -cessi, 3. *to assail.*
Incipio, incepi, inceptum, 3. *to begin.*
Increbresco, -crebui, 3. *become frequent*
Indulgeo, -ulsi, -ultum, 2. *to be indulgent*
Induo, indui, indutum, 3. *to put on.*
Ingemisco, ingemui, 3. *to groan over.*

Jacio, jēci, jactum, 3. *to throw.*
Jubeo, jussi, jussum, 2. *to command.*
Jungo, junxi, junctum, 3. *to join.*
Juvo, juvi, jutum, 1. *to help.*

Labasco, 3. *to totter.*
Lacesso, -ivi, -itum, 3. *to provoke.*
Lædo, læsi, læsum, *to hurt.*
Lambo, lambi, 3. *to lick.*
Languesco, langui, 3. *to grow languid.*
Lateo, latui, 2. *to lie hid.*
Lavo, lavi, lavātum, lautum, lotum, 1. *to wash.*

Lego, legi, lectum, 3. *to choose, read.*
Lino, levi and livi, lītum, 3. *to smear.*
Lingo, linxi, linctum, 3. *to lick.*
Linquo, liqui, * lictum, 3. *to leave.*
Luceo, luxi, 2. *to shine.*
Ludo, lusi, lusum, 3. *to play.*
Lugeo, luxi, 2. *to mourn.*
Luo, lui, luĭtum, 3. *to wash, atone.*

Malo, inf. malle, malui, *to prefer.*
Mando, mandi, mansum, 3. *to chew.*
Maneo, mansi, mansum, 2. *to remain.*
Mansuesco,-suevi, -suetum,3. *grow tame.*
Maturesco, maturui, 3. *to grow ripe.*
Mergo, mersi, mersum, 3. *to drown.*
Meto, messui, messum, 3. *to mow, reap.*
Metuo, metui, 2. *to fear.*
Mico, micui, 1. *to glitter.*

Minuo, minui, minutum, 3. *to lessen.*
Misceo, -cui, mistum or mixtum, 2. *mix.*
Mitesco, 3. *to grow ripe.*
Mitto, misi, missum, 3. *to send.*
Mŏlo, molui, molitum, 3. *to grind.*
Mordeo, mŏmordi, morsum, 2. *to bite.*
Moveo, movi, mōtum, 2. *to move.*
Mulceo, mulsi, mulsum, 2. *to soothe.*
Mulgeo, mulsi, mulsum, 2. *to milk.*

Necto, -xui and -xi, -xum, 3. *to tie, bind.*
Negligo, -lexi, -lectum, 3. *to neglect.*
Neo, nevi, nētum, 2. *to spin.*
Ningo, ninxi, 3. *to snow.*
No, navi, 1. *to swim.*
Nolo, inf. nolle, nolui, *to be unwilling.*

Nosco, novi, notum, 3. *to be acquainted with.*

Nubo, nupsi, nuptum, 3. *to be married.*

Obmutesco, obmutui, 3. *to become mute.*
Obdormisco, -ivi, -itum, 3. *to fall asleep.*
Obstupesco, -stupui, 3. *become amazed.*
Occido, occĭdi, occāsum, 3. *to fall.*
Occido, occīdi, occīsum, 3. *to slay.*
Occulo, occului, occultum, 3. *to hide.*
Offendo, -di, -sum, 3. *to knock against.*
Operio, operui, opertum, 4. *to cover.*

Pallesco, pallui, 3. *grow pale.*
Pando, -di, -sum & passum, 3. *to spread.*
Pango, pepigi, pactum, 3. *to fasten.*
Parco, peperci, parsum, 3. *to spare.*
Pario, peperi, partum, 3. *to bring forth.*
Pasco, pavi, pastum, 3. *to feed.*
Patesco, patui, 3. *to become open.*
Paveo, pavi, 2. *to fear.*
Pecto, -xi, -xum and -ctĭtum, 3. *to comb.*
Pello, pepuli, pulsum, 3. *to drive.*
Pendeo, pĕpendi, pensum, 2. *to hang.*

Pendo, pĕpendi, pensum, 3. *to weigh.*
Percello, -cŭli, -culsum, 3. *to dishearten.*
Pergo, perrexi, perrectum, 3. *to go on.*
Peto, petivi, petitum, 3. *to ask, seek.*
Pingo, pinxi, pictum, 3. *to paint.*
Pinso, -si and -sui, -sum, 3. *to pound.*
Plango, planxi, planctum, 3. *to beat.*
Plaudo, -si, -sum, 3. *to clap hands.*
Plecto, 3. *to punish.*
*Pleo, *plevi, *pletum, 2. *to fill.*
Plico, plicavi and *plicui, *plicatum and plicitum, 1. *to fold.*

Pono, posui, positum, 3. *to place.*
Posco, poposci, 3. *to demand.*
Possum, inf. posse, potui, *to be able.*
Poto, -avi, -atum and pōtum, 1. *to drink.*
Præcello, præcellui, 3. *to exc.l.*

Prandeo, prandi, pransum, 2. *to dine.*
Prehendo, -di, -sum, 3. *to grasp.*
Premo, pressi, pressum, 3. *to press.*
Promo, -mpsi, -mptum, 3. *to take forth.*
Psallo, psalli, 3. *to play on harp.*
Pungo, pupugi, punctum, 3. *to prick.*

Quæro, quæsivi, quæsitum, 3. *to seek.*
Quatio, quassi, quassum, 3. *to shake.*
Queo, quivi, quĭtum, *to be able.*
Quiesco, quievi, quietum, 3. *to rest.*

Răpio, rapui, raptum, 3. *to seize.*
Rado, rasi, rasum, 3. *to scrape.*
Rego, rexi, rectum, 3. *to rule.*
Reperio, -pperi, -pertum, 4. *to discover.*
Rĕpo, repsi, reptum, 3. *to creep.*
Revivisco, revixi, 3. *to come to life again.*

Rideo, risi, risum, 2. *to laugh.*
Rodo, rosi, rosum, 3. *to gnaw.*
Rubesco, rubui, 3. *to become red.*
Rudo, -di and -ivi, -itum, 3. *to bray.*
Rumpo, rupi, ruptum, 3. *to break.*
Ruo, rui, rutum, 3. *to rush, fall.*

Sæpio (sepio), -si, -tum, 4. *to hedge in.*
Salio, salui, saltum, 4. *to leap.*
Sancio, sanxi, sanctum, 4. *to consecrate.*
Sapio, sapi(v)i, 3. *to taste of, be wise.*
Sarcio, sarsi, sartum, 4. *to mend.*
Scabo, scabi, 3. *to scratch.*
Scalpo, scalpsi, scalptum, 3. *to scratch.*
Scando, scandi, scansum, 3. *to climb.*
Scindo, scĭdi, scissum, 3. *to tear.*

Scisco, scivi, scitum, 3. *to decree.*
Scribo, scripsi, scriptum, 3. *to write.*
Sculpo, sculpsi, sculptum, 3. *to engrave.*
Seco, secui, sectum, 1. *to cut.*
Sedeo, sēdi, sessum, 2. *to sit.*
Sentio, sensi, sensum, 4, *to feel.*
Sepelio, sepelivi, sepultum, 3. *to bury.*

Sero, serui, sertum, 3. *to join.*
Sero, sevi, sātum, 3. *to sow.*

Serpo, serpsi, serptum, 3. *to crawl.*
Sido, sīdi, 3. *to sit down.*
Sileo, silui, 2. *to be silent.*
Singultio, 4. *to sob.*
Sino, sivi, sĭtum, 3. *to allow.*
*Sisto, *stiti,*statum, 3. *to make to stand.*
Sitio, siti(v)i, 4. *to be thirsty.*

Soleo, solitus sum, 2. *to be wont.*
Solvo, solvi, solūtum, 3. *to loosen.*
Sono, sonui, sonitum, 1. *to sound.*
Sorbeo, -bui, 2. *to suck up.*
Spargo, sparsi, sparsum, 3. *to sprinkle.*
*Specio, *spexi, *spectum, 3. *to espy.*
Sperno, sprevi, spretum, 3. *to despise.*
Spondeo,spopondi, sponsum, 2.*to pledge.*
Statuo, statui, statūtum, 3. *to set up.*

Sterno, stravi, stratum, 3. *to strew.*
Sterto, stertui, 3. *to snore.*
*Stinguo,*stinxi,*stinctum, 2. *to quench.*
Sto, stĕti, statum, 1. *to stand.*
Strepo, strepui, strepitum, 3. *to roar.*
Strideo, stridi, 2. *to shriek.*
Stringo, strinxi, strictum, 3. *to tie.*
Struo, struxi, structum, 3. *to pile.*
Suadeo, suasi, suasum, 2. *to advise.*
Suesco, suevi, suetum, 3. *to be wont.*
Sugo, suxi, suctum, 3. *to suck.*

Sum, inf. esse, perf. fui, *to be.*
  Absum, -esse, -fui & afui, *be absent.*
  Adsum, -esse, -affui, *to be present.*
  Desum, -esse, -fui, *to be wanting.*
  Insum, -esse, -fui, *to be in.*
  Intersum, -esse, -fui, *to be among.*
  Obsum, -esse, -fui, *to be in the way of.*
  Praesum, -esse, -fui, *to be before.*
  Prosum, prodesse, profui, *to be useful.*
  Subsum, subesse, *to be under.*
  Supersum,-esse, -fui,*to be over,remain.*

Sumo, sumpsi, sumptum, 3. *to take.*
Suo, sui, sutum, 3. *to sew.*
Surgo, surrexi, surrectum, 3. *to arise.*

Tango, tetigi, tactum, 3. *to touch.*
Tego, texi, tectum, 3. *to cover.*
Temno, tempsi, temptum, 3. *to despise.*
Tendo, tetendi, -sum & -tum, 3. *to stretch.*
Teneo, tenui, tentum, 2. *to hold.*
Tepesco, tepui, 3. *to become warm.*
Tero, trivi, tritum, 3. *to rub.*
Tergo, tersi, tersum, 3. *to wipe.*
Texo, texui, textum, 3. *to weave.*
Timeo, timui, 2. *to fear.*
Tinguo, tinxi, tinctum, 3. *to dye.*

Tollo, sustuli, sublatum, 3. *to take up.*
Tondeo, totondi, tonsum, 2. *to shear.*
Tono, tonui, tonitum, 1. *to thunder.*
Torqueo, torsi, tortum, 2. *to twist.*
Torreo, torrui, tostum, 2. *to roast.*
Traho, traxi, tractum, 3. *to draw.*
Tremo, tremui, 3. *to tremble.*
Tribuo, tribui, tributum, 3. *to assign.*
Trudo, trusi, trusum, 3. *to thrust.*
Tundo, tutudi, tunsum, 3. *to thump.*
Turgeo, tursi, 2. *to swell.*

Unguo, unxi, unctum, 3. *to anoint.*
Urgeo, ursi, 2. *to press.*
Uro, ussi, ustum, 3. *to burn.*

Vado, *vasi, *vasum, 3. *to go.*
Veho, vexi, vectum, 3. *to carry.*
Vello, vulsi (velli), vulsum, 3. *to pluck.*
Vēneo, venivi and venii, venitum, 4. *to be on sale.*
Venio, veni, ventum, 4. *to come.*
Vergo, versi, 3. *to bend.*
Verro, verri, versum, 3. *to sweep.*
Verto, verti, versum, 3. *to turn.*
Veto, vetui, vetitum, 1. *to forbid.*

Video, vidi, visum, 2. *to see.*
Vincio, vinxi, vinctum, 4. *to bind.*
Vinco, vici, victum, 3. *to conquer.*
Viso, visi, 3. *to visit.*
Vivo, vixi, victum, 3. *to live.*

Volo, inf. velle, volui, *to wish.*
Volvo, volvi, volūtum, 3. *to roll.*
Vomo, vomui, vomitum, 3. *to vomit.*
Voveo, vovi, votum, 2. *to vow.*

IRREGULAR DEPONENTS.

Amplector, ampleciti, amplexus sum, *to embrace.*
Apiscor, apisci, aptus sum, *to obtain.*
Assentior, -tiri, assensus sum, *to agree to.*
Comminiscor, -ci, -mentus sum, *to devise.*
Expergiscor, -ci, experrectus sum, *to wake up.*
Experior, experiri, expertus sum, *to try.*
Fateor, fateri, fassus sum, *to confess.*
Fatiscor, -ci, fessus sum, *to grow weary.*
Fruor, frui, fruitus sum, *to enjoy.*
Fungor, -gi, functus sum, *to discharge.*

Gradior, gradi, gressus sum, *to step.*
Irascor, irasci, iratus sum, *to be angry.*
Labor, labi, lapsus sum, *to glide.*
Loquor, loqui, locutus sum, *to speak.*
Medeor, mederi, *to heal.*

Metior, metiri, mensus sum, *to measure.*
Morior, mori, mortuus sum, *to die.*
Nanciscor, -ci, nactus sum, *to obtain.*
Nascor, nasci, natus sum, *to be born.*
Nitor, niti, nisus & nixus sum, *strive.*

Obliviscor, -ci, oblitus sum, *to forget.*
Opperior, -iri, oppertus sum, *to wait for.*
Ordior, ordiri, orsus sum, *to begin.*
Orior, oriri, ortus sum, *to rise.*
Paciscor, -ci, pactus sum, *to bargain.*
Patior, pati, passus sum, *to suffer.*
Proficiscor, -ci, profectus sum, *to set out.*
Queror, -i, questus sum, *to complain.*
Reor, reri, ratus sum, *to think.*
Sequor, sequi, secutus sum, *to follow.*
Ulciscor, ulcisci, ultus sum, *to avenge.*
Utor, uti, usus sum, *to use.*

END OF PART III·

PART IV. DIFFICILIORA.

L

PART IV. DIFFICILIORA.

CONTENTS.

PART IV. DIFFICILIORA.

GENDER OF THE SUBSTANTIVE.

In giving in full the Gender of the Substantive, page 18, Part I., is repeated, to make each Part complete in itself.

THERE are three Genders; a Substantive must be either (a) Masculine, (b) Feminine, (c) Neuter. Some also are Common, i.e. Masculine or Feminine.

We give two common General Rules:

I. Certain classes of things are of certain Genders.

Masculine.	Males.	People.	Mountains (*most*).
	Months.	Winds.	Rivers (*most*).
Feminine.	Females.	Countries (*most*).	'
	Islands.	Cities and Trees (*most*).	
Neuter.	Indeclinable Nouns; as, fas, nefas, nihil.		
Common.	Words applicable to either sex; as,		
	Conjux, *husband* or *wife*.		
	Hostis, *an enemy.*		

II. Genders of Substantives are in a general way also known by the terminations in each Declension.

First. Feminine, in a and e; Masculine in as and es.

Second. Masculine, in us and er; Neuter in um.

Third. (a) *Masculine* terminations: o, or, os, er, es, increasing in gen., ex (not x).
(b) *Feminine* terminations: is, as, aus, x (not ex), s preceded by a consonant, es not increasing in genitive.
(c) *Neuter* terminations: ar, ur, us, c, a, t, l, e, n.

Fourth. Masculine in us; Neuter in u.

Fifth. Feminine.

But to these rules there are many exceptions (see pp. 158–167).

157

GENDER OF THE SUBSTANTIVE.

EXCEPTIONS.

DECLENSION I.

Nouns in *a* denoting Males, are Masculine ; as, poeta, *a poet.*
So also are

   Hadria, *Adriatic Sea.*   Scurra, a *buffoon.*

DECLENSION II.

A few in *us* are Feminine :

Alvus, *the belly.*	Humus, *the ground.*
Arctus, *the Bear* (constellation).	Pampinus, *vine-leaf.*
Carbasus, *fine flax.*	Pirus, *a pear-tree.* (*a*)
Colus, *a distaff.*	Sapphirus, *a sapphire.* (*b*)

Vannus, a winnowing fan.

A few in *us* are Neuter :

Pelagus, *the sea.*	Vulgus, *the common people*
Virus, *poison.*	(*generally*).

DECLENSION III.

Exceptions are numerous (see pp. 158–167).

DECLENSION IV.

A few in *us* are Feminine :

Acus, *a needle.*	Manus, *the hand.*
Anus, *an old woman.*	Nurus, *a daughter-in-law.*
Domus, *a house.*	Porticus, *a portico.*
Idūs (pl.), *the Ides.*	Socrus, *a mother-in-law.*

Tribus, a tribe.

DECLENSION V.

All are Feminine except *dies*, which is common in the Singular, but Masculine in the Plural, and *meridies*, *midday*, which is Masculine.

(*a*) And names of plants.
(*b*) And names of jewels.

GENDER OF THE THIRD DECLENSION. -

Words of the Third Declension are of various terminations and of all genders.

Some of course may be known by their meanings; as,

Pater, *a father*,
Tiberis, *the Tiber*, $\quad\rbrace$ are masculine.

Mulier, *a woman*,
Soror, *a sister*, $\quad\rbrace$ are feminine.
Venus, *the goddess Venus*,

But, as a rule, the gender in each declension must be decided by the termination.

FIRST GENERAL RULE.

Substantives are masculine which end in *o, or, os, er, es* increasing in Genitive, *ex* (not *x*).

o,	leo, *a lion.*	*er,*	anser, *a goose.*
or,	dolor, *pain.*	*es,*	pes, *a foot.*
os,	flos, *a flower.*	*ex,*	grex, *a flock.*

SECOND GENERAL RULE.

Substantives are feminine which end in *is, as, aus, x* (not *ex*), *s* preceded by a consonant, *es* not increasing in Gen.

is,	navis, *a ship.*	*x,*	pax, *peace.*
as,	libertas, *liberty.*	*bs,*	urbs, *a city.*
aus,	laus, *praise.*	*es,*	nubes, *a cloud.*

THIRD GENERAL RULE.

Substantives in *ar, ur, us, c, a, t, l, e, n* (catlen) are neuter.

ar,	calcar, *a spur.*	*a,*	poema, *a poem.*
ur,	fulgur, *lightning.*	*t,*	caput, *the head.*
us,	corpus, *a body.*	*l,*	animal, *an animal.*
c,	lac, *milk.*	*e,*	mare, *the sea.*

n, nomen, *a name.*

But there are many exceptions.

I. MASCULINE.

Substantives in *o, or, os, er, es* increasing, *ex* (not *x*) are masculine.

1. But though Substantives ending in *o* are *masculine*, those ending in *do, go, io* are *feminine*, and so are—

Caro	carnis	*flesh*
Echo	echus	*an echo*

The following however, though they end in *do, g⌐, io,* are *masculine* :

Cardo	cardinis	*a hinge*
Ordo	ordinis	*a row*
Prædo	prædonis	*a pirate*

Harpăgo	-ōnis	{ *a grappling hook*
Ligo	ligonis	*a spade*

Curculio	-ōnis	*a weevil.*
Papilio	-ōnis	*a butterfly*
Pugio	-ōnis	*a dagger*
Scipio	-ōnis	*a staff*
Septentrio	-ōnis	*the North*
Stellio	-ōnis	*a lizard*
Unio	-ōnis	*a pearl*
Vespertilio	-ōnis	*a bat*

And one in *go* is *common* :

Margo	marginis	*a border*

2. Those ending in *or* are *masculine ;* but arbor, arbŏris, *a tree,* is *feminine,* and four are *neuter.*

Ador	ădŏris	*spelt*
Æquor	æquŏris	*the sea*
Cor	cordis	*the heart*
Marmor	-ŏris	*marble*

3. Those ending in *os* are *masc.,* but two are *feminine :*

Cos	cōtis	*a whetstone*
Dos	dōtis	*a dowry*

And two are *neuter :*

Ŏs	ossis	*a bone*
Ōs	ōris	*the mouth*

4. Those ending in *er* are *masculine ;* but linter, lintris, *a wherry,* is *feminine,* and thirteen are *neuter :*

Acer	aceris	*the maple*
Cadāver	-eris	*a corpse*
Cicer	ciceris	*the chickpea*
Iter	itineris	*a journey*
Papaver	-eris	*the poppy*
Piper	-eris	*pepper*
Siler	sileris	*an osier*
Suber	suberis	*the cork tree*
Tuber	tuberis	*a swelling*
Uber	uberis	*an udder*
Ver	vŏris	*the spring*
Verber	-beris	*a whip*
Zingĭber	-eris	*ginger*

N.B.—The penultimate in the Genitive Case of words in previous list is short, so they are not marked; except ver, vēris, spring.

5. Those ending in *es* increasing in the Genitive Case are *masculine,* but seven are *feminine.*

Compes	compĕdis	*a fetter*
Merces	mercēdis	*wages*
Merges	mergĭtis	*a sheaf of corn*
Quies	quiētis	*rest*
Requĭes	requiētis	*rest*
Seges	segĕtis	*standing corn*
Toges	tegĕtis	*a mat*

And one in *œs* is *neuter :*

œs	æris	*copper* (money)

And three are *common :*

Ales	alitis	*a bird*
Comes	comitis	*a companion*
Heres	herēdis	*an heir or heiress*

6. Those ending in *ex* are *masc.,* but six are *feminine :*

Carex	caricis	*a kind of rush*
Faex	faecis	*sediment*
Forfex	forficis	*a pair of shears*
Lex	legis	*a law*
Nex	nĕcis	*a violent death*
Supellex	-lectilis	*furniture*

And ten are *common :*

Artifex	artificis	*an artificer*
Imbrex	imbricis	*a hollow tile*
Index	indicis	*an informer*
Judex	judicis	*a judge*
Obex	obicis	*a bolt*
Opifex	opificis	*a workman*
Pūmex	pumicis	*pumice stone*
Rūmex	rumicis	*sorrel*
Silex	silicis	*a flint*
Vindex	vindicis	*an avenger*

II. FEMININE.

Substantives are feminine which end in *is, as, aus, x, s* preceded by a consonant, *es* not increasing.

1. Those ending in *is* are *fem.,* but many are *masculine.*

Amnis	-is	*a river*
Annālis	-is	*a year-book*
Axis	-is	*an axle*
Canālis	-is	*a canal*
Casses	-ium (pl.)	*a snare*
Caulis	-is	*a stalk*
Clunis	-is	*a buttock*
Collis	-is	*a hill*
Crinis	-is	*hair*
Cucumis	-is (ĕris)	*a cucumber*
Ensis	-is	*a sword*

Fascis	-is	*a bundle*
Follis	-is	*a pair of bellows*
Fustis	-is	*a cudgel*
Glis	glīris	*a dormouse*
Ignis	ignis	*fire*
Lapis	lapĭdis	*a stone*
Mensis	-is	*a month*
Mugĭlis	-is	*a mullet*
Natalis	-is	*a birthday*
Orbis	-is	*a circle*
Panis	-is	*bread*
Piscis	-is	*a fish*
Postis	-is	*a door-post*
Pulvis	-ĕris	*dust*

(*see over*)

Sanguis	-gŭĭnis	*blood*
Torris	-is	*a fire-brand*
Unguis	-is	*finger or toe-nail*
Vectis	-is	*a lever*
Vermis	-is	*a worm*
Vōmis (er)	-ĕris	*a ploughshare*

For those sometimes *fem.*, see those with an asterisk, pp. 165, 166.

2. Those ending in *as* are *fem.*, but six are *masculine* :

Adamas	-antis	*a diamond*
As	assis	*a Roman coin*
Elephas	-antis	*an elephant*
Gigas	-antis	*a giant*
Mas	măris	*a male*
Vas	vădis	*a surety*

And one is *neuter* :

Vas	vasis	*a vessel.*

3. Those ending in *aus* are *feminine*, and there are no exceptions.

4. Those ending in *x* are *fem.*, but three in *ix* are *masculine* :

Calix	calicis	*a cup*
Fornix	fornicis	*an arch*
Phœnix	phœnicis	*the phœnix*

And two in *ux* are *common* :

Conjux	conjugis	*a husband or wife*
Dux	ducis	*a guide*

Note those in *ex* on p. 161.

5. Those ending in *s* preceded by a consonant are *feminine*, but thirteen are *masculine* :

Bidens	bidentis	*a hoe*
Chalybs	chalÿbis	*steel*
Dens	dentis	*a tooth*
Fons	fontis	*a fountain*
Gryps	grÿphis	*a griffin*
Hydrops	hydrōpis	*dropsy*
Mons	montis	*a mountain*
Occĭdens	occidentis	*the West*
Oriens	orientis	*the East*
Pons	pontis	*a bridge*
Rudens	rudentis	*a cable*
Tridens	tridentis	*a trident*
Triens	trientis	*a third part*

And seven are *common* :

Adeps	adĭpis	*fat*
Adolescens	-entis	*a youth*
Infans	infantis	*an infant*
Munĭceps	municipis	*a burgess*
Parens	parentis	*a parent*
Princeps	principis	*a chief*
Serpens	-entis	*a serpent*

6. Those ending in *es* not increasing are *feminine*, but two are *masculine* :

Acinăces	-is	*a scimitar*
Verres	-is	*a boar-pig*

And one is *common* :

Vates	vatis	*a seer*

III. NEUTER.

Substantives in *ar, ur, us, c, a, t, l, e, n,* are *neuter.*

1. Substantives ending in *ar* are *neuter,*—but one is *masculine :*

| Lar | laris | *household deity* |

2. Those ending in *ur* are *neuter,* but four are *masculine :*

Fur	furis	*a thief*
Furfur	furfŭris	*bran*
Turtur	turtŭris	*a turtle dove*
Vultur	vultŭris	*a vulture*

3. Those ending in *us* are *neuter,* but two are *masculine :*

| Lepus | lepŏris | *a hare* |
| Mus | muris | *a mouse* |

Nine are *feminine :*

Incus	incūdis	*an anvil*
Juventus	juventutis	*youth*
Palus	palūdis	*a marsh*
Pecus	pecŭdis	*cattle*
Salus	salūtis	*safety*
Senectus	senectūtis	*old age*
Servitus	servitutis	*slavery*
Tellus	tellūris	*the earth*
Virtus	virtutis	*virtue*

And two are *common :*

| Grus | gruris | *a crane* |
| Sus | suis | *a swine* |

4. Those ending in *c, a, t,* and *e* are *neuter,* and there are no exceptions.

5. Those ending in *l* are *neuter,* but five are *masculine :*

Consul	consulis	*a consul*
Mugil	mugīlis	*a mullet*
Pugil	pugīlis	*a boxer*
Sal	salis	*salt*
Sol	solis	*the sun*

6. Those ending in *n* are *neuter,* but eight are *masculine :*

Attagen	attagēnis	*a heathcock*
Delphin	delphīnis	*a dolphin*
Fĭdĭcen	-inis	*a lute-player*
Lien	liēnis	*the spleen*
Pecten	pectĭnis	*a comb*
Renes	renum (pl.)	*the kidneys*
Splēn	splēnis	*the spleen*
Tibīcen	-Inis	*a flute-player*

Three in *on* are *feminine :*

Gorgon	Gorgonis	*Gorgon*
Halcyon	halcyŏnis	*a kingfisher*
Sindon	sindŏnis	*fine linen*

EPITOME.

As a rule the genders must be decided by the terminations, as follows, but there are many exceptions.

Masculine : o, or, os, er, es *increasing,* ex (*not* x).
Feminine : is, as, aus, x, s preceded by a consonant, es *not increasing.*
Neuter : ar, ur, us, c, a, t, l, e, n (catlen).

MASCULINE.

1. Words ending in *o :* but those in *do, go, io* are feminine, three in *do,* two in *go,* eight in *io* are however masculine; and one in *go* is common.

MASCULINE.

2. Words ending in *or.*
But *one* is feminine,
And *four* are neuter.

3. Words ending in *os.*
But *two* are feminine,
And *two* are neuter.

4. Words ending in *er.*
But *one* is feminine,
And *thirteen* are neuter.

5. Words ending in *es,* increasing.
But *seven* are feminine,
And *one* is neuter.
And *three* are common.

6. Words in *ex* (not *x*).
But *six* are feminine,
And *ten* are common.

FEMININE.

1. Words ending in *is.*
But *many* are masculine

2. Words ending in *as.*
But *six* are masculine,
And *one* is neuter.

3. Words ending in *aus.*

4. Words ending in *x.*
But *three* in *ix* are masculine,
And *two* in *ux* are common.

Note words in ex (opposite column).

5. Words in *s* after a consonant.
But *thirteen* are masculine,
And *seven* are common.

6. Words in *es* not increasing.
But *two* are masculine.
And *one* is common.

NEUTER.

1. Words ending in *ar.*
But *one* is masculine.

2. Words ending in *ur.*
But *four* are masculine.

3. Words ending in *us.*
But *two* are masculine,
And *nine* are feminine,
And *two* are common.

4. Words in *c, a, t, e.*
There are no exceptions.

5. Words ending in *l.*
But *five* are masculine.

6. Words ending in *n.*
But *eight* are masculine,
And *three* (in *on*) are feminine.

SUBSTANTIVES IRREGULAR IN GENDER.

(Alphabetically arranged.)

MASCULINE.

Acinăces	acinacis	*scimitar*
Adamas	adamantis	*adamant*
Amnis	amnis	*a river*
Annālis	annalis	*a year-book*
As	assis	*a Roman coin*
Attagen	attagēnis	*a heathcock*
Axis	axis	*an axle*
Bidens	bidentis	*a hoe*
Calix	culicis	*a cup*
*Callis	callis	*a path*
Canālis	canalis	*a canal*
Cardo	cardĭnis	*a hinge*
Casses	cassium	*a net*
Caulis	caulis	*a stalk*
Chalybs	chalўbis	*steel*
*Cinis	cĭnĕris	*ashes*
Clunis	-is	*a buttock*
Collis	collis	*a hill*
Consul	consulis	*a consul*
Crinis	crinis	*hair*
Cucŭmis	-cumeris	*a cucumber*
Curculio	-culionis	*a weevil*
Delphin	delphinis	*a dolphin*
Dens	dentis	*a tooth*
Elephas	-phantis	*an elephant*
Ensis	ensis	*a sword*
Fascis	fascis	*a bundle*
*Finis	finis	*an end*
Follis	follis	{ *a pair of bellows*
Fons	fontis	*a fountain*
Fornix	fornicis	*an arch*
*Funis	funis	*a rope*
Fur	furis	*a thief*
Furfur	furfŭris	*bran*
Fustis	fustis	*a cudgel*
Gigas	gigantis	*a giant*
Glis	glĭris	*a dormouse*

Gryps	gryphis	*a griffin*
Harpago	harpagōnis	{ *a grappling hook*
Hydrops	hydrŏpis	*dropsy*
Ignis	ignis	*fire*
Lapis	lapidis	*a stone*
Lepus	lepŏris	*a hare*
Lien	liēnis	*spleen*
Ligo	ligonis	*a spade*
Mas	măris	*a male*
Mensis	mensis	*a month*
Mons	montis	*a mountain*
Mugil (-is)	mugўlis	*a mullet*
Mus	muris	*a mouse*
Natālis	natalis	*a birthday*
Occidens	occidentis	*the West*
Orbis	orbis	*a circle*
Ordo	ordinis	*a row*
Oriens	orientis	*the East*
Panis	panis	*bread*
Papilio	papilionis	*a butterfly*
Pecten	pectĭnis	*a comb*
Phœnix	phœnicis	*the phœnix*
Piscis	piscis	*a fish*
Pons	pontis	*a bridge*
Postis	postis	*a door-post*
Prædo	prædonis	*a pirate*
Pugil	pugilis	*a boxer*
Pugio	pugionis	*a dagger*
Pulvis	pulvĕris	*dust*
Rēnes	rēnum	*the kidneys*
Rudens	rudentis	*a cable*
Sal	salis	*salt*
Sanguis	sanguinis	*blood*
Scipio	scipionis	*a staff*
*Sentis	sentis	*a bramble*
Septentrio	-trionis	*the North*

Sol	solis	the sun	Unio	unionis	a pearl
Splēn	splēnis	spleen	Vas	vadis	a surety
Stellio	stellionis	a lizard	Vectis	vectis	a lever
*Torquis	torquis	a necklace	Vermis	vermis	a worm
Torris	torris	a fire-brand	Verres	verris	a boar-pig
Tridens	tridentis	a trident	Vespertilio	-lionis	a bat
Triens	trientis	a third part	Vomis (er)	vomĕris	a ploughshare
Turtur	turturis	a turtle dove	Vultur	vultūris	a vulture
Unguis	unguis	the nail			

A few words in *is* in this list marked * are sometimes feminine (see p. 162).

FEMININE.

Arbor	arbŏris	a tree	Linter	lintris	a wherry
Carex	caricis	a kind of rush	Merces	mercedis	wages
Caro	carnis	flesh	Merges	mergitis	a sheaf of corn
Compes	compēdis	a fetter	Nex	necis	a violent death
Cos	cotis	a whetstone	Palus	palūdis	a marsh
Dos	dotis	a dowry	Pecus	pecŭdis	cattle
Echo	echûs	an echo	Quies	quiētis	rest
Faex	faecis	sediment	Requies	requiētis	rest
Forfex	forficis	{ a pair of shears	Salus	salutis	safety
			Seges	segetis	standing corn
Gorgon	Gorgonis	Gorgon	Senectus	-tutis	old age
Halcyon	halcyonis	a kingfisher	Servitus	-tutis	slavery
Ilex	ilicis	the holm-oak	Sindon	sindonis	fine linen
Incus	incūdis	an anvil	Supellex	-lectilis	furniture
Inquies	inquietis	restlessness	Teges	tegetis	a mat
Juventus	juventutis	youth	Tellus	telluris	the earth
Lex	legis	a law	Virtus	virtutis	virtue

NEUTER.

Acer	aceris	the maple	Papaver	papaveris	the poppy
Ador	adŏris	spelt	Piper	pipĕris	pepper
Æquor	æquŏris	the sea	Siler	silĕris	an osier
Æs	æris	copper	Suber	subĕris	a cork tree
Cadāver	cadaveris	a corpse	Tuber	tubĕris	a swelling
Cicer	ciceris	the chickpea	Uber	ubĕris	an udder
Cor	cordis	the heart	Vas	vasis	a vessel
Iter	itineris	a journey	Ver	vēris	spring
Marmor	marmoris	marble	Verber	verbĕris	a whip
Os	oris	the mouth	Zingiber	zingibĕris	ginger
Os	ossis	a bone			

COMMON.

Adeps	adĭpis	*fat*		Index	indĭcis	*an informer*
Adolescens	-entis	*a youth*		Infans	infantis	*an infant*
Advĕna	-vĕnæ	*a stranger*		Interpres	-prĕtis	*an interpreter*
Ales	alitis	*a bird*		Judex	judĭcis	*a judge*
Anguis	anguis	*a snake*		Margo	marginis	*a border*
Artifex	artificis	*an artificer*		Municeps	municĭpis	*a burgess*
Auctor	auctoris	*an author*		Obex	obĭcis	*a bolt*
Bos	bovis	*an ox*		Obses	obsĭdis	*a hostage*
				Opifex	opifĭcis	*a workman*
Canis	canis	*a dog*				
Civis	civis	*a citizen*		Parens	parentis	*a parent*
Cliens	clientis	*a client*		Pollis	pollinis	*fine flour*
Comes	comitis	*a companion*		Princeps	principis	*a chief*
Conjux	conjugis	{ *a husband or wife*		Pumex	pumicis	{ *pumice stone*
Convīva	convivæ	*a guest*		Rumex	rumicis	*sorrel*
Custos	custodis	*a guardian*		Sacerdos	sacerdotis	{ *a priest or priestess*
Dama	damæ	*a deer*		Serpens	serpentis	*a serpent*
Dux	ducis	*a guide*		Silex	silicis	*a flint*
Exul	exulis	*an exile*		Sus	suis	*a swine*
Grus	gruis	*a crane*		Talpa	talpæ	*a mole*
Heres	heredis	{ *an heir or heiress*		Testis	testis	*a witness*
Hostis	hostis	*an enemy*		Tigris	tigrĭdis	*a tiger*
Imbrex	imbricis	*a hollow tile*		Vates	vatis	*a seer*
Incola	incolæ	*an inhabitant*		Vindex	vindĭcis	*an avenger*

The following five are rarely found masculine :

Dama	damæ	*a deer*		Sus	suis	*a swine*
Grus	gruis	*a crane*		Talpa	talpæ	*a mole*
		Tigris	tigrĭdis	*a tiger*		

The following six, though common, are rarely found feminine :

Augur	auguris	*an augur*		Hostis	hostis	*an enemy*
Aurīga	aurigæ	*a charioteer*		Miles	militis	*a soldier*
Hospes	hospĭtis	*a guest*		Præses	præsĭdis	*a guardian*

PECULIARITIES OF THE SUBSTANTIVE.

There are many irregularities in the Substantive which require notice.

1. Some Substantives are not declined ; as,

fas.   nefas.   nihil.   instar.

2. Some Substantives are used in the Singular number only.

Argentum, *silver.*   Ævum, *age.*
Aurum, *gold.*   Letum, *death.*
Ferrum, *iron.*   Sanguis, *blood.*
Plebs, *the common people.*   Pueritia, *boyhood.*
Justitia, *justice.*   *Aer, *air.*
Ver, *the spring.*   Æther, *the sky.*

With many more.

* A Plural occurs in Lucretius.

3. Some are used in the Plural number only.

Manes, *ghosts.*   Nugæ, *trifles.*
Liberi, *children.*   Grates, *thanks.*
Penates, *household gods.*   Arma, *arms.*
Divitiæ, *riches.*   Munia, *functions* (office).
Cunæ, *a cradle.*   Magalia, *huts.*

With many more.

4. Some Substantives want one or more cases.

The following have no Nom.; viz.:

(daps) dăpis (f.) *a feast.*
(ditio) ditionis (f.) *a dominion.*
(frux) frugis (f.) *fruit.*
(ops) ŏpis (f.) *strength.*
and others.

5. Some take two forms, though of the same declension, as

Jocus, *a jest;* plur., joci and joca.
Locus, *a place;* plur., loci, loca.
Frenum, *a bit;* plur., freni, frena.
Rastrum, *a harrow;* plur., rastri, rastra.

6. Some Substantives have a twofold declension, and so are called Heteroclīta ; *e.g.* domus, *a house.*

7. In the second declension some Substantives end in *us* and *um ;* as—

Callus, callum, *hardened skin.*
Commentarius, commentarium, *a note book.*

8. Some fluctuate between the first and second declension; as—

Menda, mendum, *a fault.*
Vespera, vesper, *the evening.*

9. Some fluctuate between the first and fifth ; as—

Barbaria, barbaries, *barbarism.*
Luxuria, luxuries, *luxury.*
Materia, materies, *matter.*
Mollitia, mollities, *softness.*

10. Some fluctuate between the second and third ; as—

Delphīnus, -i, and delphin, delphinis, *a dolphin.*
Elephantus, -i, and elephas, elephantis, *an elephant.*
Tergum, -i, and tergus, tergŏris, *a back.*

11. Some fluctuate between the second and fourth ; as—

Cupressus,	-ūs,	and -i,	*a cypress.*
Domus	domūs,	and domi,	*a house.*
Ficus,	ficūs,	and fici,	*a fig tree.*
Laurus,	laurūs,	and lauri,	*a bay tree.*
Pinus,	pinūs,	and pini,	*a pine tree.*
Eventus (4),	eventum (2),		*an occurrence.*
Suggestus (4),	suggestum (2),		*a platform for speakers.*

12. Some fluctuate between the third and fifth ; as—

Plebs, plebis ; as also plebes, plebis ; as also plebes, plebei, and plebī,
common people.

M

13. Some vary their declension in the two numbers:

Jugĕrum, *an acre;*   Sing., second declension ; Plural, third.
Vas, vasis, *a vessel;* Sing., third declension ;   Plural, second.

14. Some Substantives have a different meaning in the Singular and the Plural.

Ædes, *a temple.*	P.	Ædes, *a house.*
Aqua, *water.*		Aquæ, *medicinal springs.*
Auxilium, *help.*		Auxilia, *auxiliary forces.*
Carcer, *a prison.*		Carceres, *a starting place.*
Castrum, *a fort.*		Castra, *a camp.*
Copia, *plenty.*		Copiæ, *forces.*
Gratia, *favour.*		Gratiæ, *thanks.*
Impedimentum, *a hindrance.*		Impedimenta, *baggage.*
Littera, *a letter* (alphabet).		Litteræ, *an epistle.*
Ludus, *play, school.*		Ludi, *public games.*
Opera, *exertion.*		Operæ, *workmen.*
Ŏpis (Gen.), *help.*		Ŏpes, *power, wealth.*
Rostrum, *a beak.*		Rostra, *a platform for speakers.*
Tabula, *a board.*		Tabulæ, *writing tablets.*

With others.

15. Many have only certain cases; but these will be given elsewhere.

16. The following have a full plural, but only the ablative in the singular:

Ambage (f.), *a circuit.*
Casse (m.), *a snare.*
Fauce (f.), *the throat.*
Verbere (n.), *a stripe.*

With others.

Verbere has also, according to Ovid, a Gen. : *verberis.*

FIRST DECLENSION.

1.

The Dative and Ablative of some words end in *abus*.

Dea, *a goddess*, deabus.
Filia, *a daughter*, filiabus.
Nata, *a daughter*, natabus.
And others.

2.

The two following words have Gen. Plur. in *um*.

Cœlicola, *a dwelling in heaven*, cœlicolûm.
Terrigena, *earth-born*, terrigenûm.

3.

Two words have old Genitive in *as* remaining,

Paterfamilias, *master of a family*.
Materfamilias, *mother of a family*.

4.

Æneas, Æneas, *Æneas*.

Voc., Ænea.
Acc., Æneam or Ænean.

Greek Substantives in *e* and *es* are given on p. 177.

SECOND DECLENSION.

1.

Deus, *a god*, is irregular; p. 177.

2.

Filius, *a son*, makes—

Voc., fili (mî filî, *my son*).
Gen., filii or filî.

And proper names in *ius* are like *filius*; as, *Lœlius, Lœli;* so is also *genius*.

3.

Jocus, *a jest.*
Locus, *a place.*
Frenum, *a bit.*
Rastrum, *a rake.* } Have in Plural, Nom. *i* and *a;* Acc., *os* and *a*

4.

Pelagus, *the sea.*
Virus, *poison.*
Vulgus, *the common people.* } Have no plural.

5.

Carbasus, *fine flax*, Nom.P.carbasa,
Tartarus, *Tartarus*,   Tartara.

6.

Adulter, *an adulterer.*
Armiger, *an armour-bearer.*
Gener, *a son-in-law.*
Liber, *Bacchus.*
Liberi, *children.*
Puer, *a boy.*
Signifer, *a sign-bearer.*
Socer, *a father-in-law.*
Vesper, *evening.* } Are the only words in *er* that keep the *e* in all cases.

7.

Faber, *a smith*, Gen. Plur., fabrorum and fabrum.
Nummus, *money*, Gen. P., nummûm and nummorum.

For Greek Substantives, Delos, Orpheus, see p.177.

THIRD DECLENSION.

(*With Adjectives.*)

1. The terminations of the Substantives of this declension are many and various. Some grammars give at full length as many as *thirty* samples; but this adds considerably to what a boy *thinks* he has to learn. Three, or at most *four*, as samples, are quite sufficient.

> Nubes, *because it does not increase.*
> Lapis, *because it does increase.*
> Opus, *because it is neuter.*
> Mare, *because it makes* ia *in the Plural.*

2. But it must be *well noted* that the Genitive Singular *must* be known, and then nearly every Substantive, whatever its termination, can be gone through regularly.

3. Some Substantives have more syllables in the Genitive than they have in the Nominative, hence they are called *increasing*, the proper word being imparisyllabic (not equal in syllables), as those which do not increase are called parisyllabic (equal in syllables).

4. There is generally with learners a difficulty as to the Genitive Plural, whether it ends in *um* or *ium*. But the general rule is,

> The Genitive Plural of *increasing*
> nouns is *um* and not *ium*.

In other words, if the word increases in the Genitive Singular it does not further increase in the Genitive Plural; but there are exceptions, which will be given presently.

There are peculiarities also in the Acc. and Abl. Singular.

THIRD DECLENSION.

ACCUSATIVE AND ABLATIVE SINGULAR.

ACCUSATIVE SINGULAR.

The Accusative Singular is *im* not *em*

1. In the five words—

Amussis	*a rule*
(Ravis) ravim	*hoarseness*
Sitis	*thirst*
Tussis	*a cough*
Vis	*violence*

2. And in the names of towns and rivers in *is;* as—

| Hispălis | *Seville* |
| Tiberis | *the Tiber* |

The Accusative Singular is *im* or *em* in the nine words—

Clavis	*a key*
Febris	*fever*
Messis	*a harvest*
Navis	*a ship*
Pelvis	*a basin*
Puppis	*the stern of a ship*
Restis	*a rope*
Securis	*an axe*
Turris	*a tower*
and others.	

ABLATIVE SINGULAR IN I.

The Ablative singular has ī not ĕ—

1. In all words where the Acc. is *im* only : as siti, Tiberi.

2. In Neuter nouns that end in *e, al, ar,* as—

N. Mare	Abl. Mari
Animal	Animali
Calcar	Calcāri

3. Substantives in *ar*—the Gen. of which is not *āris (ā* long)—have *e* in the Ablative; as—

Baccar	baccăris	*a sweet herb*
Far	farris	*spelt*
Jubar	jubăris	*a sunbeam*
Nectar	nectăris	*nectar*

4. *Adjectives* ending in *is, e; er, is, e :* as—

| Tristis | *sad* | tristi |
| Acer | *sharp* | acri |

THIRD DECLENSION.

ABLATIVE SINGULAR IN ɪ AND ᴇ.

The Ablative Singular has both *i* and *e*,

1. In most words where the Accusative is *im* and *em;* as, puppi and puppe.

Restis, *a rope*, has only reste.
Securis, *an axe*, has only securi.

Also in

Avis   *a bird*
Ignis   *fire*
Imber   *rain*
Supellex   *household utensils*

2. In *Adjectives* which have in Nominative one termination; and in Comparatives; as—

Prudens   *prudent*   *ti* and *te*
Altior   *higher*   *ri* and *re*

But the following *Adjectives* have *e* only.

Cœlebs	cœlibis	*unmarried*
Compos	compŏtis	*master of*
Deses	desidis	*lazy*
Impos	impŏtis	*not master of*
Pauper	pauperis	*poor*
Princeps	principis	*chief*
Pubes	puberis	*adult*
Superstes	superstitis	*surviving*

Memor, *mindful,* has only *i.* The Participles in *ns* generally have when used as Epithets, but otherwise *e.*

NEUTER PLURAL IN IA.

The Nom., Voc., Acc. Plural of Neuter Nouns have *ia.*

1. In Substantives the Nom. Sing. of which ends in *e, al, ar* (Gen. *āris*); as—

Mare	*the sea*	maria
Animal	*an animal*	animalia
Calcar	*a spur*	calcaria

2. In *Adjectives* which have the Abl. Sing. in *i* alone, or in *i* and *e*, except Comparatives; as—

gravis, gravia; prudens, prudentia.
But
melior, meliora; altior, altiora, etc.

THIRD DECLENSION.

GENITIVE PLURAL.

The general rule, as before stated, is that words that *do not* increase in Gen. Sing. *do* increase in Gen. Plural, and have *ium ;* if they *do* increase in Gen. Sing., they *do not* further increase in Gen. Plural, and have only *um ;* as,

Hostis	hostis	*an enemy*	hostium.
Nubes	nubis	*a cloud*	nubium.

But,

Lapis	lapidis	*a stone*	lapidum.
Judex	judicis	*a judge*	judicum.

But there are exceptions.

1. The following six and others, though they do not increase in the Gen. Sing., have *um* in Gen. Plural.

Canis	canis	*a dog.*		Mater	matris	*a mother.*
Frater	fratris	*a brother.*		Pater	patris	*a father.*
Juvenis	juvenis	*a youth.*		Vates	vatis	*a prophet.*

2. The following three have *um* or *ium.*

Apis	apis	*a bee.*
Mensis	mensis	*a month.*
Sedes	sedis	*a seat.*

3. Monosyllables, the stem of which ends in two consonants, though they increase in the Gen. Sing., have *ium* in the Gen. Plural, except Lynx.

Arx	arcis	*a citadel.*
As (stem *ass*)	assis	*a Roman coin.*
Mons	montis	*a mountain.*
Os (stem *oss*)	ossis	*a bone.*

4. Several monosyllables, the stems of which end in a single consonant, though they increase in the Gen. Sing., have *ium* in the Gen. Plur.; as

Faux	faucis	*the throat.*		Mus	muris	*a mouse.*
Glis	gliris	*a dormouse.*		Nix	nivis	*snow.*
Lis	litis	*a law-suit.*		Strix	strigis	*an owl.*
Mas	maris	*a male.*		Vis	vis	*strength.*

5. The Gen. Plural generally ends in *ium,* sometimes with Poets in *um,* in words the Nom. Sing. of which is *ens :*

Cliens	clientis	*a client.*
Adolescens	-entis	*a youth.*
Prudens (Adj.)	-entis	*prudent.*

FOURTH DECLENSION.

1. The Dative Singular *ui* is often contracted into *u :* as, grad*ui*, grad*u*.

2. The following eleven words have the Dative and Ablative Plural in *ubus ;* some have both forms, *ubus* and *ibus.*

Acus	acus	*a needle*	Portus	portus	*a harbour*
Arcus	arcus	*a bow*	Quercus	quercus	*an oak*
Artûs	artuum	*joints*	Specus	specus	*a cave*
Lacus	lacus	*a lake*	Tribus	tribus	*a tribe*
Partus	partus	*a birth*	Pecu		*cattle*
	Veru	verūs	*a spit*		

3. Domus, *a house*, belongs partly to the second declension and partly to the fourth—declined see next page.

FIFTH DECLENSION.

1. All words are Feminine except meridies (*m.*) and dies, which is *common* in the Singular, but must be *masculine* in the Plural.

2. In the Gen. and Dat. Singular the *ei* is sometimes contracted into *ē ;* as, die*i* di*ē*, fide*i* fid*ē*.

3. *Res* and *dies* are the only words of this declension which have a complete plural.

4.
Acies	aciēi	*a line of battle*	Series		*a series*
Effigies	-ēi	*an image*	Species	-ei	*an appearance*
Facies	-ĕi	*a face*	Spes	spēi	*hope*

have Nom., Voc., Acc. Plural. No other words of the declension have any Plural at all, except *res, dies*, mentioned above, and Virgil gives a Plural to *glacies* (*Georg.* IV. 517).

5. In Gen. and Dat. Singular the *e* in *ei* is long after a vowel, as di*ēi*, faci*ēi*, but doubtful after a consonant, as fid*es*, fid*ĕi*.

DECLENSION OF PROPER NAMES AND IRREGULAR SUBSTANTIVES.

FIRST DECLENSION.

An abridgment

S. N. Epitome	S. Cybĕle
V. Epitome	Cybele
A. Epitomen	Cybelēn
G. Epitomes	Cybeles,Cybelæ
D. Epitomæ	Cybelæ
A. Epitome	Cybele, Cybela

S. N. Anchises	S. Æneas
V. Anchise (-a)	Ænea
A. Anchisen(-am)	Æneāu (-am)
G. Anchisæ	Æneæ
D. Anchisæ	Æneæ
A. Anchise (-a)	Ænea

S. N. Thesēïdes	P. Thesidæ
V. Thesidē(-ĕ, -ă)	Thesidæ
-A. Thesidēn (-am)	Thesidas
G. Thesidæ	Thesidum
D. Thesidæ	Thesidis
A. Thesidē (-ā)	Thesidis

SECOND DECLENSION.

S. N. Deus (God)	P. Dei, Dii, Di
V. Deus	Dei, Dii, Di
A. Deum	Deos
G. Dei	Deorum, Deum
D. Deo	Deis, Diis, Dis
A. Deo	Deis, Diis, Dis

A house

S. N. Domus	P. Domûs
V. Domus	Domus
A. Domum	Domus, domos
G. Domûs	Domuum, -orum
D. Domui or domo	Domibus
A. Domo	Domibus

SINGULAR.

N. Delos	G. Deli
V. Dele	D. Delo
A. Delon (-um)	A. Delo

THIRD DECLENSION.

S. N. Achilles -eūs	S. Pallas
V. Achille -eu	Pallas
A. Achillem, -ēn, -ĕă	Palladem, -ă
G. Achillis, -ĕī, -i, -ĕōs	Palladis, -os
D. Achilli	Palladi
A. Achillĕ	Palladĕ

S. N. Paris	S. Perĭcles
V. Parĭ	Periclēs, -ĕs, -ē
A. Parĭdem, -a, Parin -im	Periclem, -ĕă
G. Paridis,-dos	Periclis, Pericli
D. Paridĭ	Pericli
A. Paridĕ	Pericle

S. N. Sŏcrătes	S. Thales
V. Socrates, Socrate	Thales, -e
A. Socratem, -ēn	Thalem, -ēn, ētă
G. Socratĭs, -ī	Thalis, Thalētis
D. Socrati	Thalī, Thalētī
A. Socratē, -ĕ	Thalē, Thalētĕ

A cloak

S. N. Chlamys	P. Chlamȳdĕs,
V. Chlamy	
A. -dem, -a	Chlamydes, -as
G. -dis	Chlamydum
D. Chlamydi	Chlamydibus
A. Chlamyde	Chlamydibus

S. N. Sappho	N. Orpheus
V. Sapphŏ	V. Orpheu
A. Sappho, -nem	A. Orpheum, -ea
G. Sapphûs, -onis	G. Orpheï, -eos
D. Sappho, -oni	D. Orpheo,-eï,-ei
A. Sappho, -one	A. Orpheo

PECULIARITIES OF SUBSTANTIVES AND ADJECTIVES.

Acer (adj.), acris, e, *sharp.* Abl. Sing., acri ; Nom., Voc., and Acc. Plur. Neut., acria ; Gen. Plur. acrium.

Acies, aciei (f.), *a line of battle.* Only Nom., Voc., Acc., in the Plur.

Acus, -ūs (f.), *a needle.* Dat. and Abl. Plur., acubus.

Adolescens, -entis (c.), *a youth.* Gen. Plur., adolescentium.

Adulter, -eri (m.), *an adulterer.* Keeps the *e* in all cases.

Ædes (f.), in the Sing. is *a temple ;* in the Plur., ædes, -ium, *a house.*

Æneas, -æ (m.), *Æneas.* Voc. Sing., Ænea ; Acc. Sing., Æneam or Ænean.

Ambages, -is (f.), *a winding.* In Sing. only Abl. Gen. Plur., ambagum.

Amussis, -is (f.), *a rule.* Acc. Sing., amussim ; Abl. Sing. amussi.

Anchises, -æ (m.), *Anchises.* Acc., Anchisēn, or -am ; Abl., Anchise or Anchisā ; Voc. Anchise or -ă, declined, see p. 177.

Animal, -is (n.), *an animal.* Nom., Voc., Acc. Plur., animalia ; Gen. Plur., animalium ; Abl. Sing., animali.

Apis, apis (f.), *a bee.* Also, apes, apis. Gen. Plur., apium and apum.

Aqua, aquæ (f.), *water.* (Plur.) aquæ, *medicinal springs.*

Arcus, -ūs (m.), *a bow.* Dat. and Abl. Plur., arcubus, like acus.

Arma, -orum (n.), *arms.* Has no singular.

Artus, -uum (Pl.), (m.), *limbs.* Dat. and Abl. Plur., artubus, like acus.

Arx, arcis (f.), *a citadel.* Gen. Plur., arcium.

As, assis (m.), *a small coin.* Gen. Plur., assium, like arx.

Aurum, auri (n.), *gold.* Has no Plur.

Auxilium, -i (n.), *help.* (Plur.) auxilia, *auxiliary forces.*

Avis, -is (f.), *a bird.* Abl. Sing., avi and ave.

Barbaria, -æ (f.), *barbarism.* Also barbaries, barbariei.

Cælicola, -æ, *a dweller in heaven.* Gen. Plur., cælicolûm.

Cœlum, cæli (n.), (no plural), *heaven.*

Calcar, -āris (n.), *a spur.* Nom., Voc., and Acc. Plur., calcaria ; Gen. Plur., calcarium ; Abl. Sing., calcari.

Callus, -i (m.), also callum, -i (n.), *hardened skin.*

Canis, -is (c.), *a dog.* Gen. Plur., canum.

Carbasus, -i (f.), *fine flax.* (Plur.), carbasa (n.), *sails.*

Carcer, -eris (m.), *a prison.* Carceres, -um, *a starting point.*

Casses, -ium (Pl.), (m.), *a snare*. Only Abl. in Sing.
Castrum (Sing.), -i (n.), *a fort*. (Plur.) castra, -orum, *a camp*.
Chlamys, chlamydis (f.), *a cloak*. Declined (see p. 177).
Clavis, -is (f.), *a key*. Acc. Sing., -im or -em. Abl., -i or -e.
Cliens, clientis (c.), *a client*. Gen. Plur., clientium and clientum.
Cœlebs, cœlibis, *unmarried* (adj.). Abl. Sing., cœlibe.
Commentarius (m.), also commentarium, -i (n.), *a note book*.
Compos, compotis (adj.), *having the mastery of*. Abl. Sing., compote.
Copia, -æ (f.), *plenty*. (Plur.) copiæ, -arum, *forces*.
Cupressus, -i, and cupressus, -ūs (f.), *a cypress*.

(Daps), dapis (f.), *a feast*. No Nom. or Voc. Sing.
Dea, -æ (f.), *a goddess*. Dat. and Abl. Plur., deabus.
Delos, Deli (f.), *Delos*. Irr., declined at full length (see p. 177).
Deses, desidis (adj.), *lazy*. Abl. Sing., deside.
Deus, dei (m.), *a god*. Irr., declined at full length (see p. 177).
Dies, diei or diē and dii, *a day*. Common in Sing., masc. in Plur.
(Ditio), ditionis (f.), *a dominion*. No Nom. Sing.; no Plur.
Domus, -ūs (f.), *a house*. Declined (see p. 177).

Echo, echus (f.), *echo*. The other cases in *o*.
Effigies, effigiei (f.), *an image*. Has only Nom., Voc., and Acc. in Plur.
Epitome, epitomes (f.), *an abridgment*. Declined (see p. 177).
Eventus, -ūs (m.), eventum, -i (n.), *an occurrence*.

Faber, fabri (m.). Gen. Plur., fabrorum and fabrum.
Facies, faciei (f.), *a face*. Has only Nom., Voc., and Acc. in Plur.
Fas (n.), *Divine law*. Indeclinable.
(Faux) (f.) Sing., some times Abl., fauce; Plur., fauces, faucium, etc.
Febris, febris (f.), *fever*. Acc. Sing., febrim and febrem; Abl. Sing., febri and febre.
Feriæ, feriarum (f.), *holidays*. Has no Sing.
Ficus, -i, and ficus, -ūs (f.), *a fig tree*.
Fides, fidei (f.), *faith*. Gen. Sing., fidei, also fide in poets; Dat. Sing., fide in poets, or fidei.
Filia, -æ (f.), *a daughter*. Dat. and Abl. Plur., filiabus.
Filius, -i (m.), *a son*. Voc. Sing., fili; Gen. Sing., filii and fili.
Frenum, -i (n.), *a bit*. Plur. freni (m.), frena (n.).
(Frux), frugis (f.), *fruit*. Has no Nom.
Grates, *thanks* (Plur.); usually only in Nom. and Acc. Abl. (*Tacitus*).

Gratia, -æ (f.), *favour;* gratiæ, -arum, *thanks.*
Gravis, -e (adj.), *heavy.* Nom., Voc., and Acc. Plur. neut., gravia ;
Gen. Plur., gravium ; Abl. Sing., gravi.
Gener, generi (m.), *a son-in-law.* Keeps the *e* in all cases (like puer).
Genius, genii (m.), *a genius.* Declined like filius.
Glis, gliris (m.), *a dormouse.* Gen. Plur., glirium.

Hispalis, -is (f.), *Seville.* Acc. Sing., Hispalim.

Ignis, ignis (m.), *fire.* Abl. Sing., igni and igne.
Imber, imbris (m.), *a shower.* Abl. Sing., imbri and imbre.
Impedimentum, -i (n.), *a hindrance.* Plur., impedimenta, *baggage.*
Impos, impotis (adj.), *not master of.* Abl. Sing., impote.
Instar (n.), *likeness.* Indeclinable.

Jocus, -i (m.), *a joke.* Plur., joci (m.), joca (n.).
Jugerum, -i (n.), *an acre.* 2nd declension in Sing., 3rd in Plur. Nom.,
Voc., and Acc. Plur., jugera ; Gen. Plur., jugerum ; Dat. and Abl.,
jugeribus.
Justitia, -æ (f.), *justice.* Has no Plural.
Juvenis, -is (m.), *a youth.* Gen. Plur., juvenum.

Lacus, -ūs (m.), *a lake.* Dat. and Abl. Plur., lacubus, like acus.
Lælius, Lælii (m.), *Lælius.* Declined like filius.
Laurus, -i (f.), *a bay tree,* and laurus, -ūs.
Liber, Liberi (m.), *Bacchus.* Keeps the *e* in all cases.
Liberi, -orum (m.), *children.* Has no Sing.
Lis, litis (f.), *a law suit.* Gen. Plur., litium.
Littera, -æ (f.), *a letter* (alphabet) ; litteræ, -arum, *an epistle.*
Locus, -i (m.), *a place ;* loci (m. Plur.), loca (n. Plur.).
Ludus, -i (m.), *play ;* ludi, -orum, *public games.*
Luxuria, -æ (f.), *luxury;* also luxuries, luxuriei.

Mare, maris (n.), *the sea.* Abl. Sing., mari ; neut. Plur., maria.
Mas, maris (m.), *a male.* Gen. Plur., marium.
Materfamilias (f.), matrisfamiliæ and matrisfamilias, *the mother of a*
family.

Materia, -æ (f.), *timber;* and materies, -ei.
Memor, -oris (adj.), *mindful.* Abl. Sing., memori.
Menda, -æ (f.), and mendum, -i (n.), *a fault.*
Mensis, -is (m.), *a month.* Gen. Plur., mensum or mensium.
Messis, -is (f.), *a harvest.* Acc. Sing., messem or messim.
Mollitia, -æ, *softness;* and mollities, -ei (f.).
Mons, montis (m.), *a mountain.* Gen. Plur., montium.
Mus, muris (m.), *a mouse.* Gen. Plur., murium.

Nata, -æ (f.), *a daughter.* Dat. and Abl. Plur., natabus.
Navis, -is (f.), *a ship.* Acc. Sing., navim or navem.
Nefas (n.), *crime.* Indeclinable.
Nihil (n.), *nothing.* Indeclinable.
Nix, nivis (f.), *snow.* Gen. Plur., nivium.
Numus and nummus, -i (m.), *money.* Gen. Plur., numorum and numûm.

Opera, -æ (f.), *an exertion;* operæ, -arum (m.), *workmen.*
(Ops) opis (f.), *strength;* opes, opum (Plur.), *wealth.*
Orpheus, Orpheï, Orpheos (m.), *Orpheus.* Declined (see p. 177).
Os, ossis (n.), *a bone.* Gen. Plur., ossium.

Pallas, Palladis or Pallados (f.), *Minerva.* Declined (see p. 177).
Paris, Paridis or Paridos (m.), *Paris.* Declined (see p. 177).
Partus, -ūs (m.), *a birth.* Dat. and Abl. Plur., partubus, like acus.
Paterfamilias, patrisfamiliæ and patrisfamilias (m.), *father of a family.*
Pauper, pauperis (adj.), *poor.* Abl. Sing., paupere.
Pecu (-ūs) (n.), *cattle.* Dat. and Abl. Plur., pecubus, like acus.

Pelagus, -i (n.), *the sea.* Has no Plural.
Pelvis, -is (f.), *a basin.* Acc. Sing., pelvim and pelvem.
Pericles, -is and -i (m.), *Pericles.* Declined at full length (see p. 177).
Pinus, -ūs, and pinus, -i (f.), *a pine.*
Plebs, plebis, and plebes, -is, -ei (f.), *common people.*
Portus, -ûs (m.), *harbour.* Dat., Abl. Plur., portubus and portibus.
(Prex) (precis) (f.), *a prayer.* Nom. and Gen. Sing. not used.
Princeps, principis (adj.), *chief.* Abl. Sing., principe.
Prudens, prudentis (adj.), *prudent.* Abl. Sing., prudenti and prudente;
   Nom., Voc., and Acc. Plur. (n.), prudentia.

Pubes and puber, puberis (adj.), *adult.*
Puer, pueri (m.), *a boy.* Keeps the *e* in all cases.
Puppis, -is (f.), *a ship.* Acc. Sing., puppim and puppem. Abl. Sing., puppi and puppe.

Quercus, -ūs (f.), *an oak.* Dat. and Abl. Plur., quercubus.

Rastrum, -i (f.), *a rake.* (Plur.) rastri, -orum (m.), rastra, -orum (n.).
(Ravis), -is (f.), *hoarseness.* Acc. Sing., ravim.
Requies, -etis (f.), *rest.* Acc. Sing., requietem and requiem. Abl. Sing.
    requiete and requie.
Restis, -is (f.), *a rope.* Acc., restim or restem. Abl. Sing., reste.
Rostrum, -i (n.), *a beak.* (Plur.) rostra, -orum, *a platform for speaking.*

Sappho, -us and -onis (f.), *Sappho.* Declined at full length (see p. 177).
Securis, -is (f.), *an axe.* Acc. Sing., securim and securem ; Abl. Sing.,
    securi.
Sedes, -is (f.), *a seat.* Gen. Plur., sedum and sedium.⁑
Series (f.), *a series.* Has cnly Nom., Acc., and Abl. Sing.
Sibilus, -i (m.), *a hissing.* (Plur.) sibili and sibila, sibilos and sibila.
Sitis, -is (f.), *thirst.* Acc. Sing., sitim ; has no Plur.
Socer, -ĕri (m.), *a father-in-law.* Keeps the *e* in all cases, like puer.
Species, -ei (f.), *an appearance.* Has only Nom., Voc., and Acc. Plur.
Specus, -ūs (m.), *a cave.* Dat. and Abl., specubus, like acus.
Spes, spei (f.), *hope.* Has only Nom., Voc., and Acc. Plur.
(Spons), Abl. sponte (f.), *of one's own accord.*
Strix, strigis (f.), *an owl.* Gen. Plur., strigium.
Strues, struis (f.), *a heap.* Gen. Plur., struum.
Suggestus, -ūs (m.), and suggestum, -i (n.), *a platform for speakers.*
Supellex, supellectilis (f.), *household utensils.* Abl., supellectili and -e.
Superstes, superstitis (adj.), *only surviving.* Abl. Sing., superstite.
Sus, suis (c.), *a swine.* Dat. plur. subus (*Lucretius*), and suibus.

Tabula, -æ (f.), *a board;* tabulæ, -arum, *writing tablets.*
Tartarus, -i (m.), *Tartarus.* (Plur.) Tartara, -orum (n).
Tenebræ, -arum (f.), *darkness.* Has no Sing.
Terrigena, -æ (c.), *earth born.* Gen. Plur., terrigenûm.
Tiberis, -is (m.), *the Tiber.* Acc. Sing., Tiberim, Tibrim (from Tibris);
    Abl. Sing., -i.

Tribus, -ūs (f.), *a tribe.*   Dat. and Abl. Plur., tribubus.

Tristis, -e (adj.), *sad.*   Abl. Sing., tristi.

Turris, -is (f.), *a tower.*   Acc. Sing., turrim and turrem ; Abl. Sing., turri and turre.

Tussis, -is (f.), *a cough.*   Acc., tussim ; Abl. Sing., tussi.

Vas, vasis (n.), *a vessel.*   3rd dec. in Sing., 2nd in Plur ; (Plur.) vasa, vasorum.

Vates, vatis (c.), *a prophet.*   Gen. Plur., vatum.

(Verber), verberis (n.), *a stripe.*   Abl. Sing., verbere ; only Gen. and Abl. in Sing., full Plur.

Veru, verus (n.), *a spit.*   Dat. and Abl. Plur., verubus and veribus.

Vesper, vesperis (3) and -eri (2) (m.), *the evening.*   Acc. Sing., vesperum ; keeps the *e* in all cases.   Also vespera, -æ (f.).

Virus, viri (n.), *poison.*   Has no Plural.

Vis, vis (f.), *strength.*   Acc. Sing., vim ; (Plur.) Nom., Voc., and Acc., vires, virium.   Gen. and Dat. Sing., very rare.

Volucris, volucris (f.), *a bird.*   Gen. Plur., volucrum.

Vulgus, -i (n.), *common people.*   Has no Plural.

APPENDIX.

Ales, alitis (c.), *a bird.*   Abl. Sing., alite and -e ; Gen. Plur., alitum and alituum.

(Cassis, cassis) (m.), *a net, snare.*   Only Abl., casse, in Sing.   Full Plural.

Grus, gruis (c.), *a crane.*   Nom. Sing., gruis (*Phædrus*).

Lien, lienis, and lienis, lienis (m.), *milt, spleen.*

Obex, obicis and objicis (c.), *a bolt.*

Palus, paludis (f.), *a marsh.*   Gen. Plur., paludum and paludium.

Parens, parentis (c.), *a parent.*   Gen. Plur., parentum and parentium.

Poema, poematis (n.), *a poem.*   Dat. and Abl. Plur., poematis.

Renes, renum (m.), *kidneys.*   Has no Singular.

Sanguis, sanguinis (m.), *blood.*   Has no Plural.

| Amnis, *a river,* | Collis, *a hill,* | Fustis, *a cudgel,* |
| Clunis, *a buttock,* | Finis, *a boundary,* | Postis, *a door,* |

besides those mentioned and many others, have Abl. Sing. in *i* and *e.*

THE ROMAN CALENDAR.

The Roman month had three chief days, with reference to which the other days were reckoned.

These days were the Kalends (Kalendæ), which fell on the 1st;
the Nones (Nonæ),   ,,   ,,   5th ;
the Ides (Idūs),   ,,   ,,   13th.
But in

March, July, October, May,
The Nones were on the 7th day,

and the Ides on the 15th, or eight days later.

All other days were counted *backwards* from these three points; in other words, the Romans did not say such a day *after* the Kalends, Nones, or Ides, but such a day *before* these three principal days.

To express a date in Latin observe these rules :

(*a*) For days before the Kalends, add *two* to the number of days in the month, and subtract the day of the month from the result so obtained.

(*b*) For days before the Nones and Ides, add *one* to the day on which they respectively fall, and subtract the day of the month from the result.

E.g.—To express the 16th of January in Latin—

January contains 31 days; add 2 to this, and you have 33. $33-16=17$. So that you find January 16th=ante diem septimum decimum Kalendas Februarias; or, as it is usually written, a. d. XVII. Kal. Feb.

To express February 3rd. The Nones fell on the 5th; Add 1, and the result is 6; 6—3=3. Therefore, February 3rd=a. d. III. Non. Feb. *

To express May 13th. The Ides of May fell on the 15th; add 1 to this, and you have 16; 16—13=3. Therefore, May 13th=a. d. III. Id. Mai.

To express in Latin the date of a year the ordinal numerals must be used; *e.g.* A.D. 1885=Anno post Christum natum millesimo octingentesimo octogesimo quinto.

The Kalends, Nones, and Ides of January, etc., will be expressed by Kalendis, Nonis, Idibus, Januariis, etc.; or, briefly, by Kal. Jan.: Non. Jan.: Id. Jan., etc

The day before the Kalends, Nones, and Ides of January, etc., is expressed by Pridie Kalendas, Nonas, Idus, Januarias, etc.; or, briefly, Prid. Kal., Non., Id., Jan.

In leap year February 24 (a. d. VI. Kal. Mart.) was reckoned twice; and the day was called *dies bissextus,* whence the term bissextile, as applied to leap year.*

The Latin names of the months, which are adjectives (agreeing with *mensis*), are Januarius, Februarius, Martius, Aprilis, Maius, Junius, Julius (or Quintilis), Augustus (or Sextilis), September, October, November, December.

Those in -*us* are declined like *bonus;* those in -*is* like *tristis;* those in -*er* like *acer.*

---

* The intercalated day was counted between a. d. VI. and a. d. VII., and called a. d. bissextum Kal. Mart.; so that a. d. VII. answers as in ordinary years to Feb. 23rd.

N

ROMAN MONEY.

There were two principal coins, the *As* (genitive *assis*) and the *Sestertius* (a silver coin = $2\frac{1}{2}$ *asses*), the symbol for which was HS.

The *As*, or pound of 12 ounces (*unciæ*), was thus divided:

Uncia	=	1	oz., or $\frac{1}{12}$ of the As.		
Sextans	=	2	,,	$\frac{2}{12} = \frac{1}{6}$	,,
Quadrans	=	3	,,	$\frac{3}{12} = \frac{1}{4}$	,,
Triens	=	4	,,	$\frac{4}{12} = \frac{1}{3}$	.,
Quincunx	=	5	,,	$\frac{5}{12}$	,.
Semis	=	6	,,	$\frac{6}{12} = \frac{1}{2}$	,,
Septunx	=	7	,,	$\frac{7}{12}$	,,
Bes	=	8	,,	$\frac{8}{12} = \frac{2}{3}$	,,
Dodrans	=	9	,,	$\frac{9}{12} = \frac{3}{4}$	,,
Dextans	=	10	,,	$\frac{10}{12} = \frac{5}{6}$	,,
Deunx	=	11	,,	$\frac{11}{12}$	,,

The following terms were used in bequeathing property:

Heres ex asse.	Heir to the whole estate.
Heres ex sextante.	,, $\frac{1}{6}$ of the ,,
Heres ex besse.	,, $\frac{2}{3}$,, ,,

Etc., etc., etc.

Interest was reckoned monthly at the rate of so much per 100 *asses*.

Hence

Unciæ usuræ = $\frac{1}{12}$ per cent. per month = 1 per cent. per annum.

Sextantes usuræ = $\frac{1}{6}$ per cent. per month = 2 per cent. per annum.

Quadrantes usuræ = $\frac{1}{4}$ per cent. per month = 3 per cent. per annum.

Asses usuræ = 1 per cent. per month = 12 per cent. per annum.

Instead of asses usuræ we find centesimæ:

So, Binæ centesimæ   = 2 ⎫ per cent.   or 24 ⎫ per cent.
    Trinæ   „   = 3 ⎬ per month   „ 36 ⎬ per an-
    Quaternæ   „   = 4 ⎭   „ 48 ⎭ num.

The sestertius, or sesterce, as we have said, was a *coin*.

The sestertium was the name of a *sum* (= 1,000 sestertii), and is only used in the plural.

Sestertia, HS, joined with Cardinal or Distributive numbers, means so many thousand sesterces.

The Numeral adverbs joined with (or understanding) *sestertii* (gen. sing.), *sestertium*, or HS, denote so many 100,000 sesterces.

Thus, Tres sestertii   = 3   sesterces.
    Trecenti sestertii   = 300   „
    Mille sestertiûm   = 1,000   „
    Duo millia sestertiûm, *or* duo ⎫
        sestertia   ⎬   = 2,000   „
    Decem millia sestertiûm   = 10,000   „
    Centum millia sestertiûm,   ⎫
    Centena millia sestertiûm   ⎬   = 100,000   „
    Centum sestertia   ⎭
    Ter centena millia sestertiûm, ⎫
    Ter sestertiûm   ⎬   = 300,000   „
    Decies centena millia sestertiûm, ⎫
    Decies sestertiûm   ⎬   = 1,000,000   „
    Quadringenties sestertiûm   = 40,000,000   „

NOTE.—HS. X = Sestertii   decem = 10   sesterces.
      HS. X̄ = Sestertia   decem = 10,000   „
      H̄S̄. X̄ = Sestertium decies = 1,000,000   „

PARSING.

There is but little doubt that the generality of teachers, whether at public or private schools, make use of *Parsing* too much as a means of *teaching* the Grammar of a sentence, whereas it should more properly be used simply as a test of what the pupil knows. As also dictation is often improperly used as a means of *teaching* spelling, though it is a most capital exercise and test when the pupil *has learned* to spell fairly.

Much time is wasted over Parsing. The pupil has to say every-thing he knows of a word, whether it is Masculine or Feminine, Singular or Plural; and of a Verb, what Conjugation, Voice, Mood, Tense, Number, Person, etc. Careful and diligent teachers boast that they do this with their pupils every day. The pupil no doubt gets up the required form by rote, but half the time does not understand what he is about; and if asked what Gender and why, cannot answer without thinking.

The simplest form of *Parsing* is the best, as not wearying either to the teacher or the pupil. Below is an example :

Maturus fructus dulcem saporem habet.

Maturus fructus ripe fruit *habet* has *dulcem saporem* a sweet taste.

Maturus. Nominative Case, to agree with its substantive *fructus.*
Fructus. Nominative Case to the verb *habet.*
Dulcem. Accusative Case, to agree with its substantive *saporem.*
Saporem. Accusative Case governed by the verb *habet.*
Habet. Third Person Singular, to agree with its Nominative Case *fructus.*

This is all that is required to enable a pupil to understand the construction of the sentence.

It is certainly *most important* that much more than this should be known; but, according to the teaching of this little book, the pupil would know it. He would know as well as his teacher that *maturus* was an Adjective, Masculine Gender and Singular Num-ber, and declined like *bonus*, or certainly he *would* not and *could* not be doing exercises.

And so with *dulcem.* If he did not know that *dulcem* was an Adjective of two terminations, declined like *tristis*, and that *dul-*

cem in itself was Masculine or Feminine, but Masculine in this sentence because it has to agree with *saporem*, he certainly would have to shut his Exercise book and take to his Grammar again.

There must be added a word or two about this Parsing for those who wish to learn Latin by themselves, that they may teach it to others.

Maturus is the Nominative Case, simply and for no other reason than that it has to agree with *fructus*, which is Nominative. Being an Adjective, it has nothing to do with the Verb, or with anything but a Substantive.

Fructus is the Nominative Case to the verb *habet*. *Habet* standing in the sentence must have some Nominative, either expressed or understood; as *fructus* is a Nominative, then *fructus* must be taken.

Dulcem is the Accusative Case—not governed by the Verb, for being an Adjective it has nothing to do with anything but a Substantive; but it is the Accusative Case to agree with *saporem*, because *saporem* is the Accusative.

Saporem is the Accusative Case governed by the verb *habet*. *Habet* must take some Accusative Case after it—what is it but *saporem*?

Habet is the Third Person Singular, to agree with its Nominative Case *fructus* (or *maturus fructus*). *Habet* is the Singular Number because *fructus* is, and Third Person because every thing and every person but "you" or "I," "you" or "we" is the Third Person.

But were there any idea that the pupil did not know *every particular* about each word, then each word should be taken, and he should be questioned upon it in every way.

Saporem.—What Case? Why? What Declension? How do you know the Declension? What Gender? Why?

Habet.—What Part of Speech? What Voice—Mood—Tense? What Person? Why? What Conjugation? How do you know that it is the Second Conjugation?

But then a pupil taught as by this book *would* know this, and there would be no need to ask these questions once a month.

ORDER OF LATIN WORDS.

I. In short Latin sentences the *Nominative* will come first.
Pisces extra aquam cito exspirant.
Fish *quickly expire out of the water.*

II. As a general rule, the *Verb* comes last.
Milites trans hostium fertiles agros *ibant.*
The soldiers were going *across the fertile fields of the enemy.*

III. The word governed is generally placed before the word that governs it; as,

Pomum habet, not *Habet pomum*.
Urbis portas clausit, not *Portas urbis clausit.*

IV. The *Possessive Pronoun* will usually come after the word it agrees with; as,
Puer librum suum *amisit*, not *Puer* suum *librum amisit.*

V. The *Adjective* mostly comes after the Substantive with which it agrees; as,

Poeta filiam bonam *habet.*

VI. This *Adjective* may however be separated from its Substantive by a Genitive (with its Adjective) depending on that Substantive, in which case it precedes the Genitive; as,

Puer bonam poetæ *filiam videt ;*
as also
Puer bonam sapientis poetæ *filiam* videt.
The boy sees the good daughter of the wise poet.

VII. The *Adverb* will come generally next before the word to which it belongs; as,
Pisces extra aquam cito *exspirant.*

VIII. The *Preposition*, as a general rule, *must* come IMME-
DIATELY before the word to which it belongs; as in
the last sentence,
Pisces extra aquam *cito exspirant.*

IX. It may however (see p. 112)
(*a*) Go before the Adjective that agrees with the Substantive; as, *Milites* trans fertiles *agros ibant.* Or

(*b*) Before a Genitive depending on that word; as,
Milites trans hostium *fertiles agros ibant.*

X. *Conjunctions* which join words together must of necessity come between such words; as, *Mare* et *terra.*
If *que* is used instead of *et*, it will be affixed to the word
to which it belongs; as, *Mare terramque videt.*
If the conjunction join sentences together, it will come
between the sentences; as, *Multa vidit* et *plura audivit.*

XI. *Autem, enim, vero, quidem, quoque, igitur,* may *not* stand
first in the sentence; but *namque sed, equidem, ergo,
itaque, tamen,* may stand first.

XII. The Interjection will be the first word in the sentence.

There is also another way of telling the proper order for
Latin words; viz. according to emphasis. *The word which
is of first importance is first in the arrangement of words.*
Hence the emphatic words precede others. The following
will at least explain what is meant by the above rule:

1. *Will you go into the town to-morrow ?*
   Visne cras in oppidum ire?

2. *Will you go into the town to-morrow ?*
   Tune in oppidum cras ire vis?

3. *Will you go into the town to-morrow ?*
   Crasne in oppidum ire vis?

RULES OF SYNTAX.

Page 72.

FOUR GENERAL RULES.

LATIN.	ENGLISH.
A.	**A.**
Verbum Finitum cum nominativo Subjecti congruit numero et persona. 88. I.	A Verb Finite agrees with the nominative of its Subject in Number and Person. 88. I.
B.	**B.**
Adjectivum genere, numero, et casu congruit cum eo cui attribuitur. 89. II.	An Adjective agrees in Gender, Number, and Case with that to which it is in attribution. 89. II.
C.	**C.**
Substantivum casu congruit cum eo cui apponitur. 90. III.	A Substantive agrees in case with that to which it is in apposition. 90. III.
D.	**D.**
Relativum cum Antecedente congruit, genere, numero, et persona; sed casu spectat suam clausulam. 91. IV.	A Relative agrees with its Antecedent in Gender, Number, and Person; but in Case belongs to its own clause. 91. IV.

The Letter or figure at the top of each Rule refers to Syntax, Part II. The figures *after* each Rule refer to the Public School Latin Primer.

THE VERB AND ITS NOMINATIVE OR SUBJECT.

LATIN.	ENGLISH.
I.	**I.**
Finiti Verbi Subjectum Nominativus est. 93. 1.	The Subject of a Finite Verb is a Nominative. 93. 1.
V.	**V.**
Cum Subjecto composito pluralia congruunt. 92.	With a composite Subject Plural words agree. 92.
VI.	**VI.**
In diversitate personarum Verba congruunt cum Priore Persona. 92. 1.	If the Persons differ, Verbs agree with the Prior Person. 92. 1.
VII.	**VII.**
Infinitivum stat substantive, pro nominativo vel Accusativo. 140. I. 1.	The Infinitive stands substantively for nominative or Accusative. 140. I. 1.
VIII.	**VIII.**
Clausulæ pro Substantivis ponuntur. 156 (3).	Clauses are put for Substantives. 156 (3).

THE VERB AND ITS ACCUSATIVE OR OBJECT.

Accusativus est Casu Proprioris Objecti. Necnon limitandi vim habet.	The Accusative is the Case of the nearer Object. It has also the power of limiting.
I.	**I.**
Verba Transitiva regunt Accusativum Objecti.	Transitive Verbs govern an Accusative of the Object.
III.	**III.**
Intransitiva capiunt Accusativum vi cognata. 97.	Intransitive Verbs take an Accusative of kindred meaning. 97.

THE NOMINATIVE AFTER THE VERB.

Verba Copulativa, sive Finita sive Infinitiva, complementum plerumque cum Subjecto congruens habent. 94.	Copulative Verbs, whether Finite or Infinitive, generally have a complement agreeing with the Subject. 94.

This applies also to the Accusative.

THE GENITIVE AFTER THE VERB.

Page 79.

I.

Genitivus ita stat ut suppleri possit,

indoles   munus
indicium   officium 127. *b.*

I.

A Genitive so stands that *nature, token, function, duty,* can be supplied. 127. *b.*

II.

Interest, refert, Genitivum admittunt. 129. III.

Eadem pro Genitivis Pronominum usurpant hos casus, *meā, tuā, suā, nostrā, vestrā,* cum *rē* congruentes. 129. III. *a.*

II.

Interest (*it imports*), refert (*it concerns*) admit a Genitive. 129. III.

The same verbs, instead of the Genitives of Pronouns, use these cases, meā, tuā, suā, nostrā, vestrā, agreeing with rē. 129. III. *a.*

III.

Genitivus adjungitur Verbis et Adjectivis quibus significatur—

> *Potentia* et *impotentia.*
> *Criminatio, innocentia.*
> *Damnatio, absolutio.*
> *Memoria* et *oblivio.*
>
>   133. II.

III.

A Genitive is joined to Verbs and Adjectives which signify—

> *Power* and *impotence.*
> *Inculpation, innocence.*
> *Condemnation, acquittal.*
> *Memory* and *forgetfulness.*
>
>   133. II.

IV.

Ex Adjectivis et Verbis *abundandi* vel *egendi, ditandi* vel *privandi,* pleraque Ablativum capiunt, multa etiam Genitivum. 119. IX. *b.*

IV.

Most Adjectives and Verbs of abounding or wanting, enriching or depriving, take an Ablative ; many also a Genitive. 119. IX. *b.*

V.

Misereor, miseresco, Genitivum capiunt ; *miseror, commiseror* Accusativum. 135. IV.

V.

Misereor, miseresco (*I pity*), take a Genitive ; miseror, commiseror (*I compassionate*), an Accusative. 135. IV.

VI.

Memini, reminiscor, recordor, obliviscor, Genitivum vel Accusativum admittunt. 133. II. *a.*

VI.

Memini, reminiscor, recordor (*I remember*), obliviscor (*I forget*) admit Genitive or Accusative. 133. II. *a.*⁻

VII.

Piget, pudet, pœnitet, tædet, atque *miseret,* Impersonalia, Genitivum capiunt cum Accusativo. 134. III.

VII.

Piget (*it irks*), pudet (*it shames*), pœnitet (*it repents*), tædet (*it disgusts*), and miseret (*it moves pity*), Impersonal Verbs, take a Genitive with an Accusative. 134. III.

THE DATIVE AFTER THE VERB.

Pages 80, 81.

LATIN.	ENGLISH.
Dativus est casus Recipientis seu Remotioris Objecti. 104.	The Dative is the case of the Recipient or Remoter object. 104.

I.

Trajectiva, quæ sensum trajiciunt ad Remotius objectum, sunt multa Adjectiva, Adverbia, et Verba, rarius Substantiva, quibus indicatur:	Words which carry their meaning over to a Remoter Object are called Trajective, and include many Adjectives, Adverbs, and Verbs, more rarely Substantives, by which is implied—
Propinquitas et contraria.	Nearness and its contraries.
Demonstratio et contraria.	Demonstration and its contraries.
Gratificatio et contraria.	Gratification and its contraries.
Dominatio et contraria.	Dominion and its contraries.
105. I.	105. I.

II.

Inter Trajectiva sunt multa Verba composita cum Particulis, quales sunt:	Among Trajective words are many Verbs compounded with Particles, such as:
Bene, male, satis, re, *Ad, ante, con, in, inter, de,* *ob, sub, super, post, et præ.* 106. *a.*	bene, *well.* male, *ill.* satis, *enough.* re, ad, ante, con, in, inter, de, ob, sub, super, post, et præ. 106. *a.*

III.

Sum, cum compositis, præter *possum,* capit Dativum. 107. II. *b.*	Sum, with its compounds, except possum, takes a Dative. 107. II. *b.*

IV.

Est, sunt, cum Dativo, *habere* sæpe significant. 107. II. *c.*	Est, sunt, with a Dative, often imply *having.* 107. II. *c.*

V.

Dativus Propositi pro complemento ponitur, adjuncto sæpe Dativo Recipientis. 108. III.	A Dative of the Purpose is used as a complement, a Dative of the Recipient being often added. 108. III.

THE ABLATIVE AFTER THE VERB.

Page 81.

LATIN.	ENGLISH.
I.	**I.**
Ablativum regunt :	These words govern an Ablative :
(1) Verba	(1) The Verbs :
fungor, *fruor,*	Fungor, *to perform.*
utor, *vescor,*	Fruor, *to enjoy.*
potior, *dignor.*	Utor, *to use.*
	Vescor, *to eat.*
	Potior, *get possession of.*
	Dignor, *deem worthy.*
* (2) Adjectiva	(2) The Adjectives :
dignus, indignus,	Dignus, *worthy.*
contentus, fretus,	Indignus, *unworthy.*
præditus.	Contentus, *content.*
	Fretus, *relying.*
	Præditus, *endued.*
* (3) Substantiva,	(3) The Substantives :
opus, usus.	Opus, *need.*
119. IX. *a.*	Usus, *use.*
	119. IX. *a.*
II.	**II.**
Ex Adjectivis et Verbis *abun-dandi* vel *egendi, ditandi* vel *pri-vandi,* pleraque Ablativûm capiunt, multa etiam Genitivum. 119. *b.*	Most Adjectives and Verbs of *abounding* or *wanting, enriching* or *depriving,* take an Ablative; many also a Genitive. 119. *b.*
III.	**III.**
Præpositiones etiam compositæ regunt Ablativum, præsertim *ab, de, ex.* 122. XII. *a.*	Prepositions, even when compounded, govern an Ablative, especially *ab, de, ex.* 122. XII. *a.*

* It has been thought convenient to place the Adjectives and the Substantives here to make the rule complete.

VERBS WHICH TAKE TWO CASES.

Page 82.

ACCUSATIVE AND GENITIVE.

LATIN.	ENGLISH.
I.	**I.**
Genitivus adjungitur Verbis et Adjectivis quibus significatur :	A Genitive is joined to Verbs and Adjectives which signify :
Potentia et impotentia.	*Power* and *impotence.*
Criminatio, innocentia.	*Inculpation, innocence.*
Damnatio, absolutio.	*Condemnation, acquittal.*
Memoria et oblivia.	*Memory* and *forgetfulness.*
133. II.	133. II.
II.	**II.**
Piget, pudet, pœnitet, tædet, atque *miseret,* Impersonalia, Genitivum capiunt cum Accusativo.	Piget (*it irks*), pudet (*it shames*), pœnitet (*it repents*), tædet (*it disgusts*), miseret (*it moves pity*), Impersonal verbs, take a Genitive with an Accusative.—134. III.
134. III.	

The above do not necessarily always take two cases.

ACCUSATIVE AND DATIVE.

Trajectiva quæ sensum trajiciunt ad Remotius Objectum, sunt multa Adjectiva, Adverbia, et verba, rarius Substantiva, quibus indicatur :	Words which carry their meaning over to a Remote Object are called Trajective, and include many Adjectives, Adverbs, and Verbs, more rarely Substantives, by which is implied :
Propinquitas et contraria.	Nearness and its contraries.
Demonstratio et contraria.	Demonstration and its contraries.
Gratificatio et contraria.	Gratification and its contraries.
Dominatio et contraria.	Dominion and its contraries.
105. I.	105. I.

The above do not necessarily always take two cases.

VERBS WHICH TAKE EITHER OF TWO CASES.

Page 83.

GENITIVE OR ACCUSATIVE.

LATIN.	ENGLISH.
Memini, reminiscor, recordor, Genitivum vel Accusativum admittunt. 133. II. *a.*	Memini, reminiscor, recordor (*I remember*), obliviscor (*I forget*), admit Genitive or Accusative. 133. II. *a.*

GENITIVE OR ABLATIVE.

Ex Adjectivis et Verbis *abundandi* vel *egendi, ditandi* vel *privandi,* pleraque Ablative capiunt, multa etiam Genitivum. 119. IX. *b.*	Most Adjectives and Verbs of abounding or wanting, enriching or depriving, take an Ablative; many also a Genitive. 119. IX. *b.*

VERBS WHICH TAKE A DOUBLE CASE.

Page 83.

TWO ACCUSATIVES—PERSON AND THING.

I.	I.
Verba quædam, *rogandi* præsertim et *docendi,* binos admittunt Accusativos, alterum Rei, alterum Personæ.—98.	Some Verbs, especially those of *asking* and *teaching,* admit two Accusatives, one of the thing, the other of the Person.—98.

TWO ACCUSATIVES—OBJECT AND COMPLEMENT.

I.	I.
Verba quædam *faciendi, vocandi, putandi,* similia, binos habent Accusativos, alterum Objecti, alterum Obliqui Complementi.—99.	* Certain Verbs, of *making, calling, thinking,* and the like, have two Accusatives, one of the Object, the other of the Oblique Complement.—99.

TWO DATIVES—SUM WITH OTHER WORDS.

I.	I.
Dativus Propositi pro Complemento ponitur, adjuncto sæpe Dativo Recipientis.—108. III.	A Dative of the Purpose is used as a Complement, a Dative of the Recipient being often added. 108. III.

* These are called Factitive Verbs.

ADJECTIVES AND THEIR CASES.

Pages 84, 85.

GENITIVE AFTER THE ADJECTIVE.

LATIN.	ENGLISH.
I.	
Genitivus Rei Demensæ Vocabula Quantitatis et Neutra Adjectiva comitatur.—131. B.	A Genitive of the Thing Measured is joined to Words of Quantity and Neuter Adjectives.—131. B.
II.	**II.**
Genitivus objective jungitur Substantivis, Adjectivis, aut Participiis, quibus transitiva quædam vis est, præsertim si significant: *Peritiam, curam, desiderium.* Vel quidquid erit his contrarium. 132. I.	A Genitive is joined objectively to Substantives, Adjectives, or Participles if they signify *skill, care, desire,* or whatever is contrary to these.—132. I.
Genitivus adjungitur Verbis et Adjectivis quibus significantur: *Potentia* et *impotentia. Criminatio, innocentia. Damnatio, absolutio. Memoria* et *oblivio.* 133. II.	A Genitive is joined to Verbs and Adjectives which signify: *Power* and *impotence. Inculpation, innocence. Condemnation, acquittal. Memory* and *forgetfulness.* 133. II.

DATIVE AFTER THE ADJECTIVE.

Trajectiva capiunt Dativum, quum significatur: (1) Propinquitas; (2) Demonstratio; (3) Gratificatio; (4) Dominatio; et contraria. 106.	Trajective Words take a Dative when the meanings implied are: (1) Nearness; (2) Demonstration; (3) Gratification; (4) Dominion; and their contraries. 106.

THE ABLATIVE AFTER THE ADJECTIVE.

I.	I.
Ablativum regunt: Adjectiva *dignus, indignus, contentus, fretus, præditus.* 119. IX. a. 2.	These words govern an Ablative: The Adjectives dignus (*worthy*), indignus (*unworthy*), contentus (*content*), fretus (*relying*), præditus (*endued*).—119. IX. a. 2.
II.	**II.**
Ex Adjectivis et Verbis *abundandi* vel *egendi, ditandi* vel *privandi,* pleraque Ablativum capiunt, multa etiam Genitivum.—119. *b.*	Most Adjectives and Verbs of *abounding* or *wanting, enriching* or *depriving,* take an Ablative; many also a Genitive.—119. *b.*

Also the Substantives *opus* and *usus* take an Ablative. 119. IX. *a.* 3.

DIFFERENT USES OF CASES.

Page 86.

*** These "different uses of Cases" are not intended to include the Case *after the Verb or Adjective*, which has been already given.

NOMINATIVE.

LATIN.	ENGLISH.
I.	**I.**
Finiti Verbi Subjectum Nominativus est.—93. 1.	The Subject of a Finite Verb is a Nominative.—93. 1.
II.	**II.**
Substantivum casu congruit cum eo cui apponitur.—90.	A Substantive agrees in case with that to which it is Apposition. 90.
III.	**III.**
Nominativus et Accusativus in exclamando usurpantur vel sine Interjectione vel cum Interjectione. 138.	The Nominative and the Accusative are used in Exclamations either without an Interjection or with an Interjection. —138.
IV.	**IV.**
Quam cum Nominativo. 124. XIV. 1.	*Quam* with Nominative. 124. XIV. 1.

VOCATIVE.

Vocativus extra sententiam stat vel sine Interjectione vel cum Interjectione.—137.	The Vocative stands out of the sentence either without an Interjection or with an Interjection. 137.

ACCUSATIVE.

Pages 86, 87.

LATIN.	ENGLISH.

I.

Infinitivi Subjectum in Accusativo ponitur.—93. 2.

II.

Substantivum casu congruit cum eo cui apponitur.—90. III.

III.

Accusativus Respectus adjungitur Verbis et Adjectivis, præsertim apud poetas.—100.

IV.

Nominativus et Accusativus in Exclamando usurpantur vel sine Interjectione vel cum Interjectione. 138.

V.

Duratio Temporis in Accusativo ponitur.—102. 1.

VI.

Mensura Spatii in Accusativo ponitur.—102. 2.

VII.

Accusativum regunt multæ Præpositiones.—103.

VIII.

Locus, *quo* itur, in Accusativo ponitur, idque sine Præpositione, si vel oppidi nomen est, vel *domus, rus.*—101.

IX.

Quam cum Accusativo.
124. XIV. 2.

I.

The Subject of an Infinitive is put in the Accusative.—93. 2.

II.

A Substantive agrees in case with that to which it is in Apposition.—90. III.

III.

The Accusative of Respect is joined to Verbs and Adjectives, especially in poetry.—100.

IV.

The Nominative and the Accusative are used in Exclamations either without an Interjection or with an Interjection.—138.

V.

The Duration of Time is put in the Accusative.—102. 1.

VI.

The Measure of Space is put in the Accusative.—102. 2.

VII.

Many Prepositions govern an Accusative Case.—103.

VIII.

The place, whither one goes, is put in the Accusative; and without a Preposition, if it is either the name of a town, or domus (*home*), rus (*country*).—101.

IX.

Quam with the Accusative.
124. 2.

O

GENITIVE.
Page 87.

LATIN.

I.

Genitivus Auctoris et Possessoris.
127. I.

II.

Substantivum casu, etc.

III.

Genitivus qualitatis, cum epitheto.—128. II.

IV. ·

Notentur elliptici Genitivi:

parvi	minoris	minimi
magni	pluris	plurimi
tanti	quanti	maximi

quibus supple *pretii.*

128. II. *a.*

ENGLISH.

I.

Genitive of the Author and Possessor.—127. I.

II.

A Substantive agrees in case etc.—90 III.

III.

Genitive of quality with epithet.
128. II.

IV.

The elliptic Genitives may be remarked:

Parvi, *of small worth;* minoris, *of less value;* minimi, *of very little worth.* Magni, *of great price;* pluris, *of more value;* plurimi, *of high value.* Tanti, *of so great price;* quanti, *of what price;* maximi, *of very great price.* To which supply *pretii.* 128. II. *a.*

DATIVE.
Page 87.

I.

Substantivum casu, etc.

II.

Ita Dativus ponitur cum *hei !* *væ !*—139.

I.

A Substantive agrees in case, etc.

II.

So the Dative is put with hei, (*alas!*) væ (*woe !*)—139.

ABLATIVE.
Page 88.

I.

Substantivum casu, etc.

II.

Ablativus Rei Comparatæ:
(1) Pro *quam* cum Nominativo.
(2) Pro *quam* cum Accusativo.
124. XIV.

III.

Multæ Præpositiones Ablativum regunt.—122. XII. (See list.)

IV.

Ablativus Agentis expetit Præpositionem *a, ab.*—122. XII. *b.*

I.

A Substantive agrees in case, etc.

II.

Ablative of the Thing Compared:
(1) For *quam* with Nom.
(2) For *quam* with Acc.
124. XIV.

III.

Many Prepositions govern an Ablative.—122. XIL. (See list.)

IV.

The Ablative of the Agent takes the Preposition *a, ab.* 122. XII. *b.*

LATIN.	ENGLISH.

V.

Ablativus est Casus rerum quæ circumstant et adverbiali more limitant actionem. Definit etiam Tempus et Locum.—110.

V.

The Ablative is the Case of circumstances which attend action, and limit it adverbially. It defines also time and space.—110.

V. Ablativus Causæ.
VI. Ablativus Instrumenti.
VII. Ablativus Modi.
VIII. Ablativus Conditionis.
IX. Ablativus Qualitatis, cum Epitheto.
X. Ablativus Respectus.
XI. Ablativus Pretii.
XII. Ablativus Mensuræ.
XIII. Ablativus Materiæ.
111-119.

V. Ablative of Cause.
VI. Ablative of the Instrument.
VII. Ablative of Manner.
VIII. Ablative of Condition.
IX. Ablative of Quality with Epithet.
X. Ablative of Respect.
XI. Ablative of Price.
XII. Ablative of Measure.
XIII. Ablative of Matter.
111-119.

XIV.

Ablativus Temporis respondet, si rogatur, *Quando? Intra quantum tempus? Quanto tempore ante vel post?*—120. X.

XIV.

The Ablative of Time answers the questions, *When? Within what time? How long before or after?*—120. X.

XV.

Oppidorum nomina singularia ex Declinatione prima et secunda locum stationis definiunt per casus in æ, i.—121. XII. *a.*

XV.

Singular names of towns of the first and second Declension define the place of station by cases in æ, i.—121. XII. *a.*

XVI.

Ablativus oppidi Præpositione caret, cum rogatur *Unde?*
Ita *domo, rure.*
121. XI. C.

XVI.

The Ablative of a town is without a Preposition, when the question is *Whence?*
So domo (*from home*).
rure (*from the country*).
121. XI. C.

XVII.

Ablativus Loci ponitur sine Præpositione, cum rogatur, *qua via?*—121. XI. A.

XVII.

The Ablative of Place is put without a Preposition when the question is *By what road?*
121. XI. A.

XVIII.

Substantivum cum Participio coalescit in Ablativo, qui vocatur Absolutus.—125. XV.

XVIII.

A Substantive combines with a Participle in the Ablative which is called Absolute.—125. XV.

INFINITIVE MOOD.

Page 94.

LATIN.	ENGLISH.

I.

I.

Infinitivi Casus sunt Gerundia et Supina. 141. II.

Gerunds and Supines are the Cases of the Infinitive. 141. II.

II.

II.

Infinitivum, cum Gerundio, Participiis, et Supino in *um*, eosdem casus regit ac Verbum Finitum. 142. III.

The Infinitive, with Gerund, Participles, and Supine in *um*, governs the same Cases as the Verb Finite. 142. III.

III.

III.

Infinitivum stat — substantive, pro Nominativo vel Accusativo. 140. I. (1).

The Infinitive stands—substantively, for Nominative or Accusative. 140. I. (1).

IV.

IV.

Infinitivum stat — oblique, cum Accusativo Subjecti. 140. I. (3).

The Infinitive stands —obliquely, with Accusative of the Subject. 140. I. (3).

V.

V.

Infinitivum stat — prædicative, in narrando, pro Verbo Finito. 140. I. (2).

The Infinitive stands—Predicatively, in narration, for a Finite Verb. 140. I. (2).

VI.

VI.

Infinitivum stat — prolata constructione Verbi vel Adjectivi. 140. I. (4).

The Infinitive stands—carrying on the construction of Verb or Adjective. 140. I. (4).

GERUNDS.

Page 95.

LATIN.	ENGLISH.
III.	**III.**
Accusativus Gerundii Præpositionibus adjungitur. 141. II. (1).	The Accusative of the Gerund is joined to Prepositions. 141. II. (1).
IV.	**IV.**
Genitivus Gerundii Substantivis et Adjectivis additur. 141. II. (2).	The Genitive of the Gerund is joined to Substantives and Adjectives. 141. II. (2).
V.	**V.**
Dativus Gerundii Nominibus et Verbis additur. 141. II. (3).	The Dative of the Gerund is joined to Nouns and Verbs. 141. II. (3).
VI.	**VI.**
Ablativus Gerundii causæ vel modi est aut Præpositioni jungitur. 141. II. (4).	The Ablative of the Gerund is of cause or manner, or is joined to a Preposition. 141. II. (4).

SUPINES.

II.	II.
Supinum in *um* Accusativus est post Verba motus. 141. II. (5).	The Supine in *um* is an Accusative after Verbs of motion. 141. II. (5).
Iri cum Supino efficit Infinitivum futuri Passivi. 141. II. (5). *a.*	*Iri* with the Supine forms the Infinitive of the Future Passive. 141. II. (5). *a.*
III.	**III.**
Supinum in *u* pro Ablativo Respectus est. 141. II. (6).	The Supine in *u* is for an Ablative of respect. 141. II. (6).

RULES NOT ARRANGED IN THEIR PROPER ORDER.

GERUNDIVE ATTRACTION.

I.

In Gerundiis Transitivis usitatior est Attractio Gerundiva; cujus constructionis regula est hæcce:

Trahitur Objectum in Gerundivi casum, Gerundivum in numerum et genus Objecti. 143.

I.

In Transitive Gerunds the Gerundive Attraction is more usual; the rule for which construction is the following :

The Object is attracted to the case of the Gerundive, the Gerundive to the Number and Gender of the Object. 143.

PARTITIVE GENITIVE.

Genitivus Rei Distributæ Partitivis adjungitur, quæ, quantum licet, Genitivi sumunt genus. 130. IV.

A Genitive of the Thing Distributed is joined to Partitive words, which, as far as may be, take the Gender of the Genitive. 130. IV.

ABLATIVE OF SEPARATION.

Ablativus Separationis et Originis etiam sine Præpositione Verbis et Participiis adjungitur. 123. XIII.

The Ablative of Separation and Origin is joined also with a Preposition to Verbs and Participles. 123. XIII.

THE END.

Butler & Tanner, The Selwood Printing Works, Frome, and London.

Price 2s. 6d.

By the Same Author.

In the Press.

EASY EXERCISES FOR BEGINNERS,

AS A

COMPANION VOLUME

TO

₦EW EASY LATIN ₱RIMER.

BY THE SAME AUTHOR.

Ninth Edition. 12mo. Price 1s. 6d. Cloth.
A SHORT AND EASY LATIN BOOK.

Fourth Edition. 12mo. Price 3s. 6d. Cloth.
A FIRST EASY LATIN READING BOOK.

Third Edition. 12mo. Price 3s. 6d. Cloth.
A SECOND EASY LATIN READING BOOK.

Fifth Edition. 12mo. Price 2s. 6d. Cloth.
A SHORT AND EASY GREEK BOOK.

Second Edition. 12mo. Price 5s. Cloth.
A FIRST EASY GREEK READING BOOK.

12mo. Price 5s. Cloth.
A SECOND EASY GREEK READING BOOK.

Third Edition. 12mo. Price 1s. 6d. Cloth.
FIRST GREEK READER FOR USE AT ETON.
Drawn up at the request of the Lower Master of Eton College, and
now in use at Eton, Harrow, Merchant Taylors', etc.

12mo. Price 2s.
FIRST BOOK OF HOMER'S ILIAD.
In graduated lessons, with full notes and vocabularies.

Just Published. 12mo. Price 2s. 6d. Cloth.
SELECTIONS FROM THE LATIN AUTHORS.
PROSE AND VERSE.
In Separate Parts. Price 1s. 6d.

SWAN SONNENSCHEIN, LE BAS & LOWREY, PATERNOSTER SQUARE.

"FEW living classical scholars have done so much or nearly so much as
Mr. FOWLE has done to smooth the way of the classical scholar by a series
of elementary works, which for *accuracy in detail* and *perfection of method*,
as well as *practical utility*, are, as a whole, unsurpassed by similar works
in this country. The present volume ('Selections from the Best Latin
Authors') was commenced years ago, and the delay ought to be forgiven
on account of the excellence of the work now that it is completed. Before
pointing out in detail the excellences of this most useful and charming
book we venture to express our regret that its value is somewhat lessened
in our opinion by the want of order which pervades it. The divisions made
are simply two, prose and poetry. The prose begins with Eutropius and
ends with Tacitus, and the poetry begins with Catullus and ends with
Martial. At the end of the prose selections, as well as at the end of the
poetry selections, the editors give their 'Helps for Construing,' which are
helps in reality as well as in name. Their tone is scholarly and thorough,
and no real difficulty, either in the text of the author or in his allusions, is
shirked. We can scarcely conceive a work more capable of introducing a
student to the profitable reading and study of the Latin authors' prose
and verse than this admirable and scholarly work of Messrs. FOWLE and
WHITAKER. We may add that it contains a short but the best summary of
Latin writers we have seen anywhere."—*School Board Chronicle.*

By the Same Author.

THE SATURDAY REVIEW

March 27th, 1875.

SOME STEPPING-STONES TO SCHOLARSHIP.*

" In the interest of both parents and pupils, we think it right to draw attention to two or three succinct and well-considered aids to the attainment of classical knowledge, in the way of grammar, composition, and collateral matters, which now lie on our table.

" Of these we place in the first rank two volumes differing in grade and scope, yet of the same practical character, excellently fitted, the one for grounding the merest tyro, the other for giving him, when grounded, an insight into the principles and philosophy of the grammar he has laid in by rote. The first is *A Short and Easy Greek Book*, by Mr. EDMUND FOWLE ; the other an annotated Greek Accidence, by Mr. Evelyn Abbott, now a tutor, we believe, at Balliol ; and it has seldom been our fortune to light upon Greek grammars in which economy and retrenchment of space went so thoroughly along with lucidity and solidity of information. Mr. FOWLE's book, indeed, combining grammar, exercises, and vocabulary in the space of one hundred and forty pages, distinctly aims at not only being, but also (which is a harder task, though it may appear paradoxical to say so) at seeming to the learner's eye as easy as possible. To this end each subject has been confined to one, or at most two, pages, and a vast amount of thought and pains has been bestowed upon such arrangements of declensions, division of a declension, tenses, and tables of verbs as obviate wearisome repetition, and establish a sequence readily appreciable by the learner. A further recommendation is that Mr. FOWLE's book runs in the lines of Wordsworth's Greek Grammar, and, in a less degree, in those of Mr. St. John Parry's, one or other of which is in use at most of our larger schools. And, though the nature of the *Short and Easy Greek Book* peremptorily excludes philological and philosophical explanations, which the pupils for whom it is designed would be certain to ignore, it is remarkable how seldom we have been able to trace the slightest omission of essential matter, and how often an impression is produced that the author has weighed with nicety the claims of this or that detail to be included as of vital elementary importance. . . . Yet Mr. Abbott's aim and object is also simplification. . . . When we come to the declensions of substantives, both writers are found practically limiting these to three, with a division of a third into five classes, and Mr. FOWLE has laudably simplified the intricacies of the vocative singular and dative plural of this last by a few simple rules. . . .

" In a note to his compendious account of the comparison of adjectives, Mr. FOWLE makes a reservation that ' this formation of comparatives and superlatives is only given for the sake of learning the language, and that it is not to be supposed that it represents the original growth of the words' ; and so elsewhere he distinguishes between the easy way for beginners and the more philosophical way, as regards forming the tenses. . . . We may add that a great enhancement of the usefulness of Mr. FOWLE's manual is that it contains a series of simple and progressive exercises upon the steps of grammar as the pupil masters them, thus superseding the necessity of a 'Delectus,' and insuring the pupil's safe footing as he goes forward. Similar praise may be bestowed on his *Short and Easy Latin Book* and his two graduated Latin Readers, leading the pupil up to selected passages of Cæsar, Ovid, and Virgil. His constant attention to the abridgment of labour, and the acquirement of aptness in translation by progressive vocabularies and pertinent footnotes, shows a clear sense of his mission as an instructor," etc., etc., etc.

---

* *A Short and Easy Greek Book.* By Rev. Edmund Fowle. Longmans. 1874.

The Elements of the Greek Accidence, with Philological Notes. By Evelyn Abbott, M.A., of Balliol College, Oxford. Rivingtons. 1874.

A Short and Easy Latin Book. Fourth Edition. 1873. *A First Easy Latin Reading Book.* Second Edition. 1874. *A Second Easy Latin Reading Book.* 1873. By Rev. Edmund Fowle. Longmans.

REVIEWS OF THE LATIN AND GREEK BOOKS.

"It is no exaggeration of Mr. Fowle's merits as an educational author to say that, since the days of Dr. Kerchever Arnold, no such advance has been made in the quality and usefulness of classical school books as that achieved by Mr. Fowle in the easy series of Latin and Greek manuals which he has published. It was our lot to be the very first to recognise the great and special merit of these works, and we are glad to see," etc., etc.—School Board Chronicle.

"The grand and distinctive merit of these books is the admirable skill with which the author has carefully excluded all the more difficult and advanced matters, and yet has prepared the way for their later acquirement. This *faculty of exclusion and simplification amounts almost to genius.* It requires no little skill to confine every subject within the limit of one or, at the most, two pages, and at the same time to prepare the pupil for the study of larger and more comprehensive treatises, by a perfectly natural and easy growth; *and yet this has been achieved by Mr.* Fowle *with perfect and unerring skill.*"—The Schoolmaster.

"*It is impossible to speak in terms of too high satisfaction of Mr.* Edmund Fowle's 'First Easy Latin Reading Book.'"—John Bull.

"Among those who have lately published excellent working methods for elementary teaching, *one of the highest places ought to be reserved for Mr.* Fowle. His little book is one of the most striking instances we could find of a thoughtful adult mind making the way easy for the young learner. It is always dangerous to assert an absolute superlative; but it seems to us that this little Latin Reading Book for beginners is one of the best that has ever come into our hands."—Quarterly Journal of Education.

"The Rev. Edmund Fowle's 'Second Easy Latin Reading Book'

(Longmans') carries a step farther the plan of elementary teaching so ably sketched out in his 'Short and Easy Latin Book,' and 'First Easy Latin Reading Book.' Everything, however simple, that the pupil ought to know, is put before him in the plainest and most direct language."—Guardian.

"It is a common complaint amongst tutors that there is a great want of good elementary Greek books. We do not think they have *any further ground of dissatisfaction since the appearance of Mr.* Fowle's *most admirable manual.*"—Oxford Undergraduates' Journal.

"Mr. Fowle's earlier educational works have been noticed in our columns with well-merited praise. The volume before us lacks nothing of the striking excellences which marked its valuable predecessors. It is simple in the extreme, very gradual in its steps, clear in expression, and shirks no difficulty. The passages selected are from the purest models of the purest Latinity."—Schoolboard Chronicle.

"The same good work which the Rev. Edmund Fowle has done for beginners in Latin by his 'Short and Easy Latin Book' he has now performed for those beginning Greek, in his companion volume, 'A Short and Easy Greek Book.' The arrangement is excellent, and there is the same simplicity and adaptation to the special difficulties of beginners which made Mr. Fowle's previous work so great a success."—John Bull.

"The early study of the Greek language has many thorny steps, and we think any boy fortunate who has such sedulous care given as is here shown to help him over them. It must be a very idle or a hopelessly stupid boy whom such a system as this would not bring, as old Lily said, 'past the wearisome bitterness of his learning.'"—Literary Churchman.

"This very easy and carefully selected reading book is framed on the model of the author's Latin Reading Book, which we have commended so cordially in our columns. *We speak our fullest conviction of the merits of the work when we declare it to be by far the easiest and most useful introduction to Greek* when a pupil has once mastered the rudiments of his Greek Grammar."—EVENING STANDARD.

"The author of these books, who is a classical scholar of high attainments, has performed a difficult and important task with complete success, . . . and too much cannot be said in praise of his work. While his books are free from the defects of works of a similar kind, they are marked by striking excellences."—WORCESTER JOURNAL.

"*They remain now, as when they were published—the simplest and, in our opinion, the most effective of any classical primer we know.*"—LITERARY CHURCHMAN.

"The study of language is no easy matter, . . . *but some teachers have the gift to lighten the student's labour; and such a man is* Mr. FOWLE, who has the ability to clear away difficulties, and thereby smooth the way to the attainment of a thorough knowledge of a language. *No one but a practical teacher could do what the author has done;* and in this respect his Greek Book

is quite as easy as his Latin."—BRIGHTON GAZETTE.

"It has seldom been our fortune to light upon a Greek Grammar in which economy and retrenchment of space went so thoroughly along with lucidity and solidity of information. . . . A vast amount of thought and pains has been bestowed upon such arrangements of declensions, divisions of a declension, tenses, and tables of verbs, as obviate wearisome repetition and establish a sequence appreciable by the learner."—SATURDAY REVIEW.

"We have examined these books in a somewhat sceptical spirit, fancying that amid the shoals of books of a similar character issuing daily from the press there could be no possible ground for granting them even a conditional welcome; but Mr. FOWLE has converted our scepticism into something like a well-assured and hopeful faith. The first of the two contains a very concise grammar, chiefly valuable for what it does NOT contain, and at the same time ingeniously putting the information it does contain in the form most adapted for comprehension and retention by the youthful pupil; and this grammar is followed up by some very easy exercises, admirably adapted to the slow and painful steps which can be taken by the child. *The book reveals one every page the experience of one who has not only worked with children, but felt for them.*"—SCHOOLMASTER.

SWAN SONNENSCHEIN, LE BAS & LOWREY, PATERNOSTER SQUARE.

By the Same Author.

12mo, cloth, price 2*s.*; free by post 2*s.* 2*d.*

Cheaper Edition, boards, 1*s., free by post,* 1*s.* 2*d.*

THE

S¢HOOLBOY'S FIRST BOOK

OF

E*A*SY POETRY.

EXTRACT FROM PREFACE.

M*Y* objection to nearly all those Books of Poetry which have fallen into my hands is, that there are so few pieces suitable for children, from nine to fourteen years of age, to commit to memory —some are too easy, and some too difficult. I believe that all the pieces in the present selection are of very nearly the same difficulty—not childish, I hope, but at the same time simple in the matter and in the versification.

Another objection to nearly all the selections I have seen is that they contain the same stock pieces—very pretty many of them, and very suitable, but too well known for me to care to give them in my Book. I append a list of many such pieces which will *not be found* in the present publication.

The present book would not do, certainly, to be the only Poetry Book in use in a school, or the younger generation would grow up without knowing many of our old favourites; it is therefore not intended to take the place of books now in general use, but to supplement them.

S*WAN* S*ONNENSCHEIN*, L*E* B*AS* & L*OWREY*, P*ATERNOSTER* S*QUARE*.